TRIGGER WARNING

Look for these heart-pounding thrillers
by William W. Johnstone,
writing with J. A. Johnstone,
available wherever books are sold.

THE DOOMSDAY BUNKER

BLACK FRIDAY

TYRANNY

STAND YOUR GROUND

SUICIDE MISSION

THE BLEEDING EDGE

THE BLOOD OF PATRIOTS

HOME INVASION

JACKKNIFE

REMEMBER THE ALAMO

INVASION USA

INVASION USA: BORDER WAR

VENGEANCE IS MINE

PHOENIX RISING

PHOENIX RISING: FIREBASE FREEDOM

PHOENIX RISING: DAY OF JUDGMENT

TRIGGER WARNING

WILLIAM W. JOHNSTONE
with J. A. Johnstone

PINNACLE BOOKS
Kensington Publishing Corp.
www.kensingtonbooks.com

PINNACLE BOOKS are published by

Kensington Publishing Corp.
119 West 40th Street
New York, NY 10018

PUBLISHER'S NOTE
Following the death of William W. Johnstone, the Johnstone family is working with a carefully selected writer to organize and complete Mr. Johnstone's outlines and many unfinished manuscripts to create additional novels in all of his series like The Last Gunfighter, Mountain Man, and Eagles, among others. This novel was inspired by Mr. Johnstone's superb storytelling.

ISBN-13: 978-0-7860-4050-6
ISBN-10: 0-7860-4050-5

First printing: September 2018

10 9 8 7 6 5 4 3 2 1

Printed in the United States of America

First electronic edition: September 2018

ISBN-13: 978-0-7860-4051-3
ISBN-10: 0-7860-4051-3

Chapter 1

A short, sharp cry in the night made Jake Rivers look up from the book he was reading.

To be honest, he was glad for the distraction. He was on the verge of throwing the book against the wall of his dorm room in disgust. Since it was a hard copy, a thick trade paperback he had bought in the university bookstore for an outrageous price, and not something he was reading on his phone or tablet, he could have done that without breaking anything. Although the book was heavy enough it might have dented the Sheetrock.

The window next to Jake's desk was open to let in the warm autumn air. Olmsted Hall had been built more than seventy years earlier, before air-conditioning, and updated and remodeled many times, but the windows still opened, which Jake liked. He dropped the book on the desk, switched off the lamp he'd been using for light, and stood up to move closer to the window.

From here on the second floor, he had a good view of Nafziger Plaza, the large, park-like area in the center of Kelton College's campus. Three residence halls—Pearsol, Olmsted, and Colohan, running north to south—bordered the western side of the plaza. The administration building was at the northern end, the main science building, Terrill Hall, to the south. The big Burr Memorial Library was directly across from where Jake looked out the window. He could see the lights along the front of it through the trees.

He spotted movement in the shadows under those trees. Someone ran toward the dorms along one of the concrete walks. But another figure pursued and caught the first one, grabbing an arm to sling the fleeing person to the ground. Another cry. Definitely female.

Jake had some more reading to do for class—as much as he despised the book he had just tossed onto the desk—but it could wait. He headed for the door of his room.

He wasn't really aware of it, but he was smiling as he went out.

It didn't take him long to get down the stairs. A group of students was sitting in the lobby talking about something—he heard the words "microaggression" and "privilege" and "cisnormative"—but Jake didn't even glance at them as he went by, and none of them called out to him. He didn't have any friends here, and whatever the subject under discussion, none of them wanted his opinion on it.

He was just a big, dumb brute, after all.

As he strode quickly out into the night, keen eyes searched the area under the trees where he had seen the two figures a couple of minutes earlier. At first he didn't see anything, but then he spotted movement again. *There.*

"Damn it, Annie, just be reasonable! I'm not going to let go of you until you start thinking straight."

"Stop, Craig, just stop." The words gasped out as the woman clearly fought to hold back sobs. "I told you it was over."

Jake was still moving toward them, but he stopped as he heard what the woman said. A grimace tugged at his mouth. Lovers' quarrel. None of his business. That was an old-fashioned attitude, and he knew it. But almost everything about him was old-fashioned, including his dislike of a woman being mistreated.

Of course, if he *did* step in to help her, more than likely she would stick up for her boyfriend and turn on *him* instead, accusing him of perpetuating the patriarchy and the myth of women needing to be rescued. He already got enough of that crap every day. He started to turn away . . .

Then the son of a bitch had to go and slap her.

Jake heard the crack of open hand on flesh and stopped in his tracks. He swung around, took several more steps until he could see the two of them fairly well in some stray beams of light filtering through the trees from the library. Couldn't make out too many details because the light wasn't that good. But she was petite and blond while the guy was good-sized, with dark hair and a short beard. Something was odd about the shape of his head, and after a second, Jake got it. The guy's hair was long enough that he'd pulled it up into a bun on the top of his head.

Jake ran his left hand over his own buzz cut. He'd had fairly long hair once, half a dozen years earlier, but he had never worn it in a bun. And if he ever grew it back out, he still wouldn't.

The guy started tugging on the woman, who was actually crying now. Jake said, "That's enough, Craig. Let her go."

Both of them jumped a little in surprise. Jake moved pretty quietly all the time, without thinking about it anymore. More than once people had accused him of sneaking up on them, when all he was doing was going about his business.

"Hell, man, don't do that. Do I know you?"

"Nope. I just heard you from my window up there."

Jake gestured vaguely toward Olmsted Hall.

"What, you've got super-hearing or something? We weren't being that loud. Sorry if we bothered you, man. We'll keep it down. Anyway, we're on our way back to our place. Be gone in just a second—"

"It's not our place," the woman said. Annie, that was what Craig had called her. "It's *my* apartment. You need to get your stuff and leave."

"I'm not going anywhere," Craig snapped. "That Julika girl's been filling your head full of crap. Anyway, she just wants you for herself, you know that, don't you?"

He still had hold of Annie's arm. Jake said, "You haven't let go of her."

Craig looked around at him and said in an annoyed tone, "Are you still here? This is none of your business, man." He paused. "Are you one of the football players?" Kelton College had a football team, but it hadn't won a game in three years.

"You're big enough, but Olmsted's not the athletic dorm—"

"I'm not a football player, and you need to let go of the lady."

"You don't have to call me a lady," Annie said. Just as Jake had expected, she sounded halfway offended.

"I'm trying to help you—"

"That's no excuse for perpetuating stereotypes and spreading toxic masculinity."

Jake couldn't hold back a sigh. Even scared and in trouble, Annie couldn't stop herself from parroting some of the garbage that had been forced into her head. Not for the first time in the past half-dozen years since he'd enlisted, Jake found himself wondering if the people he fought to defend really deserved it.

He'd always concluded that they did, but sometimes it wasn't easy to convince himself.

Craig said, "All right, we're going." He turned and tried to pull Annie along with him.

"No!" she said. "Let me go!"

"You heard her," Jake said as he stepped closer.

Craig finally released Annie's arm, but only so he could ball that hand into a fist. He twisted toward Jake and threw a punch. Jake moved his head out of the way and said, "Stop it, man, while you still can."

"I'm not scared of you!" Craig shouted. "I don't care how big you are! I know Krav Maga!"

He had just started some sort of fancy martial arts move when Jake hit him with a left hook to the belly. Craig's eyes got so wide Jake could see the whites of them even in the bad light. As he started to double over, Jake swung a right cross to the jaw that snapped Craig's head over. Craig went down hard, pounding his face against the concrete walk.

"You killed him!" Annie screeched.

"No. I could have, but I just knocked him out. Didn't even break his jaw. He'll be all right."

She came at him, hissing and spitting. Jake didn't know many cops, but he had known some MPs and they felt the same as their civilian counterparts about handling domestic disturbances. Those calls were the worst, and this encounter was a living example of it. All he'd tried to do was help this woman, and now she wanted to claw his eyes out because he'd hit her boyfriend.

He should have stayed with that weighty tome about how capitalism was the worst economic system and America was the most evil country in the world. Instead he had to raise his arm and fend off the punches she was throwing at him. Although the blows were ineffective enough, he probably could have just stood there and taken them without any harm being done.

"You . . . you *fascist*!" she screamed. "You oppressor!"

"Hell, lady," Jake said, knowing the word would get under her skin again, "how'd you know I used to be in the army?"

He decided he might as well turn and walk away and let her do her worst. He was about to do that when Craig groaned. The sound made Annie break off her attack and drop to her knees beside him. She lifted him into a half-sitting position and held him against her. He seemed like he was still too groggy to know what was going on.

Jake heard a sudden rush of footsteps behind him and turned to see several black-clad figures charging him. He couldn't make out their faces, and when they yelled, "Fascist! Fascist!" and the words were muffled, he knew why.

They were wearing hoods over their heads.

Then they were on him, swinging bicycle chains with locks on them, metal pipes, and other objects turned into clubs, and this peaceful night on the small, elite college campus turned into a fight for his life.

Chapter 2

Jake had battled against superior odds many times, but usually he'd been heavily armed and hadn't been forced to take his enemies on bare-handed.

The thing to do in a situation like that was to take an opponent's weapon away from him. Which was what Jake did when one of the black-clad attackers swung a pipe at his head. He ducked, let the pipe go over his head, and then came up with his left forearm under the guy's chin, forcing his head back sharply.

Not sharply enough to break the idiot's neck, though. These were kids. Arrogant, small-minded bullies, but still kids. They didn't deserve to die for being stupid enough to believe the pack of lies they had been fed by their teachers, the media, Hollywood, and more than half of Washington, D.C.

Jake reached up, closed his right hand around the pipe, and wrenched it free of the attacker's grip. He twirled it, jabbed the end into the kid's stomach, and sent him staggering backward, gagging and retching. Moving too fast to see in the shadows, Jake let his instincts and a faintly heard sound guide him. He lifted the pipe as another of the figures slashed at him with a chain. The chain wrapped around the pipe, and Jake used it to jerk the guy toward him. Jake's left fist shot out in a straight jab that popped the cartilage in the guy's nose. He howled in pain.

Jake pivoted, swung pipe and chain, and coiled the chain around another attacker's ankle. A quick tug yanked the guy's legs out from under him and dropped him hard on his back on the concrete. That knocked all the breath out of him and left him gasping for air.

A second later, somebody landed on Jake's back and wrapped wiry arms and legs around him.

"I got him!" a female voice yelled. "Kill the fascist! Down with oppressors! Kill him!"

The pipe and chain clattered on the walk as Jake dropped them. He reached up and back, got hold of the attacker clinging to his back like a spider monkey, and tore her loose. She didn't weigh much. He bent forward, swung her over his head, and tossed her onto the ground, being careful to make sure she didn't land on the concrete or hit a tree. She screeched, "Rape! Rape!" as she rolled over on the grass, and he wished for a second that he hadn't been quite so careful.

"An-ti-fa! An-ti-fa!"

The chanting made him look around. He frowned as he saw that the commotion had attracted several dozen students. His frown deepened as he realized they were cheering on the black-clad attackers.

"Wait a minute!" he shouted, knowing he was wasting his time but too angry right now to care. "I didn't do anything wrong! I was just trying to help a woman—"

"Toxic! Toxic!"

"Racist!"

"Nazi! Nazi!"

The whole world had gone freakin' crazy, he thought.

The black suits were on their feet again and regrouping. As they got ready to charge him, Jake flashed back for an instant to things he had seen in the past: men in black hoods spouting Arabic as they held a Western journalist and sawed his head off with a big knife; more black-hooded figures forcing a scared child with a bomb strapped to him down a street while they threatened to kill his mother if he didn't blow up himself and some American soldiers; those same evil men or others just like them shooting at him and his buddies . . .

Then the memories went back even further to old, grainy, historical newsreel footage he had seen, row upon row of young men in spiffy uniforms and high black boots marching through the streets of a city, lifting their arms in a salute to the madman in front of whom they passed in review, on their way to wipe out anyone who didn't think exactly the same way they did. They had disarmed the citizenry, taken over all the newspapers and radio and colleges and universities and made it a crime punishable by death to say or even think anything they disagreed with . . .

And the mass graves and the smoke rising from the crematoriums and later an even worse evil rising in the East, with more millions dead for no reason other than opposing what the party leaders said and did . . . The starvation, the booted marchers coming down the street, the knock on the door in the night followed by wails of grief and anguish . . .

And these people surrounding him now, the bullies in their black hoods and the ones who chanted for them, believed in and supported that hideous evil, all while calling *him* a Nazi and a fascist . . .

They kept using those words, Jake thought wryly as all that flashed through his mind, but he didn't believe the words meant what these people thought they did.

Then they charged him again.

Jake reached down and picked up the pipe and chain. He unwrapped the chain, held it in his left hand, and clutched the pipe in his right. He was sick and tired of this. Maybe it was time he actually fought back, no matter what the consequences.

"Drop 'em! Drop those weapons, damn it!"

The shouted command came from behind him. He turned, saw the half-dozen uniformed campus cops converging on him. He said, "Wait! I'm not the one—"

"Phelps, deploy Taser!"

He heard a stun gun fire, felt the fierce jab as the first set of needles pierced his shirt and lanced into his flesh to deliver their jolt of electricity. He staggered as the shock coursed through him, but he didn't go down.

"Carter! Taser!"

Another set of probes hit him and seemed to turn the blood in his veins and arteries into streams of fire. Agony wracked him as his muscles clamped hard as stone. He knew that he was falling but didn't feel it when he crashed to the concrete. Consciousness fled from him.

But not before he heard the gleeful, jeering cries from the spectators.

"Down—with—Nazis! Down—with—Nazis!"

"Damn it, Jake, what am I gonna do with you?"

Frank McRainey leaned back in the chair behind his desk, sighed, and shook his head. He was the chief of the campus police, and clearly he didn't appreciate being called to his office late in the evening like this, when he should have been home with his family.

Jake sat in the chair in front of McRainey's desk. His muscles still ached a little from being hit with the stun guns, but he didn't show that discomfort in his face or voice as he said, "I don't know, sir. I'm sure there are plenty of people who think you should turn me over to the police and have me arrested."

The balding, baggy-eyed campus cop frowned and said, "Was that riot your fault?"

"Well . . . there was one of me and how many of them? What conclusion would you draw from that, sir?"

"Don't get mouthy, son," McRainey snapped. Then he couldn't help but chuckle. "At least you didn't kill any of them. There's that to be thankful for."

"I tried not to hurt anybody any more than I

had to. I was just trying to stop that guy Craig from hurting the girl, at first, and after that I just defended myself."

"And quite efficiently, too, from what I hear," McRainey said, nodding. "I'm not going to charge you with anything. Not yet, anyway. Once the activists and the lawyers and the media start putting pressure on President Pelletier, there's no telling what he'll insist on, just to get them all off his back."

He took his phone out of his shirt pocket, tapped a few icons on it, and then turned the screen so Jake could read the headline on the news site the older man had called up.

FAR RIGHT EXTREMIST ATTACKS COLLEGE STUDENTS

"That's not even close to correct," Jake said. "I didn't attack anybody. I just defended myself, like I told you. And I'm not far right, far left, or far anything else. I just want to go to school and get an education, sir."

"You've been here two months. I'll bet you're getting more of an education than you ever bargained for." McRainey put away his phone, then leaned forward and clasped his hands together on the desk. "Why *are* you here, Jake? Is it just because of your grandfather?"

Jake hesitated. Most people here at Kelton didn't know who his grandfather was, but McRainey was a family friend and had known Cordell Gardner as a young man. McRainey had known Jake's father Phillip, too. He just didn't speak of him. Neither did Jake.

Jake didn't even use his father's name anymore. He had changed his legally to Rivers, his mother Donna's maiden name. He had worried a little about what Cordell would think about that, but the old man not only hadn't been offended, he had encouraged Jake to make that move . . . just as he'd encouraged him to join the army and then to come here to Kelton College.

Problem was, the army wasn't what it once had been, and Kelton College sure as hell wasn't.

"Jake?" McRainey prodded.

But Jake was lost in the past.

CHAPTER 3

Six months earlier

"Well, what else are you going to do with yourself, boy? Pull!"

Cordell Gardner tracked the clay pigeon with the shotgun, leading it perfectly as he squeezed the trigger. The pigeon exploded into small fragments as the buckshot hit it.

"I hadn't really thought about it," Jake said.

He and his grandfather were standing at the edge of a large field that Cordell Gardner used for skeet shooting. The roof of the old man's house, which was big but somehow not ostentatious, was visible over the trees behind them. Gardner's estate sprawled over a lot of East Texas acres and included tennis courts, stables, and a nine-hole golf course, even though Gardner didn't play tennis, ride horses, or have any use for golf. Sometimes his guests did, though, and he'd been raised to be hospitable.

He broke the shotgun open, took fresh shells from his pocket, and thumbed them into the gun.

"You'd better start thinking about it," he told Jake. "You didn't reenlist, so now you have to do something else with your life."

"Why?" Jake asked bluntly. "I could just sit around and wait for you to die so I'll inherit that fortune of yours."

Gardner threw back his head and laughed. He was a big old man, although not as big as Jake's six-four and two hundred and fifty pounds. The shock of hair on his head was snow-white, which made the deep, permanent tan on his weathered face seem even darker than it really was. He had an air of vitality about him despite his age and seemed to be nowhere near dying.

"How do you know I haven't disowned you?"

"You wouldn't do that," Jake said. "I'm too much like you."

Gardner grunted.

"Might be a good reason to, right there. Pull!"

One of the old man's groundskeepers, who also served as his assistant when he came out here to shoot, triggered the trap that flung a target into the air. Gardner blew it to pieces, then turned and held out the shotgun to Jake.

"Want to give it a try? You used to be pretty good at this."

Jake took the gun and loaded it with the shells his grandfather handed him. He said, "It's been a long time."

"Like riding a bicycle. It'll come right back to you." Gardner turned to look at the groundskeeper. "Send two this time, Benny."

"You want to make it tough on me?" Jake asked.

"Just setting a bar."

That wasn't all of it. Jake knew the old man still had a strong competitive streak. He wasn't necessarily trying to show Jake up, but if Jake missed one or both of the targets and then his grandfather took the gun back and broke both the next time, he would get a considerable amount of satisfaction out of that.

Jake was contrary enough that he didn't want to give the old man that much satisfaction. He set his stance, held the shotgun ready in the gun-down position, and nodded.

"Pull!" Gardner called.

The targets flew spinning into the air. Jake brought the shotgun smoothly to his shoulder, tracked the leader, squeezed off one barrel, shifted his aim just slightly, and fired again.

Tiny fragments of both targets pelted to the ground, all that was left of them.

Gardner frowned and asked, "How long's it been since you did any target shooting, boy?"

"At targets like that? Seven years. Maybe eight."

Gardner just shook his head in admiration.

"You've got a knack for it. Always have. Never saw a boy who could handle a gun like you, even when you were a little kid. You could shoot like a grown man when you were twelve years old. Drive like a grown man when you were fourteen. I'd ask some of the mamas of your high school buddies what else you could do like a grown man, but I don't think I want to know."

Jake handed back the shotgun and said, "Driving just got me in trouble."

"Street racing, you mean."

Jake shrugged.

"The cops frowned on it. I would've wound up

in jail more than once if it weren't for you and your lawyers."

Gardner pursed his lips and said, "Yes, and it was a mistake saving you from your own foolishness. I should've let you spend some time behind bars. Might've taught you a lesson. But at least I realized I was about to make the same mistakes with you that I made with your father and stopped in time to keep from ruining you the same way."

Jake didn't want to talk about his father, but the old man had brought it up.

"Most people don't consider it being ruined to be a rich, successful lawyer."

His grandfather snorted.

"Most people never knew what a sorry, no-account scoundrel Phillip Gardner really was. It pains me to say it, but he was my son, so I've got the right. Of course, I blame myself—"

"You didn't shove that cocaine up his nose."

"I might as well have."

Jake turned.

"If all we're gonna do is blow clay pigeons out of the air and talk about a bunch of old crap I'd just as soon forget, I'm out of here."

Gardner went after him, put a hand on his arm.

"Wait. I just want to know what your plans are, Jake?"

"Maybe I don't have any," Jake said, stopping and turning to look at his grandfather.

"Then why don't you go back to school and try to figure out what you want to do with your life? I know you too well, boy. You may joke about sitting around and doing nothing, but that's not in you. Never has been. Maybe the army didn't work out, but there's something else waiting out there for you. I know there is."

"Didn't work out?" Jake repeated. "Two tours in the Middle East and a chestful of medals and ribbons isn't working out?"

"You did a good job, sure. A great job, even. But did it satisfy you?"

Jake scowled. The old man knew good and well that it hadn't. Something was still missing in his life. It always had been, no matter how many skills he mastered, no matter how much excitement and risk he sought out.

But college? *That* was supposed to fulfill him? The idea was plain crazy.

"Look, I know you're smart," Gardner went on. "You already had more than half a college degree in your pocket when you were a senior in high school."

"Yeah, and I never finished senior year, did I?"

"Not because you couldn't have. Hell, you would've been the valedictorian!"

"Salutatorian," Jake corrected him. "That math team girl would've edged me out by a few percentage points. But it didn't matter. By graduation I'd already enlisted, to get out of trouble with the law. Your idea, as I recall."

"And you got your GED *and* your bachelor's degree before you got out. That took a lot of work, as well as playing the system for all it's worth."

"You taught me well," Jake said with a smile.

"I'd like to think so. But now it's time to let somebody else teach you. You know I've got ties to Kelton College—"

"You've built how many buildings and endowed how many fellowships and scholarships for them?"

Gardner made a dismissive gesture.

"I never had a chance to go to college, but I always wanted to. I've done all right for myself—"

"A few billion dollars' worth of all right."

The old man waved that off, too.

"But maybe I would have done even better . . . more importantly, maybe I would have been a better *person* . . . with a real education. You can do that, boy. Go get your master's degree. Hell, get your doctorate." He grinned. "You could be Dr. Jacob Rivers."

"Doctor of *what*?"

"I don't care. Whatever strikes your fancy. That's what college is for, to find out what you're good at, and what you enjoy."

"And here I thought it was a place where parents paid thousands of dollars for their kids to get drunk, do drugs, and have sex."

"Maybe some of them," Gardner snapped, "but it's not that way at Kelton. It's one of the finest academic institutions in the country. That's why a smart fella like you will fit right in. You'll see, Jake. Just give it a try, that's all I ask."

It was hard for Jake to argue with his grandfather. When his parents had split up, Cordell Gardner had been a rock, not only for Jake but for his mother—Cordell was very fond of her, as well. As bad as things had been, they would have been worse if Gardner hadn't been around. Jake really would have wound up in jail, his life a total waste like his dad's had turned out to be.

"Kelton College, eh?"

"That's right. It's in Greenleaf, outside of Austin."

"I know where it is."

"Beautiful little old town, beautiful campus, pines all around . . . You'll love it there, son."

Jake had his doubts about that, but he heard himself saying, "We'll see."

"You won't regret it," Cordell Gardner said with a grin on his rugged old face.

Chapter 4

But Jake *had* regretted it, almost immediately. His grandfather had said he would fit right in.

Nothing could have been further from the truth.

His bachelor's degree was in biology. He had thought briefly that he might become a veterinarian, because he'd always liked dogs and had worked some with them overseas. But inevitably, that would have meant dealing with a lot of dying animals that he couldn't save, and he knew he just didn't have the heart for that. It would take too great a toll on him.

Maybe some sort of research, though. The idea of sitting in a lab all day didn't appeal to him, but there were other kinds of research. Going out into jungles and such, discovering new species, things like that. That didn't sound so bad.

And objectively, Jake knew his grandfather was right about one thing: he *was* smart. If one field of study didn't pan out the way he wanted, he'd just do something else. With Cordell Gardner's money behind him, plus the small inheritance he had gotten from his maternal grandfather, who had owned a trucking company in New Orleans, he didn't really have to worry about making a living.

Kelton College was a liberal arts school, though. There was a science department, of course, including a program that offered a master's degree in biology, but it was a small part of the school's focus, which was heavily geared toward literature, theater, music, philosophy, sociology, and especially political science. But only politics of a certain stripe . . .

Just looking at the names of some of the courses listed in the catalog had him frowning and figuratively scratching his head.

Gender, Culture, and U.S. National Identity.

Feminist Critique of Christianity.

Social Justice and American Racism.

The Psychological Impact of Male Microaggression.

Countering Warmongering and Oppression in American Culture.

Understanding Multiphasic Gender Constructs.

Jake had never seen such a load of useless baloney in all his life. Where were the regular courses? He flipped over to the English section.

Heteropatriarchy in American Literature.

LGBTQIAPK Tales: A Seminar

He had to look that one up. The abbreviation—which, evidently, today's college students instinctively understood—meant Lesbian, Gay, Bi, Trans, Queer, Intersex, Asexual, Pansexual, and Kink. Whatever floated anybody's boat was okay with Jake, as long as it didn't involve force, coercion, or kids, but a whole college course devoted to stories about such things?

One glance into the political science section

landed him on a course called *The Toxic American Political Axis: Republicans, Nazis, and Fascists.*

Jake closed the catalog. He was grateful that he wouldn't have to mess with any of that sort of course, since he was going for his master's degree in biology.

He found out different when he met with his faculty advisor.

"Kelton College requires a diverse course load even for specialized advanced degrees," the professor said. A brass nameplate on his desk read DR. MTUMBO.

The guy was as pale as anybody Jake had ever seen. Tall, balding, gawky, with a receding chin, he looked like a big white bird. Jake couldn't help himself. He said, "Dr. Mtumbo?"

The man sniffed.

"I identify as African-American. My ancestors were colonialists named Montambault who lived for a time in French Equatorial Africa before immigrating to this country. I simply adopted a more appropriate spelling to honor the unfortunate people they oppressed and exploited."

"Oh," Jake said. He supposed that made perfect sense . . . to the guy on the other side of the desk. "And you teach . . . ?"

"Microbiology."

"I'll probably be in some of your classes then."

"I look forward to it," the professor said, not sounding the least bit sincere. He pushed a printed list across the desk to Jake. "At any rate, here is the suggested course of study for the degree you're pursuing."

Jake picked up the list and scanned it, then said, "A lot of these courses don't appear to have anything to do with biology. I mean, economics, political theory, socialization . . ."

"A Kelton College graduate is a well-rounded graduate." It sounded like a slogan and probably was, although Jake wasn't going to waste time looking for it in the college's brochure or catalog.

"So I have to take these to get a master's in biology?"

"They're prerequisites for any advanced degree."

"Ooookay."

Dr. Montambault—Jake just couldn't think of him as Mtumbo, although he realized that was "insensitive" of him—clasped his skinny fingers together and said, "You've already been admitted to this institution, Mr. Rivers, but if I may speak frankly, I'm can't really see why. No offense, but you simply don't strike me as Kelton College material, despite your academic record, which is, for the most part, exemplary."

"Except for that part about dropping out of high school as soon as I turned eighteen and joining the army, eh?"

Montambault looked like he had just bitten into a sour crabapple as he said, "We don't have a large number of veterans among our student body. We've found that a *military background*"—the look got even more sour—"doesn't prepare a person for our rigorous curriculum and stringent standards of personal behavior. We have a very strict code of conduct and accountability here at Kelton."

"More strict than the army and Marines?"

The professor opened a drawer in his desk and took out a sheaf of stapled-together pages, at least seven or eight sheets thick. He placed them on the desk and pushed them over to Jake.

"This is our speech code. As part of our commitment to diversity, Kelton College guarantees all students a safe and inclusive learning environment, so you shouldn't use any of the words or phrases listed in here."

Jake frowned.

"I seem to remember reading something about a right to free speech . . ."

Montambault tapped a fingertip against the pages.

"Bringing up the First Amendment is listed in here. You shouldn't do that. It shuts down productive discussion. You shouldn't say anything about the Second Amendment, either. *Especially* the Second Amendment." Before Jake could respond, he took a booklet from the drawer and added it to the speech code. "Our sexual guidelines."

"An abridged version of the Kama Sutra?"

Montambault glared.

"Sexist comments like that are also violations of the speech code. No, this sets out the proper steps that are required to be taken before any sort of sexual contact to ensure that all such contacts are consensual."

"No means no, eh?"

"Exactly."

"So yes means yes."

"No, yes also means no because of our heteropatriarchal, phallocentric culture."

"So no means no and yes means no." Jake spread his hands. "They're college students. How do they get it on if everything means no?"

The professor looked exasperated and impatient.

"Just study the guidelines, Mr. Rivers. I'm sure it will all become clear to you. Until it does, I would advise you to be very circumspect in your interactions with other students."

"Female students."

"*All* students. Not everyone accepts the antiquated concept of binary gender, you know. Remember LGGBDTTTIQQAAPP. That means—"

Jake held up a hand to stop him.

"That's all right. I don't need it defined. But I thought it was LGBTQIAPK."

Montambault blew out a scoffing breath.

"That's outdated. The college experience is a very fast-paced one these days, Mr. Rivers. You'll have to learn to keep up. Education is all about change. Hope and change. And resistance. And social justice."

Jake realized he might as well be talking to one of the brick walls of the buildings on campus. He said, "I appreciate the help, Doctor. Are there any more, uh, guidelines I need to have?"

"Not at the moment. When you work out which courses you're going to be taking, come back to see me and we'll go over them to make sure they fit your course of study."

Jake stood up.

"Sure. Now maybe you can tell me where to find the housing department."

"You aren't going to live off-campus? There are some decent apartments to rent in town . . ."

"No, I realize I'm a little older than most students, but I want to get the full college experience. You *do* allow graduate students to live in the dorms?"

"One floor of Olmsted Hall is reserved for graduate students. I'm not sure if there are any openings."

"I'll check into it," Jake said. He planned on keeping his relationship to Cordell Gardner quiet, but he wasn't above using it to his advantage if necessary. And the old man had it in his head that college was the same sort of place it had been fifty years earlier, when he had wanted to attend but couldn't. So that meant Jake ought to live in a dorm, as he saw it. Given the amount of money his grandfather had forked over to Kelton College, Jake figured they would find a place for him.

"The housing office is in the administration building, at the far end of Nafziger Plaza," the professor said. "On the second floor."

"Thanks." Jake turned to go.

"Mr. Rivers . . . are you *sure* you want to attend Kelton College? I ask for your own benefit. I'm just not certain you're ever going to be happy here."

"Are you kidding?" Jake grinned. "I plan on loving it."

Chapter 5

"Jake?" The college experience hadn't been great so far, despite his sarcastic comment to Dr. Montambault. But now he was in enough trouble to land him in the office of the campus police chief. McRainey was glaring at him.

"Sorry, sir," Jake said. "I guess I got a little distracted there."

"If you don't want to tell me what you're doing here, I guess it's none of my business. As long as you pay your tuition and fees and abide by the rules, you're as welcome as any other student."

"I don't know that I'd go so far as to say that. I don't vote the right way, and I'm a soldier. That's enough to make me *persona non grata* at a place like Kelton." Jake ventured to add, "I'm a little surprised to find you working here in the middle of all these . . ."

"Special little snowflakes?" A sound came from McRainey that was part disgusted snort, part tolerant laugh. "Here's the thing, Jake. Kelton charges an arm and a leg, and because of that, nearly all the kids who go here come from wealthy families. I mean really wealthy. Like your grandfather, only a lot of them are even richer. And those mamas and daddies want their kiddos to be safe. In fact, they insist on it. So the college is willing to pay me a hefty salary to make sure they stay that way. More than twice as much as I ever made as a real cop in Houston. I can put up with a lot of derp for that kind of money."

Jake grinned. "Derp? I'm surprised you know the word."

"Hey, I work on a college campus. I hear a lot of stuff. Of course, I'm usually three or four years behind the times, anyway. That's not bad for an old guy like me."

"I guess. So you're letting me go?"

"I'm releasing you on your own recognizance while I investigate the incident. That's the best I can do tonight. And I can't guarantee that the administration won't come down on you harder later on. In fact, I can almost promise they will. But they won't kick you out. Cordell's money means too much to them for that." McRainey stood up. "Come by sometime tomorrow. I'll have your statement ready for you to sign by then. Between now and then, try to stay out of trouble, okay?"

"Hey, I'm a peaceable man."

"Yeah, Wild Bill Elliott used say the same thing just before he beat the crap out of Yakima Canutt."

"Who?"

"Google 'em! Now get out of here."

Jake left the chief's office and went out into the lobby of the campus police department, which was located in an unassuming little building tucked away in a corner of the campus. Behind the counter stood a burly uniformed officer in his thirties. His head was shaved, either because he thought it made him look intimidating or because he had lost most of his hair already and didn't want to call attention to that fact.

"The chief's letting you go?" he asked with a scowl.

"That's right," Jake said. "You have a problem with that, Officer Granderson?"

"You resisted arrest. We should have held you for the Greenleaf cops."

"How did I resist arrest? You ordered your guys to tase me as soon as I turned around toward you."

"You displayed weapons in an aggressive manner."

"The pipe and chain. I was holding them down at my sides."

"It looked to me like you were getting ready to attack us with them," Granderson insisted. "I ordered preemptive action to protect the safety and well-being of my fellow officers." The scowl turned into an ugly grin. "I bet it hurt like hell, didn't it?"

"I've grabbed live wires before," Jake said with a shrug. "No big deal."

"Yeah, you thought no big deal when you were layin' there on the ground twitching and drooling."

Jake felt anger bubbling up inside him, but Chief McRainey had just warned him to stay out of trouble, and besides, a jackwagon like Cal Granderson wasn't worth it. Jake just said, "I've been released pending the results of an investigation into tonight's incident."

"You could've killed somebody. They ought to boot you out of here."

"I was outnumbered at least ten to one. The way that mob was forming, it could have been twenty or thirty to one in no time. And you blame me for what happened?"

"You assaulted two students for no reason. You resorted to violence."

"What about those goons in the black hoods who wanted to bust me up?"

"Fascism should be resisted by all available means."

"You're a cop!" Jake said, frustration making his voice rise. "Those Antifa kids hate you, too!"

"Authority figures or not, some of us are on the right side of history," Granderson said with a sneer.

The chief's door opened.

"Jake? You're still here? Go back to the dorm! Don't you have studying to do?"

Jake thought about the book he had tossed aside to go to the aid of the young woman named Annie. That had been a mistake, all right. He should have stuck with the socialistic drivel.

He held up his hands and said, "I'm going, I'm going."

"Do I need to have an officer escort you back to Olmsted Hall?"

"No, I'll be all right."

"I'm more worried about anybody you happen to run into."

"No trouble, I swear," Jake said.

McRainey didn't look convinced, but he didn't say anything as Jake left the building, and neither did Granderson.

The night was still warm and pleasant. As Jake walked along concrete paths, under trees, past stately old brick buildings instead of the chrome-and-glass monstrosities found in so many other places, he could almost believe he had been transported back in time to a college the way it used to be . . . or the way it was in movies, anyway. He almost expected to run into some blond ingenue.

Instead, when he was in a particularly dark, shadow-filled stretch of sidewalk, two shapes stepped out in front of him and brought him to an abrupt stop. Some faint sounds from behind told him the jaws of the trap had just closed on that side, as well.

"Hello, fellas," Jake said. "Are you the campus patrol, come to see that I get back to my dorm safely?"

A muffled voice, disguised even more by whispering, said, "Shut up."

"Got the hoods on, don't you? I don't get it. If you think you're standing up for what's right, why not show your faces? Why not take credit for being on the right side of history?"

"Earlier, that was a show for the cell phones," the spokesman rasped. "Those videos are already up on social media and have tens of thousands of views. The big bad alt-right warrior brought down by the people."

"Brought down by a bunch of volts of electricity, you mean."

The hooded figure ignored the comment and went on, "This is for keeps now. We don't want your kind here, Nazi. And if it takes putting you in the hospital to make you leave, we'll do it."

"I'm not a Nazi or a fascist," Jake snapped. "Go

buy a damn dictionary. The Nazis were socialists. *Your* side."

"A convenient lie."

"Study some history, you damn fool! Or go on spouting your precious narrative, I don't care. Just get out of my way."

"Not this time." The man chuckled under the hood. "You see, we're not kids playing at being revolutionaries."

That was true, Jake realized suddenly. He couldn't make out many details in the poor light, but there was something fundamentally different in the way these guys stood and moved. Something . . . *professional.*

Most of the members of the various Antifa groups really were kids. Spoiled, brainwashed, vicious little monsters . . . but still kids.

Jake had read enough about the movement, though, to have come across rumors that within the groups—terrorist cells, if somebody wanted to call them what they really were—individuals had been planted by the liberal billionaires who funded such madness. Men and women with military, paramilitary, and mercenary backgrounds who had done things that would make the kids cry and wet themselves just to think about. They were there to keep the useful idiots in line, to make sure they showed up where they were supposed to and rioted right on cue, and also to take care of any actual dirty business that came up.

Like getting rid of a former army Ranger who, for some reason, they considered more of a threat than he really was. Hell, Jake thought, all he wanted

was to be left alone. If they would do that, he would be alternately disgusted and amused by the kids' antics but would largely ignore them, as long as they ignored him.

But that wasn't to be. These guys were actual threats, and the odds were four to one. Jake was willing to bet they were armed, probably with pipes. Maybe they wouldn't kill him, but they would beat him damn close to the point of death.

They would try, anyway.

"I'm a peaceable man," he said again, under his breath, more to himself than to his enemies.

"What was that?"

"I said, I'm a peaceable man."

Didn't mean anything to the hooded figures. The spokesman snapped, "Get him!"

Chapter 6

The men behind him closed in first. Jake had to turn to meet their attack, which cost him a fraction of a second.

But he was fast enough to overcome that and darted aside from the pipe that streaked down toward his head with deadly force. It almost got his shoulder, which could have been disastrous, but it barely missed and raked down the outside of his upper right arm instead.

The hooded men hadn't been lurking here in the shadows, waiting for him, just so they could beat him up. They meant to kill him. Just because he hadn't eagerly swallowed and regurgitated their line of political bull. "Wrongthink" was a capital offense in their minds.

Well, despite his promise to Frank McRainey, Jake was in no mood right now to pull any punches himself.

The man who had just tried to crack his skull open was off balance because the blow had missed. As he stumbled forward a little, Jake kicked him in the right kneecap and heard the bone pop. The man screeched in pain under the hood. Jake gave him a hard, two-handed shove in the chest that sent him flying back into his partner.

In a continuation of the same move, Jake launched himself off the sidewalk, hit the grass, somersaulted over, and came up on his feet again. That took him out of easy reach of the two who had been in front of him, including the spokesman for the attackers.

They were still close, though, and they came at him fast, veering apart to come at him from different angles. Jake could tell by the way they moved that they'd had some training, maybe military, maybe police academy. Or else their group, funded by liberal money, had paid somebody with experience to teach them a few things.

Jake went down again, used a leg sweep to take one man's legs out from under him, and rolled to avoid the pipe wielded by the other one. He came up, blocked an attempted backhand with his right forearm, and hammered his left fist into the hooded face.

The guy's head rocked back. Jake stepped in, slid his right arm under the man's right arm, got his left hand on the elbow, and broke it with a hard, pinching twist. The man said, "Ahhh!" and dropped the pipe. It thudded to the ground at Jake's feet.

He dived again and snatched up the fallen pipe as he rolled over. He brought it up just in time to block another swipe. The pipes clanged together loudly. Would that be enough to make somebody call the campus cops and report it? Jake didn't know, and he didn't want to wind up in McRainey's office yet again tonight, so he figured it would be best to wrap this up quickly.

The two men he still faced might have something to say about that, however. Broken Kneecap and Broken Elbow were out of the fight, but their comrades swarmed Jake as he scrambled to his feet, slashing with the pipes they held. He was forced to give ground, as for a moment it was all he could do to block the blows aimed at him. The pipes rang together like an anvil chorus.

One of the blows got through and slammed against Jake's side. Pain exploded through him. He didn't think it broke a rib, but it hurt like hell, that was for sure, and made him stumble. Both attackers surged forward to seize this momentary advantage.

Jake's back bumped against something, stopping him. One of the trees in Nafziger Plaza, he realized. In a way, he was grateful for that. It protected his back, so one of the hooded men couldn't circle and try to come at him from that direction.

And it meant that this was where he would make his stand. His lips drew back from his teeth in a grimace.

"Come on, you sons of bitches," he said.

They redoubled their attack, but that frenzied effort proved to be a mistake. As much as anything else, they got in each other's way, and during the split second when they were trying to recover from that awkwardness, Jake sensed as much as saw an opening and lashed out with the pipe in his hand.

It landed on a man's right shoulder and brought a cry of pain. Jake flicked the pipe up and to the right in a short, sharp backhand that traveled only a few inches but packed enough force to break the man's jaw. Jake heard bone crunch under the impact. It was a satisfying sound.

As the injured man sagged, Jake kicked his feet out from under him. The man toppled over into his companion, just as Jake intended. That man shoved Broken Jaw away and started to retreat. In fact, the sudden prospect of an even fight didn't seem to appeal to him at all.

He turned and ran.

Jake could have let him go, but that thought never occurred to him. He took off after the guy.

They had surrounded him like jackals eager to pull down a helpless victim and feast.

But not all "victims" were helpless. And they weren't even victims.

They were hunters and killers.

The fleeing man hadn't reached the sidewalk when Jake left his feet in a flying tackle from behind his quarry. He crashed into the man and brought him down. Both of them landed hard. The jolt sent fresh explosions of pain from Jake's battered side through the rest of his body.

The man had tried to escape, but that didn't mean all the fight had gone out of him. He brought an elbow back and around and slammed it against Jake's jaw. That gave him enough wiggle room to squirm free.

When he had a little distance between them, he aimed a kick at Jake's face. Jake saw it coming and grabbed the man's foot, stopping the kick before it could land. He gave the foot a hard wrench that forced the man to roll over.

Jake tried to pounce on the man's back. If he

could get the guy in a sleeper hold, this fight would be over in a hurry. The man kept moving, though, and avoided Jake's dive. This time the kick he pistoned out landed on Jake's upper left arm and twisted him around. That arm went numb for a moment and hung uselessly from his shoulder, so he couldn't use it to block the blow when the man clubbed both hands together and swung them with stunning force at Jake's head.

The two-handed blow caught him above the left ear and stretched him out. It was a good thing his skull was so thick, he thought vaguely as he tried to recover. Before he could do so, the man landed on him and dug a knee into his belly. That didn't do any damage to the slabs of muscle there, but it did force the air from Jake's lungs and disorient him a little more.

He got his right hand up, planted it on the man's face. The hand slid because of the hood. Jake dug his fingers into it and ripped upward. The hood came off.

The shadows in the plaza were so thick Jake still couldn't see his enemy's face, but he could feel the guy's hot breath panting on him now. He threw the hood aside, grabbed the man's hair at the back of his head, and jackknifed his body in the middle so he could head-butt the guy in the face. Cartilage crunched and blood spurted as the man's nose flattened under the impact.

That stunned him enough for Jake to grab his shoulders and fling him aside. Both of Jake's arms were working well enough now that he was able to grab the man's right leg and lever it up until something gave with a sharp snap. The man let out a thin shriek of agony that Jake choked off with a hand around his throat.

Jake hovered over him and increased the pressure. The man was in too much pain from his broken or dislocated hip to fight back anymore, but the lack of air and the desperate need to breathe made him spasm ineffectively.

"I could kill you right now, you know that, don't you?" Jake said in a hoarse half-whisper. "All it would take to crush your windpipe is a little more pressure. Then I could walk away and you'd lay there and suffocate, and there wouldn't be a damn thing you could do to stop it."

Instead of doing that, Jake eased up a little. The man gasped in some air.

Then used it to rasp, "F-Fascist!"

Jake squeezed again.

"Are you really that stupid? You think a real fascist, a real Nazi, would let you live right now? I've been listening to you idiots for years now, yammering about how any politician you don't like is literally Hitler. When all along it's been *your* side that's been acting like the brownshirts and going after anybody who doesn't agree with you! Free speech! But only if it's speech you approve of, speech that fits your precious narrative! Anything else gets shut down, with violence if need be. Hell, you like the violence. Makes you feel big and powerful. Punching Nazis feels great . . . only *you're* the Nazis." Jake lifted the guy's head by the throat and banged it against the ground. "Are you listening to me? Damn it, you've got me so mad I'm the one who's yammering now. So just listen to this: if the other side was as bad as you believe it is, if we *wanted* death camps, then by God, we'd have death camps by now. But we're still willing to live and let live, if you'll just let us. If you won't . . . well, do you want a civil war? Because that's how you get a civil war. And it won't be nearly as much fun as you think it will be."

The guy wasn't struggling anymore. Jake didn't know whether he'd heard all of that. He was a little disgusted with himself for running off at the mouth that way. But his side hurt, and he was frustrated and angered by the sheer stupidity and cognitive dissonance of almost everything he had seen and heard since coming to Kelton College.

Then he hoped he hadn't killed the guy. He wouldn't lose any sleep over it—the four hooded men had been trying to kill him, after all, and he felt justified in using deadly force against them in return. But if this one, or any of the others, were dead, it could sure as hell turn out to be a hassle.

He let go of the man's neck and was relieved to hear the rough breaths in his throat. Jake stood up and looked around. The plaza remained dark and quiet. The fight hadn't been loud enough to make anybody call the cops. That was good, because Jake didn't think he could stomach another encounter with Cal Granderson tonight.

He went to the other three men who were sprawled here and there and bent over to yank the hoods off their heads, too. They were all breathing. A couple had passed out, but one was still conscious and whimpering in pain.

"Don't . . . don't hurt me," he begged.

"Don't try to bully somebody who's willing and able to fight back," Jake told him. "Better yet, don't bully anybody. People have a right to believe whatever they want to believe."

"S-social justice—"

"Is bull. There's just justice. And sometimes it's a bitch, just like karma."

Jake walked off and left the man there sobbing.

He took deep breaths as he walked along the sidewalk in front of the library. The place was closed by now, although some lights were still lit over its long, columned porch. Jake took inventory of his condition. The twinges he felt as he inhaled told him he might have bruised ribs—he definitely had bruised muscles—but he didn't believe anything was broken. He worked his shoulders. Sore but good to go there, too. The damage he had taken in the fight was minimal, he decided.

That thought was running through his mind when someone stepped out from behind one of the columns on the library porch and said, "I saw what you did back there."

Chapter 7

Jake stopped short. Instantly, he took in several details about the person who had just spoken to him, enough that he was reasonably sure he wasn't about to be under attack again. Although he couldn't be certain about that, he reminded himself. After all, women could be dangerous, too.

Even women as attractive as this one. Maybe *especially* women as attractive as this one. A guy might stand there thinking about how hot she was and never even realize she was about to kill him.

But in this case, she didn't make any threatening moves. She just stood there with her hands in the hip pockets of the jeans she wore and looked at him. It was a casual stance, but it might have been calculated to make her breasts stand out a little more prominently against the shirt she wore. If that was the case, it worked.

The hair that tumbled around her shoulders shone reddish-gold in the light. Jake couldn't see her eyes, but he was willing to bet they were brown. A deep, rich brown.

He didn't need to be thinking about that. Other things were more important.

"Are you going to take out your phone and call the cops?" he asked.

"Would you try to stop me if I did?" she asked.

He shook his head.

"That would be entirely up to you. I'd like to point out, though, that I'm the one who was attacked, and there were four of them against one of me. If that's not self-defense—"

"The same situation as earlier this evening, right?" she interrupted him. "When you allegedly assaulted those two students and then got into a fight with the Antifa patrol?"

"Patrol?" Jake repeated scornfully.

"That's what they say they're doing, patrolling the campus for any signs of extremist, right-wing aggression and oppression."

Jake snorted.

"They must not stay very busy. How many people on this campus aren't progressive idiots? A dozen? Two dozen? I'd say we're all outnumbered." He paused. "And I apologize if you're a progressive idiot."

"You're an obnoxious young man, aren't you? In addition to being a violent one."

"I speak my mind too bluntly sometimes, I suppose. Free speech," Jake added dryly. "As for the violence, I'm as peaceful as a kitten as long as nobody backs me into a corner."

"But then you fight to win, no matter what it takes."

Jake shrugged.

"Never saw any point in being any other way."

For a long moment, she regarded him in silence,

standing at the edge of the porch with six broad steps between her and Jake on the sidewalk. Then she said, "I'm not going to call the campus police."

"Appreciate that."

"You're already liable to be in enough trouble from the earlier altercation, even though it wasn't your fault."

"You admit that?"

"I know those two—Craig and Annie—and their relationship is fraught with drama, as the literature professors might say. They fight and break up and get back together almost daily. The real problem is, Craig actually is abusive, and Annie is a textbook example of an enabler. I've talked to her, tried to get her to see that, but it hasn't done any good." A sad smile touched her lips. "These students consider themselves so progressive and forward-thinking and woke, but a lot of the time they're just like young people have always been, making foolish choices about whose pants they're going to get into."

"You sound awfully world-weary and cynical for somebody who's pretty young, herself."

"I'm older than you," the woman said.

Jake shrugged.

"By six or seven years, maybe. I'm Jake Rivers, by the way."

"I know who you are. You're not exactly the run-of-the-mill Kelton College student. There are rumors among the faculty that you must be related to some big donor, but nobody seems to know exactly who it is, or if they do, they're keeping it to themselves."

"You're a professor?"

"Criminal justice. Dr. Natalie Burke."

"I'd say that you don't look like a criminal justice professor—"

"But that would be sexist, exclusionary, patriarchal, and oppressive," she said sternly. "Haven't you read the speech guide?"

"I looked at it," Jake hedged. "I was more interested in the sexual-conduct guidelines."

"Yes, well, we don't have to worry about that. And you even bringing that up is harassment, you know."

Jake held up both hands, palms out.

"I surrender, Doctor. What can I say, I'm an evil cisnormative heterosexual. I can't help myself." He smiled. "Say, does that mean I'm mentally ill? That cuts me some slack. I'm a disadvantaged, oppressed minority. On *this* campus, for damn sure."

Dr. Burke laughed. She looked a little ashamed of herself for doing so but couldn't seem to help it. She slipped her phone from one of the hip pockets of her jeans.

"I'm terrible. I should have already gotten help for those poor young men you attacked. That's the way they're going to spin it, you know. They'll tell anyone who'll listen that it was all your fault."

"My word against theirs," Jake said. "Assuming nobody comes forward to back up their story."

She held up the phone.

"What about video evidence?"

"It'll just show for sure that I was defending myself, assuming it actually exists."

"It doesn't," Dr. Burke admitted. "And I was the last one out of the library tonight and had other things on my mind, so I didn't notice exactly what happened. All I can testify to is that I found those injured men in the plaza and called 911. And that's what I'm going to do . . . now."

"Good night, Doctor," Jake said.

"Good night, Mr. Rivers."

He walked a few more yards to another sidewalk that cut across the plaza to Olmsted Hall. When he glanced back, Dr. Natalie Burke wasn't in sight. The trees must be hiding her, as the porch columns had earlier.

He was a little confused. It had seemed at times as if the woman was actually flirting with him. If that was true, it was one hell of an odd time and place for her to be doing that. At the same time, she had been right about one thing: despite everything else swirling around them, political tomfoolery and the like, people still had universal emotions and were driven by them at times.

And she had said that she taught in the criminal justice department, he recalled. Maybe she wasn't *quite* as caught up in the so-called progressive movement as some. Then, remembering how he had read where some criminal justice experts always blamed society for creating the predators, or the victims for being preyed upon, and he wasn't so sure again.

The whole encounter had him baffled. Maybe she would throw him under the bus, maybe she wouldn't, but either way, there was nothing he could do about it now.

He used his keycard on the front door of Olmsted Hall and went inside without encountering anyone else. It was late enough that the lobby was deserted and nobody was behind the desk. At this time of night, everybody was studying, sleeping, killing time on the Internet, or having sex . . . following the proper guidelines, of course.

Jake went up to the second floor. Only a few hours had passed since he heard the frightened cry through the open window and went out into the night, but it seemed much longer to him. He pulled his T-shirt over his head, tossed it on the bed, and went into the bathroom. The mirror revealed large bruises on his side, shoulders, and arms. He looked like he had been through a fifteen-round fight. Getting whacked with lead pipes would do that.

He went back over to the desk and picked up the book he was supposed to read for his economics class. After everything that had happened, forcing himself to concentrate on it wasn't easy, but he gave it a shot.

After a few minutes of trying to digest the turgid, academic writing that had the evils of capitalism as its central thesis, he was almost wishing he was getting hit by lead pipes again. It might not hurt his brain as much.

CHAPTER 8

The confrontation between Jake and the Antifa "patrol" was big news for a couple of days. It was all over the Internet and the cable news channels, and the various cell phone videos shot by people in the almost-mob got millions of views in total, on all the different social media platforms. In almost all the news stories, Jake was referred to as "alt-right," "far right-wing," "extremist," "white supremacist," "Nazi," or accused of being a member of the KKK—even though the trouble had had no racial component whatsoever. The fight with fists, pipes, and chains was hysterically headlined as a "mass shooting" by one of the Boston papers. *The New York Times* decried the "right-wing brutality," while sneeringly implying that such was to be expected because, after all, Kelton College was in *Texas*, and everybody knew what sort of presidential candidates those *Texans* voted for.

With all of that going on, it was no surprise that reporters were waiting for Jake as soon as he stepped out the front door of Olmsted Hall one morning. He was big enough that he could shoulder his way through the crowd without having to stop and say anything. He was extremely careful how he did it, though. The tiniest action that could be construed as the least bit aggressive would be portrayed as the violent attack of an alt-right lunatic against a free press.

But there wasn't a single word about the four men Jake had left scattered around Nafziger Plaza in various states of injury, at least not that he saw or heard. Maybe the Kelton College administration had hushed up that incident for some reason that was beyond Jake at the moment.

As it was, he had more than enough unwanted attention. It made it difficult for him to get to class, and once he was there, he had trouble concentrating because the other students, and usually the professors, as well, were staring at him with a mixture of fascination and fear. He was like some exotic zoo animal, he thought. They lived in such a philosophical and political bubble that they couldn't even begin to comprehend how someone could fail to share their views on everything.

And that exotic animal comparison was apt in another way, because they all seemed to be worried that he would attack and try to rip their throats out for no reason, with no warning.

The twenty-four-hour news cycle's insatiable thirst for fresh content meant that some new, outrageous story would be along soon, and so it was in this case, and three celebrity sexual harassers, two corrupt congressmen (both Democrats, although little mention of that was made), and a transsexual beauty queen of color later, nobody cared about that right-wing barbarian Jake Rivers anymore. Jake was glad of that.

Then he received an email telling him to be at President Andrew Pelletier's office for an appointment at ten o'clock the next morning. The email further advised him that he could be accompanied by legal counsel if he so chose. Jake did not choose to do so. Whatever boom they wanted to lower on him, he didn't much care. If they kicked him out, at least he could tell his grandfather that he'd tried to fit in and get the "college experience" the old man wanted him to. And Pelletier and the rest of the administration could deal with whatever fallout that brought from Cordell Gardner.

That's what Jake told himself, anyway, as he walked toward the administration building the next morning. Deep down, though, he bristled at the thought he was going to be punished for something that wasn't his fault.

Nobody ever said the world was fair, though, he reminded himself.

There were no reporters clamoring around this morning, all of them having moved on to other stories, so he noticed when someone stepped up beside him, hurrying to keep up with his long-legged strides.

"You look different this morning," Dr. Natalie Burke said.

"Why?" Jake said. "Because I'm wearing a suit?"

"You look like a professional wrestler pretending to be a businessman before a match."

"Babyface or heel?"

"Oh, you are definitely a babyface, Mr. Rivers."

That made him laugh.

"I wouldn't have pegged you as the sort to watch rasslin'."

"My dad loved it. I watched it with him. It's silly, but entertaining. At its best, almost existential."

"Yeah, I can see how big, sweaty, oiled-up guys throwing each other around is existential. You look different, too, by the way."

"Because I'm wearing a dress?"

"I guess that's it."

"A meeting of the faculty in my department with the department chairman this morning. We have to at least pretend to take it seriously."

"Am I allowed to say you look nice?" Jake asked. "Or is that a microaggression?"

"Coming from someone as big as you, I'm not sure a microaggression is possible. But I'll allow it. Why are you dressed up?"

"I'm getting called on the carpet in the president's office," he said. "I figure they're going to kick me out."

"Really?" She added quickly. "I didn't say anything about what happened the other night, I swear."

Jake slowed to a stop outside the rear entrance to the administration building. The side that faced Nafziger Plaza was actually the back of the building, which fronted on the next street over. He frowned and asked Dr. Burke, "Have you heard anything about those four guys? Anything at all?"

"The ones who jumped you on your way back to the dorm?" She shook her head. "No. Not a thing."

"All of them should have spent at least one night in the hospital. I'd think a couple of them would still be there, maybe more than that. Why didn't the press make a big deal out of it?"

"Because the school wants it kept quiet for some reason?"

"That's the only thing that makes sense, but why would they do that? Liberals never hush up *anything* that might make a conservative look bad."

"Not everything in life breaks down into terms of liberals and conservatives, you know," she said.

"That's right, now it's nice, forward-thinking progressives and evil, extremist fascists."

"Someone has to be forward thinking. If everyone thought backwards, the world wouldn't be a very good place."

"One person's forward is another person's backward."

She smiled.

"That's almost perceptive."

"I mean, I look at Antifa, and I see jackboots and goose-stepping . . ."

Dr. Burke glanced up at the clock set into the administration building tower.

"And I see that I have to hurry or I'll be late for that meeting. It was good talking with you again, Mr. Rivers. If you're still here next semester, maybe you should consider signing up for my course. There might be a career for you in criminal justice."

"I'll think about it," he promised. He stood there and waited while she walked on into the building, for no other reason than he wanted to watch her walk away in that dress. He couldn't get in trouble for just *thinking* about violating the guidelines.

Actually, he probably could, he amended, but

what were they going to do to him because of it? Kick him out? He figured he was gone anyway.

He went into the building and along the main hall to the suite of offices where the president's and vice presidents' offices were located. The secretary behind the desk in the reception office gave him one of those half-fascinated, half-scared looks and said, "I was told that you should go right on in, Mr. Rivers."

Jake smiled and said, "I didn't even tell you who I am. I guess that's not really necessary these days, is it?"

She just smiled weakly back at him and didn't say anything, just pointed along a short, carpeted hallway toward the door at the far end.

Jake opened the door without knocking and went in. The office was fairly large and comfortably furnished but not ostentatious. Several photographs on the wall to Jake's left were of the man who got to his feet behind the desk. In them he was shaking hands with different Democrat politicians, none of them white and/or male. Which the man behind the desk was. Other than the white hair, he bore a faint resemblance to the young Abraham Lincoln, pre-beard. Jake would have bet that Andrew Pelletier enjoyed that resemblance and even cultivated it.

"Mr. Rivers," he said, in the smooth, deep tones of an actor playing a college president. "Come in. Close the door."

Jake glanced around as he eased the door shut behind him. The two of them were alone in the office. He said, "I thought you'd have a couple of vice presidents and the college's legal team here."

Pelletier shook his head.

"No, I just wanted to have a talk with you, man to man."

Jake felt a stirring of concern inside. Maybe he had underestimated this man.

Maybe Pelletier was more dangerous than he had thought.

Chapter 9

"As of right now, there are seventeen lawsuits pending against Kelton College as a result of the incident three days ago," Pelletier said when both of them had sat down. "And I'm told that within the next few days, at least that many will be filed against you personally, Mr. Rivers."

"I didn't do anything wrong," Jake said. "I guess I'll just have to take my chances in court."

Pelletier smiled, but it wasn't a friendly or pleasant expression.

"You have the funds to defend yourself against such a legal barrage?"

"Well . . . no, I don't suppose I do."

"So you're counting on your grandfather to help you."

Jake didn't say anything. He didn't want to get the old man mixed up in this, but that might be unavoidable.

"We're going to settle the lawsuits," Pelletier went on after a moment. "The college's lawyers assure me that this will cost less in the long run than fighting them." His lip curled in an expression of distaste. "Besides, to be honest, I don't have the stomach to defend the actions of a person like you, Mr. Rivers."

Jake leaned forward and frowned.

"A person like me?" he repeated. "What do you mean by that, sir?" He figured he already knew the answer, but he thought he might as well go ahead and make Pelletier say it.

"I find your attitude and actions repellent and reprehensible, young man. Kelton College is supposed to be a haven of learning for all students, regardless of ethnicity, national origin, gender, lifestyle, or philosophy. We value diversity and a welcoming inclusivity. This entire campus is a safe space, if you will. And then *you* . . ." Pelletier looked like he wanted to spit. "You come in here with your far-right, nationalist, patriarchal, sexist, bigoted, supremacist leanings and make our entire student body and faculty extremely uncomfortable."

"Now hold on just a minute!" Jake couldn't hold in his anger, even though he suspected the college president was trying to goad him into losing control. "You can't be saying that I'm the only student enrolled here who's not some whiny little snowflake!"

Pelletier sniffed.

"Name-calling will gain you absolutely nothing, young man. Any other students who share some of your oppressive and unacceptable beliefs at least have the sense not to give voice to them where they would offend the sensibilities of other, more correct-thinking students and faculty."

"So the right of free speech only extends to liberals?"

The older man waved that off.

"This isn't the time or place to argue the wisdom or even the necessity of a constitution put into place by white slaveholders. I'm saying that I've received a number of complaints about you, Mr. Rivers, even before this latest incident. Your wild-eyed raving has disturbed many of our faculty and students."

"Wild-eyed raving?" Jake sounded astonished—because he was. Ever since he had arrived on campus, started his classes, and realized what sort of place Kelton was, he had bitten his tongue and held in what he wanted to say many more times than he could count.

Pelletier picked up a piece of paper from the desk in front of him, looked at what was evidently a list printed on it, and said, "You were heard to cast doubt on the validity of Keynesian economics."

"I'm taking an econ class. We're supposed to discuss things like that."

"You told another student that in your opinion, all lives matter."

"Are you saying they don't?"

Pelletier ignored that question and went on, "You claimed to be proud of your military service."

"Why wouldn't I be? This modern army isn't always what I wish it was, but what's wrong with serving your country and being proud that you did?"

Pelletier didn't answer that one, either. Instead he glared at Jake and said, "In a history class, you expressed admiration for Ronald Reagan."

"I said he was a lot better president than a lot of the bozos who came after him. Do students give up the right to have an opinion when they go to school here?"

"Of course not!" Pelletier bristled. "As long as—"

"As long as they're the *right* opinions," Jake broke in. "The politically correct opinions. The ones that fit your precious narrative."

Pelletier slapped the paper back down on the desk.

"Young man! You will *not* speak to me in such a disrespectful tone, do you understand? I am still the president of this college!"

Jake drew in a deep breath so sharply that his nostrils flared. He sat there until his hands unclenched from fists and his pulse wasn't hammering quite so hard in his head. Then he said, "I apologize, sir. You're right. I should respect the office."

"But not the man," Pelletier snapped. He made another curt gesture. "Never mind. Let's get down to business. I want you to withdraw from this institution."

"You're kicking me out for no good reason except you don't like my politics? I think I could fight *that* with a lawsuit!"

"You've violated our code of conduct in numerous ways." Pelletier lifted his chin and sniffed again. "I think we would be perfectly justified in expelling you, and any court would agree with our action. However, I would prefer that you withdraw of your own accord."

Jake sat back and grinned.

"You're trying to keep my grandfather from getting too upset with you. You don't want to lose all the donations he makes to the school."

"I have the utmost respect for Cordell Gardner—"

"And even more respect for his money." Jake

paused and thought for a second, then went on, "If I withdraw, you can tell my grandfather it was my own decision. Then you can turn around and imply to all the people suing you that you forced me out, in the hope of getting more favorable terms when you settle those suits. You're trying to play it both ways."

Pelletier glared but didn't deny the accusation. Instead, he said, "Are you going to withdraw or not, Mr. Rivers?"

"Not," Jake said. "I'll stick it out."

"Very well," Pelletier said, clearly not pleased with the decision. "You'll get no support from this institution in dealing with your own legal problems. We're washing our hands of you."

"Careful," Jake said. "That's a Biblical reference. Remember what Pilate said when the Jews asked him what to do about Jesus? You wouldn't want anybody to accuse you of being a Christian. That's a dirty word these days, isn't it?"

"We're done here."

"Yeah, I think we are." Jake got to his feet and started to turn toward the door, then stopped. "What about those other four guys?"

"What four . . . guys? What are you talking about?"

"The fight in the plaza."

"When you attacked that young couple and then fought with that group of peaceful bystanders?"

Peaceful bystanders? A bunch of hooded goons with chains and pipes?

Clearly, though, Pelletier was talking about what had happened earlier in the evening, not the clash when Jake was on his way back to Olmsted Hall from Frank McRainey's office. And he seemed genuinely puzzled, as well.

But why make things worse for himself, Jake thought. Maybe, despite the fact that he had thought them incapable of it, those four sons of bitches had been able to haul themselves off after all. In that case, as long as Natalie Burke hadn't reported it, it was possible nobody else knew about that second fight, and there wasn't a cover-up after all. Might as well let it stay that way, he decided.

"Never mind," Jake said. "If there's nothing else, sir, I have a class in twenty minutes."

"You're determined to remain enrolled here?"

"Yes, sir, I am."

"Then please try not to cause any more trouble."

"I never set out to cause it," Jake said. "But I'm not going to run away from it, either."

"Good Lord. You sound like John Wayne."

Jake grinned and said, "I'll take that as a compliment," as he opened the office door and went out.

CHAPTER 10

Matthias Foster peered over the sights of the heavy double-action revolver in his hand and squeezed the trigger. The gun boomed and the heavy recoil tried to make the barrel rise up, but Foster's strong, two-handed grip controlled it. He fired again, fast but not rushing, then again.

The target, set up twenty yards away in front of a thick barrier of earth and wooden beams, showed three holes, grouped close together a bit low and left from the bull's-eye.

Foster lowered the revolver onto the wooden counter in front of him where a number of other pistols—some revolvers and some semi-automatics—lay waiting. He knew he might well be trusting his life to some of these weapons, whether he held them or not, so he intended to check the sights and firing mechanisms of all of them.

He left the protective, wraparound plastic goggles on but lowered the ear protectors so they wrapped around his neck from behind.

"This one just needs a little adjustment to the sights," he told the woman who stood beside him holding a tablet. Using a stylus, she made a note on the screen. She wore custom earbuds with speakers built into them, as well as noise-suppression circuitry, so her ears were protected from the sound of guns going off but she could still hear what her companion was saying without removing the buds.

"We've been at this for a while, Matthias," she said.

A smile appeared on his handsome face.

"Preparation, my dear Lucy. Proper preparation is the key to success. Forgive me for sounding like a motivational speaker."

He didn't look like a motivational speaker. He wore jeans and a faded blue work shirt with the sleeves rolled up over wiry but strong-looking forearms. His head was topped by a shock of wavy brown hair. In an earlier day, he would have been considered movie-star handsome. His deep tan testified that he spent a lot of time outside. He could have been a farmer or ranch hand. His voice was deep, powerful, cultured, with a touch of the didactic about it.

"Of course," the woman called Lucy replied. "But we have other things to do to get ready, too, besides just testing guns."

"You're right," Foster agreed. "We have other powerful weapons on our side. Our brains"—he touched his forehead—"and our hearts." His fingertips rested for a second on his chest. "Those are a higher caliber than any mechanical weapon we might employ, and we must test them as well." He laughed. "God, I sound pretentious at times, don't I?"

Lucy smiled and said, "Some people respond to that."

"True. And it's also true that, facing such a great undertaking as we are, we need to test our resolve." He was looking past her as he said it. "Here comes such a test now."

Lucy turned and gazed along the dirt road that led to the outdoor shooting range nestled in the Central Texas hills. A cloud of dust rose from the road as a vehicle approached. This range was on private property and the entrance was guarded, so no one could be driving along that road who wasn't supposed to be here. Even so, a tiny shiver of apprehension went through her.

The vehicle, a nondescript white SUV with a layer of grime on it, came into sight. As it came closer, Foster gestured toward the tablet in Lucy's hand and said, "Tell Khaled to get to work on those as soon as he can."

"Of course. Would you like me to go, Matthias?"

He shook his head.

"No, stay here. You might find this interesting."

Lucy set the tablet on the long, open-air counter that was covered by a metal roof supported by wooden posts. She and Foster both turned toward the SUV as it came to a stop twenty yards away. Lucy reached up and started to take the earbud out of her right ear, but Foster stopped her.

"Leave them in," he said. "You might need them again later."

Lucy looked puzzled but shrugged in acceptance of what he said.

Four men got out of the SUV and walked toward them. All were in their twenties: one black, one Hispanic, two white. All wore the same sort of casual clothes as Foster and Lucy. The black guy and one of the white guys wore sunglasses, as well. The other white guy and the Hispanic had gotten out of the SUV's backseat.

"Jimmy, Hank," Foster greeted the two in sunglasses with a nod, then smiled at the other two. "Carlos, Ben."

Ben, a rangy young man with blond hair, grinned. "We here to get in some target practice, Matthias?"

"That's right," Foster answered. "We need to be sure that everybody can handle what's expected of them, once we get this thing started. There won't be any turning back, you know."

"Nobody wants to turn back," Ben said. "We're all committed to the cause, aren't we, guys?" He turned his head to look at the three young men who had come out here with him.

"Sure we are," the black guy, Jimmy, said. "The only way to stop those fascists from taking over the country and ruining it is to fight back against them with something they'll understand."

"Force," Carlos said. "The same sort of oppression they deal out to us."

"You know they'd put us all in death camps if they thought they could get away with it," Hank added.

Ben nodded and said, "Sure they would. Racist, sexist, homophobic bigots, that's all they are. Every single one of them. If you're not part of the solution, you're part of the problem."

Foster laughed.

"That's an old, old line, buddy. Where'd you read that?"

"It was in one of your posts online, wasn't it?" Ben asked with a frown.

"You know what, maybe it was. I say so many things, it's hard to keep track of them. And you know what they say, there's truth behind every cliché."

Ben turned toward the range counter with the guns spread out on it.

"So let's do some shooting."

"Hold on, hold on," Foster said as he held up a hand. Still smiling, he went on, "I need to ask you about something first."

"Sure. Just don't ask me if I'm committed, because I am. I am ready to go through with this, I give you my word on that."

"So I can trust you?" Foster asked.

"Absolutely. One hundred percent."

"Then I know you'll tell me the truth when I ask you why you drove into Austin last night."

Ben frowned a little.

"You didn't say we couldn't. We're supposed to go on about our business normally until the time comes, right?"

"That's not exactly an answer."

"Well, I just needed to buy a few things, that's all. There are more places to shop in Austin than there are in Greenleaf."

"You went to a shopping center, all right," Foster said, "but you didn't go into any of the stores."

Ben was starting to look angry now.

"How the hell do you know that? Have you been having me *followed*, Matthias? I thought you trusted all of us. You wouldn't have brought us in on this if you didn't."

"I do trust you. I trust you to tell me who that guy was you met in the parking lot, and what was on that flash drive you gave him."

"I don't know what you're talking about," Ben said with a stubborn shake of his head. "I didn't meet some guy, and I didn't give anybody a flash drive."

"Really?" Foster reached in his pocket, took something out, and flipped it through the air to Ben, who reached up and caught it instinctively. He lowered his hand, opened it, and stared at the little flash drive in his palm. Foster went on, "Sorry if it's a little sticky. It got some blood on it."

Lucy's eyes widened. She took half a step back toward the counter with the guns on it and said, "Matthias, what . . . what is this?"

He lifted a hand toward her gently.

"Nothing for you to worry about," he said in reassuring tones. "I'm just trying to find out how loyal Ben is to the rest of us."

"You know damn well I'm loyal," Ben said angrily. He waved his left hand toward the counter. "Didn't I help you get some of those guns right there? Didn't I put my own ass on the line by delivering drugs for you?"

"Weed," Foster said with a scornful note in his voice. "Hell, in some states what you did wasn't even illegal, man."

"Getting those untraceable guns was."

"And I appreciate it. We all do. But I still want to know about that flash drive. It's encrypted, so we couldn't get into it . . . yet . . . but we'll crack it sooner or later, if I decide to go to that much trouble. Not sure that would be worth it, since I've got a hunch there are a bunch of names on there. My name, and Hank's and Jimmy's and Carlos's. Maybe even pretty little Lucy's. What about it, Ben?"

"I still don't know what you're talking about. I don't know what else to tell you, Matthias."

"All right." Foster laughed and spread his hands. "What the hell. Whatever's on that drive, it can't hurt us, and neither can the guy who had it. So it's all moot, right? You're still with us. If you'd really betrayed us, you'd be in the wind by now. You wouldn't have come out like this. You don't have the stones for that, my friend. No offense."

Ben grunted.

"Yeah, I think maybe I *am* offended. But I don't care. You've gotten things mixed up, Matthias, and you'll realize that sooner or later."

"Maybe. Yeah, I'm sure you're right." Foster turned to the counter, picked up a 9mm semi-automatic pistol, and tossed it to Ben. "There you go. Let's see what you can do with that target practice you were talking about."

Ben had caught the pistol deftly. With practiced ease, he thumbed the button in the side of the weapon, dropped the magazine from the butt, and looked at it to be sure it was loaded. He slid it back into place, pulled the slide back to eject the round that was in the chamber, and then let it go back forward to load another round.

Then he stepped over to the counter to face the targets, but he stood there only for a second before he turned quickly and pointed the gun at Lucy's head. She gasped in surprise and fear and took a step back.

"Drop them now!" Ben said. "All the guns you've got on you, throw them on the ground! I'll kill her! I will!"

None of the other men seemed surprised. Foster, in fact, was smiling as he shook his head and said, "No, you won't. You're one of the good guys, Ben. FBI, Homeland . . . Hell, maybe even a Texas Ranger. You're not just about to shoot some innocent girl in the head, and we all know it."

Ben grimaced and swung the gun toward Foster. He jerked the trigger.

Nothing happened.

"A gun being loaded doesn't do any good if the firing mechanism has been disabled," Foster said. "You should have checked that, too."

Wide-eyed with sudden terror, Ben threw the inoperative pistol aside and tried to twist toward the other guns on the counter. Before he could reach any of them, Jimmy, Hank, and Carlos opened fire with the pistols they had drawn from under their shirts. The bullets, some .45 caliber and some 9mm, plowed into Ben's back and pitched him forward. He fell short of the counter and lay on his face, twitching as blood pumped from the holes in his back. The spasms lasted for maybe ten seconds and then stopped.

Foster hadn't fired a weapon of his own. He stepped over to Lucy, who was pale and shaken, and lifted a hand to cup her chin as he smiled.

"I'm sorry about that," he said. "But you know I never would have let him hurt you."

"I was . . . bait," she said.

"Not exactly. He could have tried to shoot any of us. I just wanted him to show his true colors . . . and he did. And now we know." He put his arm around Lucy's shoulders. "Come on. The guys will take care of cleaning this up. You and I can go back to town and leave them to their work."

"Somebody might have heard all those shots."

"It's a shooting range. That's what we do here." Foster smiled. "Target practice."

CHAPTER 11

When Jake answered a knock on the door of his dorm room the evening of his abrasive meeting with President Andrew Pelletier, he was surprised to see his grandfather standing there in the hall. "Cordell," he said, using the old man's first name like he often did, "what are you doing here?"

"I came to see you, of course. And to bail your stubborn ass out of trouble. You gonna let me in?"

Jake stepped back out of the doorway.

"Sure. Come in." Even though he was several inches taller and considerably heavier than his grandfather, he still felt a little intimidated by the old man. "I guess you, ah, heard about the trouble a few days ago."

"Be hard not to," Gardner said as he closed the door behind him. "I don't do that, whatchacallit, social media stuff myself, but everybody who works for me does. You made yourself famous, boy. Or infamous, depending on who's doin' the talking."

"I didn't do anything wrong," Jake said firmly. "I was defending somebody else, at first, and after that I was sticking up for myself. I seem to remember both of my grandfathers telling me that's what

I'm supposed to do. When somebody else starts a fight—"

"You make damn sure you finish it," the old man growled. "Yeah, I can't argue with that. My secretary showed me some of those videos people shot on their phones. You did the right thing, son. Even so, I was gonna let you handle it yourself. Let you navigate those treacherous waters. Figured you'd learn more that way." Gardner swept back the lapels of his Western-cut jacket and hooked his thumbs behind his belt. "But that was before I found out you were about to have a whole swarm of locusts descend on you. Lawyers, I mean."

"Yeah, I figured that out," Jake said with a smile. "They plan on coming in and stripping me clean just like locusts."

Gardner blew out a disparaging breath.

"You don't have a whole lot to be stripped away from you. You're not rich . . . yet."

"I don't care if I ever am," Jake said.

"Spoken like a boy whose family has always had plenty of money."

Jake would have argued with that, just on general principles, but he supposed it was true. His father had been a very successful lawyer in Houston, and they had always had plenty of money, or at least so it seemed. Then drugs, booze, and hookers had leeched off most of the available funds, which revealed just how fragile a foundation the family's finances had been built upon. Seeing his mother go through that was one of the reasons Jake had taken her last name and cut all ties with his father.

He didn't know where the man was now or if he was even still alive, although Jake suspected that Cordell Gardner kept up with his son, disowned or not.

"What do you want?"

The old man laughed harshly.

"You sound like you're not glad to see me."

"I'm always happy to see you, you know that. But *I* know that you're not in the habit of just dropping in on people without a good reason."

"That's true, I suppose," Gardner said with a shrug. "Like I said, I heard rumors you were about to get hit with a bunch of lawsuits. Considering what I saw in that video, I'm not surprised."

"No charges were filed against me," Jake pointed out. "The college didn't even take any real action against me. The president just urged me to withdraw."

"You told him where he could stick that, I imagine."

"Something like that."

"Well, no charges were filed against you because there's too much evidence that you *were* acting in self-defense when that mob of hood-wearin' bullies attacked you. The stuff that came before, the trouble with that fella who was beating up his girlfriend, there doesn't seem to be any footage of that floating around, so it would be hard to prove anything in court. Your word against theirs. But that's why there are civil suits, so things you can't prove in criminal court might get addressed by a jury. The burden of proof's a lot lower, and hell, most civil cases are decided by the emotional state of the people in the jury box, not by the evidence."

"So what do you think I should do?"

Gardner snorted.

"I think you should say thank you to the old man who got you out of this mess. I got some contacts in the county courthouse to look into the matter, found out who was going to file suit against you, and sicced a fleet of lawyers on 'em to make settlement offers. Some accepted the offers right off the bat, and the others got spooked into it when my paper-pushers started playin' hardball. I'm not sayin' that there might not be more crawling out of the wood-work later on, but for now, anyway, it's over."

"Just like that?" Jake stared. "You bought them off?"

"I took the most efficient, least-expensive way in the long run. Oh, there were still some of the little bully boys you gave a thrashin' to who wanted to take you to court and punish the big bad fascist, but once they had some dollar signs dangled in front of their faces, their progressive beliefs faded like a freak dusting of snow in Corpus Christi."

Jake shook his head in amazement. His pride made him say, "I didn't ask you for help, you know."

"I don't sit around waitin' for family to come begging," the old man snapped. "Now, what's this about Pelletier asking you to withdraw?"

Jake waved a hand.

"Forget it. I didn't go along with his suggestion, so it doesn't matter. I'm going to stick it out and get my master's degree."

"Decided you want to finish your education and improve your mind, did you?"

"No, I'm just too damn stubborn to let anybody run me off, especially a bunch of whiny little snowflakes."

That made a grin break out on Gardner's rugged face. He clapped a hand on Jake's upper arm and said, "There you go, boy! I never liked anybody trying to tell me what to do, either."

Jake felt a little awkward about it, but he said, "I do appreciate what you did. Don't get me wrong about that. I would have fought every one of those bastards in court—"

"Damn right."

"But I can't afford much in the way of lawyers. The only thing is . . . Won't they think they beat me, since they took the settlements and got paid?"

"They can think whatever they damn well please. A bunch of pajama boys struttin' around and thinking they're tough doesn't mean a blasted thing to me." Gardner smiled. "And some of them—the most obnoxious of the bunch—are going to get hit with some lawsuits of their own in the next week or so. If they can sue you for defending yourself against them, *you* can sue *them* for attacking you in the first place."

"Won't the settlements make it seem like I was admitting that I was wrong? With that on the record, lawsuits like you're talking about would be hard to win."

"Yeah, they would, if we pressed it. I just want them to get served with that paperwork, see the figure the suit is asking in damages, and dribble down their legs while they're countin' the zeroes."

Jake looked at his grandfather for a moment, then laughed.

"You are a vicious old man."

"How do you think I made so much money?"

Jake didn't answer that. Instead he said, "Why don't we go out and get a beer? You can bring your driver and your bodyguards along."

"Spend the evening in some college hangout? Thanks, but no thanks."

"It's not exactly the malt shop anymore," Jake said.

"Maybe not, but I'll still pass." The old man pointed to the desk, where open books were spread out and a computer and a tablet were both on. "And you've got some studying to do, from the looks of it. Get back to work. I didn't go to all that trouble just to have you flunk out."

"Don't worry about that."

"I'm not. I know you're carryin' a 4.0 average."

"You have spies everywhere, don't you?"

Gardner just grinned, waved, and left the room.

Jake went back to the desk and tried to concentrate on what he'd been working on, but it wasn't easy. He was both relieved and annoyed that his grandfather had stepped in to save him from a barrage of lawsuits that would have sucked up all his time and money and ensured that he wasn't able to continue at Kelton College. His pride was a little wounded, but his practical side knew it was a good thing.

Another knock sounded on the door. Jake pushed

his chair back, stood up, and stepped across the room to open it. He expected to see his grandfather standing there again and said, "Changed your mind about getting that beer, I—"

"Actually, I didn't, because nobody's asked me to go and get a beer," Dr. Natalie Burke said. "But now that you mention it, I think it sounds like an excellent idea."

Chapter 12

Jake didn't want to be impolite and stare, but it was difficult not to do so. Dr. Burke—or rather, Natalie, since *Doctor* sounded too stuffy for somebody who looked like she did—wore a pair of tight, tan jeans and a long-sleeved green silk shirt. Her hair fell in reddish-gold waves around her pretty face.

Still, he didn't want to be rude, so he used her title as he said, "I didn't expect to see you here, Dr. Burke."

"Why? Do you think there's something inappropriate about it? Female students and faculty have to follow the same guidelines as the males, as far as relationships are concerned."

"I didn't know we *had* a relationship, other than being acquainted. And aren't you forgetting about the gender-fluid and all the other two dozen alternative lifestyles?"

She laughed.

"So you *have* read the guidelines."

"Yeah, but I haven't exactly *studied* them rigorously."

"That's all right. If you happen to violate one of

them, someone will let you know, in no uncertain terms. Possibly even with a megaphone."

"And the scarlet letters R, B, S, and H?"

Natalie frowned a little and cocked her head to the side for a second before she understood. Then she said, "Ah. Racist, bigot, sexist, homophobe. You left out C for cishet. You *are* cishet, aren't you?"

"That's what they used to call straight?"

"That's right."

"Then yeah, you can add the C in there." Acting on impulse, he added, "What about that beer? Unless it's frowned upon for faculty and students to fraternize."

"Do you care about being frowned upon?"

Jake shook his head.

"Not really."

"Well, neither do I."

"Let me get my jacket."

Jake didn't much like going out without being armed, especially after the recent troubles. As a private institution, Kelton College had the right under the law to prohibit carrying weapons of all kinds. Public universities, which received tax funds, had to abide by the law of the State of Texas that allowed citizens to bear arms. The news media, the academic world, and the left in general had freaked out over that legislation, shrieking that the state's colleges and universities were going to become the site of frequent bloody shoot-outs.

Of course, that hadn't happened, just as all of the liberals' doomsday predictions about all sorts of things from global warming to the population explosion had failed to come to pass. When a provision was added to the law allowing Texans to carry openly, it was the end of the world as we know it, according to some. People would be blasting away at each other constantly. That couldn't be allowed to happen. Just think of the *children.*

Instead, Jake could count on the fingers of one hand how many times he had seen someone open carrying in normal, day-to-day life. Everyone he knew who had been carrying concealed continued to do so, as he himself did in the places where he was allowed to . . . and where, technically, he wasn't allowed to. With an inside-the-waistband holster and the comfortably fitting shirts he wore, nobody had to know he was armed unless it was necessary.

He also had several small but deadly combat knives he carried on occasion. He knew some older men, including his grandfather, had carried at least a pocketknife every day of their lives for fifty years or more, until the rise of the nanny state and its metal detectors had created too much of a hassle for them.

Jake had a couple of guns in his dorm room. They weren't supposed to be there, but he wanted to have them handy anyway. He didn't try to take one of them with him tonight, though. Instead, as he slipped his jacket on, he felt the comforting weight of the folding knife in one of the pockets. The blade, when it was opened, was a little less than three inches long, but in the hands of an expert—and Jake was an expert—that was more than enough to be deadly.

He smiled at Natalie as he closed the door behind them and started along the hall toward the stairs, which Jake habitually took instead of the elevator, both for the exercise and because he didn't care for tight, enclosed places.

"Where would you like to go?" he asked Natalie.

"The Shamrock is close," she said. "Is that all right with you?"

"Sure," he said. The Shamrock was only a couple of blocks off-campus. It advertised itself as an authentic Irish pub but was really only about as authentic as any bar and grill that was owned by a corporation could be.

Still, it was pleasant enough, or had been the one time Jake was in there, the beer was good, and the bar food wasn't bad. The lighting was subdued enough that it would be nice to sit with Natalie in one of the booths and talk. They were likely to be noticed, but he didn't care for his own sake—he had never been the type to give a damn what anybody thought about him—and since she was the one who'd suggested the place, she was probably all right with that, too.

Jake got beers for them at the bar, and they took them to an empty booth toward the back of the big room laid out around a horseshoe bar. They sat down across the table from each other, and Natalie raised her bottle.

"To a world that will someday be normal again," she said.

"That's an odd toast," Jake said, "but I can't argue with it."

They clinked bottles together and drank.

"If you want normal, though, you're not going to find it on a college campus," he said. "Not these days. If Kelton is any example—and from what I read online, it is—those places are hotbeds of crazy."

Natalie shrugged and said, "They've changed a lot, even in the short time that I've been teaching. Things that seemed over-the-top and ridiculous a dozen years ago are commonplace now."

"You've been teaching a dozen years? I find that hard to believe."

She smiled and said, "Maybe I'm a little older than I look. If you call me a cougar, though, I'll report you for hate speech."

"Wouldn't dream of it," Jake said. To tell the truth, even though she was older than him, they seemed about the same age. He had always been an old soul, his grandfather had told him once. And everything he and his mother had gone through with his father had aged him even more.

"You suddenly look very solemn," Natalie said. "This is supposed to be the banter part of the evening."

"Sorry. I was just thinking about some things. Family, mostly."

She drank some more from the beer bottle and then said, "I know who you are."

Jake cocked an eyebrow and said, "I told you my name, so . . ."

"I should have said, I know who your grandfather is. I told you the first time we met that there are rumors about you, about how you must be related to somebody important. I'd say Cordell Gardner certainly qualifies."

Jake's forehead creased.

"How'd you know about that?"

"I teach criminal justice, remember? You have to know a little about police procedure and how to poke around and find out things."

"I don't like to talk about it," he said, shaking his head. "I don't want people thinking I'm getting breaks or being treated differently because of who my relatives are."

"But you are," Natalie said. "And that's just the way of the world, Jake. People who have more wealth and power, or whose families have more wealth and power, *are* treated differently. Some people who are obsessed with trying to make everything in the world fair don't like that, but there's nothing really they can do about it. They've been trying to for hundreds of years but haven't been able to."

"Maybe so, but I don't have to take advantage of it."

Although that was just what he was doing, Jake thought with a trace of a bitter taste in his mouth that had nothing to do with the beer. He was going to allow his grandfather to make those lawsuits go away, even though it still felt to him like he was admitting that he had done something wrong. The old man was a bottom-line sort of guy, though. The cheapest and most efficient way to accomplish anything was the best way, as far as he was concerned.

"Why don't we change the subject, at least sort of?" Natalie suggested. "Still on family. Tell me about your parents and your brothers and sisters."

"No brothers or sisters. I'm an only child. My father was a lawyer in Houston. My mother . . . well, my mother married my father. I hate to sum up anybody like that, but it's about all you can say about her."

"Is she from Houston as well?"

He shook his head.

"New Orleans. Her father owned a trucking company there that carried freight all over the country. He passed away a long time ago."

"But your folks are still alive?"

"My mother is. I honestly don't know about my father."

Natalie nodded.

"I caught it when you said he *was* a lawyer. What happened?"

Jake gestured with the hand that held the beer bottle.

"Big scandal. He got disbarred because it came out he'd been heavily involved with drugs and had a lot of gambling debts. He was paid off to tank some big cases he worked on. He probably should have been sent to jail, but they wound up just not letting him practice law anymore. My mother divorced him and took back her maiden name. I decided to follow her example. I'd lost all respect for my father, and I didn't want to be carrying around his name. So I got it legally changed and took the name of my maternal grandfather instead. Big Joe Rivers was a good man, for all I've heard about him. I barely remember the man, myself." He scowled across the table. "And how the hell did you get me talking so much about myself? I never do that!"

She smiled and said, "I'm easy to talk to, I guess."

"You are, at that."

"Any other relatives?"

"Determined, aren't you?"

"Nosy."

"Well, you've run up against a brick wall now. My mother had two brothers, but they're both dead. One went nuts and died in an asylum—I know, I'm an insensitive lout, but at least I didn't call it a loony bin—and my other uncle was killed in an explosion."

Natalie raised her eyebrows and said, "An explosion?"

"Yeah. The blast blew up him and his wife. I was too little to know anything about it at the time, but later on I heard rumors that it was mob-related."

"That's terrible."

"I'm sure Uncle Barry and his wife thought so when they got blown up."

"And now *you're* being terrible. I think I've heard enough about your family."

"And I've said more than enough about 'em, that's for sure. Tell me about yours instead."

"My family?" She smiled. "I come from a long line of madmen. We're Irish, you know."

"The best kind of mad," Jake said as he grinned and raised the bottle in his hand.

CHAPTER 13

They split an order of potato skins to go along with the beers they drank—three for Jake and two for Natalie. She really didn't talk much about her family, and he didn't prod her for information. That was her business. Just because he had let down his guard and spilled some of the more sordid details of the Rivers and Gardner clans, that didn't mean she had to do likewise.

She did share some amusing stories about her teaching career, mostly concerning the difficulty of navigating the hazardous waters of academia. Over the past few years, especially, it had gotten more and more difficult to say or do anything without offending somebody.

"I swear, there's a special interest group for *everything*," she said. "And if you do something to upset one of them, then all the others pile on you as well. You wind up with a firestorm on social media."

"A tale told by an idiot, full of sound and fury, signifying nothing," Jake quoted. "That's kind of the way I look at social media most of the time."

"That's a wise approach. I imagine it helps keep you sane."

"Well," Jake said with a smile, "there's probably a lot of debate in some circles about just how sane I really am."

"The administration takes social media very seriously, though, and the news media as well. They can't stand any bad publicity, so if there's very much of an uproar about anything . . . well, they cave, to be blunt about it."

"How does that make the faculty feel?"

Natalie blew out a breath.

"Most of the faculty agree with the professionally outraged. They're part of the whole deal. More than once, I've had faculty members come to me with letters of support they were all signing because of some so-called microaggression against black students or gay students or Muslim students." She laughed, but there wasn't much humor in the sound. "A while back, the Union of African-American Students refused to let students who were actually from Africa join."

Jake frowned.

"Wait. What?"

"That's right. Black students who came here from Africa specifically to go to college at Kelton were told they weren't black enough to join the African-American students' group."

"Well, that's kind of . . . odd."

"Then the Islamic Students' Association demanded that prayer rooms be set aside for them in every building on campus. I can almost understand that one, since they pray at certain times, but they wanted the space in *every* building." Natalie shrugged. "The administration complied, of course, although it wasn't easy. This is an old campus, without much room to spare. But they kicked up a fuss and got what they wanted." She drank some of her second beer. "Then there was the business about the rainbow."

"People are offended by rainbows now?"

"No, no, that wasn't it," Natalie said, raising a finger. "The Gay Students Alliance—well, that's not the official name of the group, that has about a dozen letters in it now, but people call it the Gay Students Alliance—anyway, they painted a rainbow mural on the side of an older building they knew was scheduled to be demolished. Then they demanded that the building be protected and claimed that tearing it down would be a hate crime. It was just a storage building next to the old power plant, and it's in such bad shape that it's not being used for anything anymore. If a strong enough wind came along, it would likely fall down on its own. But now it's a monument to the gay, lesbian, transgender movement, as well as the other stuff that gets lumped in with that these days."

"I suppose the administration went along with that, too."

"Of course," Natalie said. "President Pelletier and the others didn't dare be perceived as anything less than one hundred percent supportive of the movement."

"I guess all people have rights," Jake said with a shrug.

"Certainly they do. Don't get me wrong. I don't want to see anyone being discriminated against.

But they lose their minds over the smallest things, things that were never meant to harm or disadvantage anyone. Like tearing down an old building that's no good to anybody. The alliance knew that was scheduled to happen, so they picked it for their mural just to force a confrontation."

"So it gets them publicity and makes them look like the good guys while the college comes off as heartless and homophobic."

"Exactly. I've seen it happen over and over again. No matter who gets offended over what, they pitch a hissy fit and demand safe spaces."

Jake smiled.

"You know who Audie Murphy was?"

"The name's vaguely familiar," Natalie said with a puzzled frown, "but I can't place it."

"Farm boy from here in Texas. He went off to fight in World War II and wound up as the most decorated soldier in the history of the country. After the war he became an actor, mostly in Western movies. A better actor, generally, than most people gave him credit for."

"What does he have to do with what we're talking about?"

Jake took another drink and smiled.

"When all these college kids started getting upset with everything and demanding safe spaces, I heard somebody say something I've never forgotten: When Audie Murphy was nineteen years old, like a lot of these precious little snowflakes . . . his safe space was behind a .50 caliber machine gun."

"Well, that's cute," Natalie said with a smile of

her own, "but it wouldn't mean anything to the students here. They're opposed to war, most of them have never even touched a gun, let alone fired one, and just the idea of guns makes them feel a little queasy."

"People sleep peacefully in their beds at night only because rough men stand ready to do violence on their behalf."

"Another quote. Orwell, right?"

Jake shrugged.

"He usually gets credit for it, but I believe there's some question about whether or not he actually said it. That doesn't really matter. It's true, whether these kids want to accept it or not."

"These kids," she repeated. "And exactly how old are you, Jake?"

"Twenty-four," he said, then took another pull of the beer. "But my grandfather claims I have an old soul."

"Well, as long as you don't start telling them to keep off your lawn, I suppose you're all right."

"I know I'm kind of out of date," Jake admitted. "I've never cared that much about fitting in, though."

"There's nothing wrong with going your own way. Most people, whether we like to admit it or not, act like sheep a lot of the time."

Jake raised an eyebrow.

"I thought I was supposed to be the cynical one."

"I teach criminal justice, remember? You can't study the kinds of awful things people do to each other in this world without getting a little . . ." She trailed off and shook her head. "Never mind.

This was supposed to be drinks and some light conversation, maybe a little flirting. We didn't set out to solve all the problems of the world."

"Solving the world's problems is above my pay grade," Jake said. "Now, the flirting, that I might be able to handle."

"I'll just bet you can," she said.

By the time they left the Shamrock, Jake was as comfortable with Natalie Burke as he had been with any woman for quite some time. The fact that she was older, and a professor, while he was a graduate student, didn't bother him. As far as he could tell, she wasn't put off by those things, either. After all, he reminded himself, *she* was the one who had shown up at his dorm room tonight. She never had said why she was there, however.

He knew he was risking things turning awkward, but his curiosity led him to say, "Why did you come to Olmsted Hall tonight, anyway?"

"To see you, of course," she answered in a straightforward manner. "I wanted to talk to you again. You're an interesting person, Jake Rivers. I'm not sure what to make of you, and mysteries have always intrigued me."

"Have you figured it out?"

"Figured *you* out?" She laughed. "Not at all. You're full of contradictions. You're a warrior, but you're also a philosopher. You quote Shakespeare. You're young, but you look down on people your age and venerate soldiers from a war that was fought three generations ago. You're quiet-spoken and gentle, and yet you've been one of those rough men ready to do violence on other people's behalf. When you need to be, you still *are* a rough man."

"I don't go out of my way to look for fights."

"Exactly. You're like . . . a warrior monk."

That made him throw back his head and laugh as they walked along the concrete path at the edge of Nafziger Plaza toward his dorm.

"Believe me, I am *nothing* like a monk," he told her.

She stopped in a patch of shadows, and so he did, too. He couldn't see her face very well as she spoke, but he could hear the husky intensity in her voice as she said, "You mean you're not celibate?"

"That, too," he said.

Unless he had read all the signals wrong, she wanted him to kiss her, so he put his hands on her shoulders and leaned toward her. She tipped her head back, and despite the poor light, he had no trouble letting instinct guide him so that his lips found hers. She rested the fingertips of her left hand on his chest and slipped her right arm around his waist.

It was a good kiss, with just enough heat and urgency that they both tightened the embrace, but with the natural restraint of a first kiss. It definitely held the potential for more, Jake thought.

After a long moment, he drew back. He started to make some comment about hoping he hadn't broken any of the college's rules, but then he sensed that this wasn't the right time for that. He didn't want to break the mood that seemed to have come over both of them.

Instead, he said quietly, "That was very nice."

"It was, wasn't it?" Natalie agreed. "But maybe we should do it again, just to be certain?"

"It never hurts to be sure," Jake said. He lowered his mouth to hers again.

That was when the rush of footsteps came from the darkness behind them, and Jake knew that hell was about to break loose, yet again.

CHAPTER 14

Natalie let out a startled "Oh!" as Jake gave her a push that sent her staggering back away from him. He didn't see or hear any attackers coming from that direction, so his instincts told him that was the safest place for her. As soon as he had done that, he whirled to face the shadowy figures charging toward him. No more than a shaved instant of time had passed since his keen ears picked up the first warning sounds of danger.

It was too dark here under the trees to tell how many of them were coming at him. All he knew for sure was that he was damned tired of being jumped like this . . . and especially at such a pleasurable moment as the one he'd just been sharing with Dr. Natalie Burke.

He heard the faint swish of something coming at his head and ducked. Unfortunately, one of the attackers had lunged in from the side and brought a weapon of some sort around at a lower trajectory, and Jake ducked right into its path. The blow didn't strike him full force, just clipped him on the side of the head, but it was enough to make stars explode behind his eyes for a second and sent him stumbling to the side.

One of the men caught him around the waist with a flying tackle, and since he was already off-balance, the collision was enough to jolt him off his feet.

He landed hard on his right hip. Pain shot through him from the impact with the unrelenting concrete sidewalk. He ignored it as he grappled with the man who had driven him down. Reaching out blindly, Jake felt his hand close over what felt like a cloth-shrouded jaw.

Those damn black-hooded Antifa fanatics! They were after him again, even though he had put the last four in the hospital. At least he supposed he had. There had never been any official word about them, as far as he knew.

With the heel of his hand under the man's chin, he shoved up as hard as he could. The man had to let go of him and jerk away, or else Jake might well have broken his neck with that thrust. Jake rolled to put some distance between them, but as he did, another of the attackers stepped up and launched a kick that slammed into Jake's ribs. They still ached from the previous fracases, and this vicious blow was enough to make agony roll through him like a flood tide.

In order to kick Jake, though, the man had to get close to him, and Jake shoved the pain aside so he could take advantage of that. He reached out swiftly and closed his left hand around an ankle. A hard yank and twist threw the man to the ground. He yelped in alarm as he went down.

Feet scuffed on the sidewalk as more of the indistinct, black-clad, black-hooded figures closed in around Jake. He knew he couldn't allow them to keep him on the ground. If they did, they could kick and stomp him into submission. They might even do enough damage to seriously injure or even kill him.

His hand dipped into a jacket pocket and came out with the folding knife. His thumb found the opening in the top of the blade and flicked the knife open. He came up on one knee and brought that hand around in a long, sweeping, curving stroke. The blade met resistance more than once, and each time the razor-sharp edge cut through whatever it encountered. A couple of screams sounded from the men who had been looming over Jake, only to encounter more trouble than they evidently expected.

Jake powered to his feet, still slashing back and forth with the knife. The attackers gave ground. They had to, if they didn't want to get sliced to ribbons. Jake sensed as much as heard one of them coming at him from behind and bent sideways at the waist. He had his balance now, so he was able to snap a side kick that sunk the heel of his work boot into the man's belly. The man folded up and collapsed, and a second later Jake heard him retching.

As Jake returned to an upright position and stood there, braced for more trouble with his chest heaving, not from exertion as much as from emotion, he tried to calm the rage that had burst into white-hot fire inside him. All the resentment and disgust that had been building up since he had come here to Kelton College had broken free. He knew he could have killed somebody if one of those knife strokes had opened up a throat, but right at the moment, he didn't care. *They* had attacked *him* . . . again! . . . and whatever happened to them was on their own heads.

At the same time, the still-logical part of his brain knew how heavily stacked the odds against him were. Not in terms of battling these attackers. He would take on however many of them wanted to come at him, one at a time or all at once, and trust to his own abilities to keep him alive.

But would his abilities enable him to triumph in what came afterward? If he killed any of them, he would be arrested and probably charged with murder. The survivors would claim he had attacked them for no reason at all, and they would all back up each other's stories. The college administration would make no effort to defend him. Indeed, President Pelletier and the other members of the administration would be glad to see him convicted, imprisoned, and out of their hair. The news media would try him in the court of public opinion and find him guilty, guilty, guilty . . . of being a conservative, and oh, yeah, of murder, as well. Jake knew his grandfather would provide him with the best lawyers money can buy, but it might not be enough.

The unfairness of it grated at Jake. These Antifa lunatics could try to kill him—the blow that had clipped his skull could have fractured it just as easily, if it had struck him with full force behind it—but he couldn't defend himself without risking life imprisonment. The system was broken and had been for a long time. The axis had tilted toward the monsters for so long that most people now regarded the situation as normal.

Jake knew all that . . . but he also knew that in life, you had to deal with things as they were, not how you wished they could be.

So when the waves of rage inside him had subsided a little, he said hoarsely, "Back off. I don't want to hurt anybody."

"Too late," one of the men said. The hood muffled and disguised his voice, but Jake could tell that it was drawn thin with pain, probably from a knife slash. "You've already cut us up, you son of a bitch. You have to pay for that."

Jake hoped that Natalie had run away when she realized he was being attacked again. He thought he vaguely remembered hearing the swift rataplan of her footsteps on the sidewalk just as the fight was getting started. As long as he didn't have to worry about keeping her safe . . .

Slanting beams of light suddenly pierced the shadows and darted over Jake and the black-clad figures around him. Rapid footsteps sounded again. A strong, familiar voice called, "Hold it right there! Drop any weapons you have and get on the ground!"

"Let's go!" the man who seemed to be the leader of the Antifa thugs ordered. Some of them were limping heavily from the damage Jake had done with the knife, but they all managed to run away from the campus police officers charging toward the scene from the far end of Nafziger Plaza.

Jake had recognized Frank McRainey's voice. He stayed where he was and allowed the flashlight beams to roam over him. The way he was turned, the campus cops couldn't see what he was doing as he closed the knife and slipped it back into his pocket. Violating the prohibition against carrying weapons on campus was only a misdemeanor, and otherwise, the knife was perfectly legal. Jake was willing to pay a fine if it meant having the means to save his life or the life of some other innocent person.

If he got busted for carrying the knife on campus, though, and word of it got out, the media would use that ammunition to make him look like even more of an alt-right, neo-Nazi lunatic. And the college might decide to use it as justification for expelling him.

Jake wasn't giving up the knife, though. He would wait and see how this played out.

He recognized McRainey in the vanguard of the officers who rushed up to him. Keeping his hands in plain sight now, in a nonthreatening manner, he said, "It's me, Chief McRainey. I'm not going to give you any trouble."

The chief was the only person on the force who carried a firearm, but the others were armed with stun guns and batons. Jake didn't want Cal Granderson getting carried away and hitting him with a stun gun again. That was no fun.

Granderson was one of the officers who had responded. He looked like he was almost hopping up and down with excitement as he yelled at Jake, "Get on the ground!"

"I think we can dispense with that, Cal," McRainey

said, always the voice of reason. "Jake doesn't appear to be armed, and he's not resisting."

"He's been fighting again!" Granderson said. "Look at him! That's disturbing the peace, Chief. Maybe assault! Who did he attack this time?"

"I didn't attack anybody," Jake said calmly. "I was walking back to Olmsted Hall when some of those Antifa goons jumped me again."

"Antifa," Granderson said with a sneer obvious in his voice. "You blame everything on Antifa, Rivers. You scared of them or something?"

"That's enough," McRainey said before Jake could answer. "What happened to the men who attacked you, Jake?"

"You mean you believe him?" Granderson asked.

The chief made a curt gesture for him to shut up, then turned back to Jake, who said, "They took off when they saw you coming."

"How many of them were there?"

"I'm not sure. I never got a good look, and anyway, I didn't have time to count them. Five or six, I'd say as a guess."

"Are you hurt?"

Jake's head and ribs hurt from the blows they had absorbed, but he said, "Nah, I'm fine. It didn't amount to anything more than a scuffle, thanks to you coming along when you did."

He wanted to get out of here and back to the dorm before this blew up into more trouble than it was worth.

"Well, you can thank Dr. Burke for calling us. She said she was with you when those guys showed up."

"Yeah, that's right." Jake looked around. "Where is she now?"

"I don't know. The dispatcher just talked to her on the phone." McRainey gave Jake a shrewd look. "Is there something going on I ought to know about?"

"I don't know what it would be. You're not the morality police now, are you, Chief?"

"On a college campus?" McRainey snorted. "We'd sure as hell be overworked if we were."

Jake could tell that Granderson was just busting at the seams to get a comment in. He couldn't resist poking the campus cop.

"Something you want to say, Cal?"

Granderson opened his mouth, then shut it after McRainey gave him a stern look. He settled for shaking his head and glaring at Jake.

McRainey told Granderson and the other officers, "You guys go on back to the office. I'll escort Mr. Rivers to his dorm to make sure he gets there all right and there isn't any more trouble."

"Thanks, Chief," Jake said, even though he was pretty sure the hooded thugs wouldn't be back tonight.

"Aren't you going to search him?" Granderson protested.

"Why? The incident turned out not to be serious. There's no need to search Mr. Rivers or to detain him any further."

Granderson didn't look happy about that at all, but he turned around and left with the other officers as they headed back to the campus police building.

McRainey fell in step beside Jake as they walked toward Olmsted Hall. After a couple of seconds, he said quietly, "Son, you are just asking for trouble."

"How?" Jake wanted to know.

"The ice under you is already about as thin as it can get after those earlier incidents. The administration will throw you under the bus before you can blink, if you give them the slightest excuse . . . like carrying a weapon on campus."

"Nobody said I was carrying a weapon."

"You want to deny it?"

"Is that an official question?"

McRainey blew out a breath.

"I know you, Jake," he said. "You play by your own rules and figure you can take care of yourself, and ninety-nine percent of the time, you're right. But getting on the wrong side of ninety-nine point nine percent of the student body and about that many of the faculty the way you have, you're bucking heavy odds. Messing around with a professor is just going to make it worse for you."

"Who said anything about me messing around with a professor?"

"Dr. Burke sounded mighty worried about you when she called. You're not in any of her classes. I'm not sure how the two of you even know each other. But where were you before you started back to Olmsted Hall this evening?"

Jake shrugged.

"The Shamrock."

"Were you alone?"

Jake knew it wouldn't take much effort on the

chief's part to find out the answer to that, so he told the truth.

"No. As a matter of fact, I was having a few beers with a friend. Dr. Burke."

"Yeah, that's what I thought. Look, Jake, I'm not trying to give you trouble. I'm just saying that you can only break so many rules in life before it starts to catch up with you. Just be careful, that's all."

They had reached the steps of Olmsted Hall. Jake said, "I always am, Chief."

McRainey just made a scoffing sound, shook his head, and turned to walk off.

Jake walked up the steps to the dorm's front porch, wondering what had become of Natalie. He knew she probably was all right, since she had called the campus police, but he would have liked to be sure. He couldn't call her, though, because he didn't have her number. He'd meant to ask for it but had never gotten around to it. That was another way he was out of step with his own generation. Most people his age, if they had any interest in someone else, would have gotten their number right away.

His phone buzzed in his pocket before he could go inside. He pulled it out, checked the display, and saw that he'd gotten a text message from a number he didn't recognize. When he read it, he saw it said, *Are you all right? N.*

That was her, he thought. He wasn't sure how she had gotten *his* number, but she had already proven to be resourceful. He tapped out, *Fine. You?*

All good. I'm glad you weren't hurt. And now you have my number, so I'll be expecting you to call me.

Jake sent her back a thumbs-up, not knowing what else to say, then put the phone in his pocket and went on into the dorm.

A thumbs-up, he thought, shaking his head at his own ineptitude.

Chapter 15

Matthias Foster walked out of the apartment's kitchen carrying three beer bottles in one hand and two in the other. He distributed the bottles among the four people waiting for him in the living room. Jimmy, Hank, and Carlos were in armchairs. Lucy sat at one end of the sofa with her legs pulled up under her. Foster kept one of the beers and sat down beside her. "Rivers is going to be a problem," he said.

"We need to take that son of a bitch *out*," Jimmy said. He held up his left arm, which sported a bandage around the forearm. "He cut me pretty bad. I had to get a dozen *stitches*, man. If we didn't have a doctor of our own, we'd have guys in the ER right now and the cops asking questions. And we were lucky it wasn't worse. Somebody could've gotten killed. As it was, we've got men laid up again."

"He's just one man," Lucy said. "I don't see how he can do any real damage to the plan."

"One dangerous man," Foster said. "We've seen that demonstrated twice now, close up. He could've killed Jimmy or one of the boys with him." Foster paused. "Of course, if Rivers *had* killed somebody, he'd be in jail now, and we wouldn't have to worry about him."

The others frowned at him but didn't say anything. After a moment, Foster laughed.

"Hey, I'm just screwin' with you. I don't want any of our group getting killed." Foster's expression grew more solemn. "Listen, though. We knew going into this that it was serious business. Dangerous business. There's a very good chance not everybody will come out alive on the other end. But the reward will be worth the risk. We're all agreed on that, right?"

Carlos said, "We know the deal, Matthias. And we're in."

"Yeah, we're in," Hank added.

"All the way," Jimmy said. "But if somebody's gotta die, I want to make sure it's that bastard Rivers. I still think we ought to do something about him before the time comes."

"We've gone after him twice, just to test him and find out how much of a badass he really is," Foster pointed out. "Now we know. He's not going to take us by surprise and *Die Hard* us. If he tries, we'll be ready for him. That's why we have to make sure where he is and keep track of him."

"Still think we should just go ahead and kill him right off the bat," Jimmy muttered sullenly.

"What about the rest of the students?" Hank asked. "There could be somebody else who might take us by surprise."

Foster made a face and shook his head.

"The chances of that are so small I'm not really worried about it. You know what they're like. They're not violent. They *abhor* violence. Just ask them, they'll tell you. Oh, they can form a mob quickly enough, if anybody offends them and violates their safe spaces, but as long as we keep them spread out, they won't do that. They won't do anything unless the odds are on their side. They think they're noble, but they're just cowards." He laughed again. "They're about to learn a valuable lesson, though."

"What's that?" Lucy asked.

"In a world full of wolves, there *are* no safe spaces."

The next day, Jake had a break of several hours in the middle of the day without classes, so he got in his pickup and drove out into the country east of Greenleaf to visit his friend Keith Randall.

Randall owned an outdoor gun range and firearms and self-defense training school, and Jake tried to get out there at least once every couple of weeks to put some rounds through his guns. He had his 1911 with him today, along with a hammerless .32 S&W wheel gun.

He had gotten the revolver out one day while he was at the range, and Randall's twelve-year-old daughter had looked at him with contempt and said, "I hope you're planning on throwing that at somebody, instead of shooting at them. You'll do more damage that way."

"It's not the size of the gun, it's what you know

how to do with it," Jake had responded, then immediately wished he hadn't said such a thing to a twelve-year-old girl. He needed to watch his phrasing in the future.

If she'd been offended, though, she hadn't shown it. She'd just snorted disgustedly, shook her head, and gone back to the AR-15 she was sighting in.

Today, Randall checked Jake in, then followed him out to the range, knowing that Jake didn't mind having other people watching him shoot.

As Jake was loading the 1911, Randall asked, "How are things in Greenleaf these days? Everybody doing their part to keep the place weird?"

Jake grunted and pulled his ear and eye protection into place, then steadily and methodically emptied the gun into the target twenty yards away. He lowered the gun and let the echoes die away, then went on, "You don't fool me, Keith. You know there's been trouble there on campus."

Randall grinned and said, "Yeah, the way the news media played it up, it was all-out war between those anarchists and the second coming of the Third Reich. Only come to find out, the Nazi horde was just one guy: you."

"You've got the numbers right but everything else flipped around," Jake said. "It was me against a mob, all right, but they're not anarchists. Just the opposite, in fact. They want everything controlled by the government . . . and the government controlled by them."

"That kind of makes them the Nazis, doesn't it?"

Jake cocked an eyebrow.

"Ya think?" He paused, then went on quietly, "You don't know about this, Keith, because for some reason there hasn't been anything in the news about it, but I've been jumped twice since that big fight. They haven't been just brawls, either. The first time they were out to hurt me, and last night I think they would have killed me if they could."

Randall stepped closer and frowned.

"Are you kidding me? Jake, that . . . that's unacceptable! What happened? How did you keep from getting hurt? You're not hurt bad, are you?"

"I'm fine," Jake said, shaking his head. "I guess I put up more of a fight than they expected. I gave better than I got, and they took off."

"You didn't see who—"

"Guys in black hoods, like those Antifa kids. I'm pretty sure that wasn't what this was, though. Antifa is a bunch of amateurs. Would-be badasses playing at being revolutionaries. I caught at least a hint of professionalism from the guys who attacked me."

"Have you told the cops?"

"Frank McRainey knows about what happened last night, but I downplayed the whole thing, so as far as he knows it was connected to the trouble several nights ago. He may suspect that it's more than that, but he doesn't have any way of knowing for sure. He wasn't there, didn't see how those guys handled themselves."

"But you haven't said anything to the town cops?"

"Kelton College is the most important business in Greenleaf, you know that," Jake said. "The mayor and the city council will go along with whatever

President Pelletier and the Board of Regents want. And what they'd like more than anything else is for me to just go away. The only reason they haven't booted me out before now is that they don't want to tangle with my grandfather."

"Well, you can't blame them for that," Randall said. "Nobody in his right mind would want a scrap with Cordell Gardner. But look, Jake, if you've got a target on your back, you can't just go around waiting for people to take shots at it. You're about as good at taking care of yourself as anybody I've ever seen, but you're surrounded by enemies in a place like that."

Jake laughed and said, "Pretty ineffectual enemies."

"Mostly, maybe. But not all of them."

"No," Jake agreed, thinking of the men who had jumped him when he was on his way back to Olmsted with Natalie. "Not all of them."

As Jake sat in his microbiology class later that afternoon, he wished he was back out on Keith Randall's gun range. That had been a lot more fun than listening to Dr. Montambault drone on and on. Despite wanting to please his grandfather, Jake was feeling more and more like maybe grad school hadn't been such a good idea after all.

That opened up the question of what he would do with his life, but a possible answer was nagging at the back of his brain.

Earlier that day, when he'd been finishing up his

practice, another guy had arrived at the range and taken a position several places down the line. Jake hadn't paid much attention to him at first, but then he had heard the swift, evenly paced way the man shot and looked at the target, only to see an incredibly tight grouping around the center of the silhouette printed on the hanging piece of paper. Jake had no false modesty about his own abilities—he was a damned good shot and he knew it—but he didn't think he had ever put that many rounds quite so close together. This guy was *good.*

That realization had led Jake to take a closer look at the man firing. His hair was mostly gray, and age had weathered his rugged features. However, he carried himself with a youthful vitality that belied his obvious years. He might have been seventy, but he moved, stood, and shot like a man in the prime of his life. Jake had a sense that, age difference or no age difference, he wouldn't want to tangle with the man.

When Randall walked by, Jake had angled his head toward the older man and asked quietly, "Who's that? I don't think I've seen him around here before."

"His name's Rivera," Randall replied. "He's been coming here to shoot for a few months. I don't know a thing in the world about him except that he's one of the best with a gun I've ever seen. He might be retired law enforcement. FBI, maybe."

"Not many of those lawyers-with-guns can shoot like that. Most LEOs can't, either. No reason to get good at it when you only have to shoot a few rounds each year to qualify."

Randall shrugged.

"Maybe some sort of private operator, then. Security specialist. You can go ask him if you want to."

Rivera was loading a fresh magazine into a Browning Hi-Power. Jake watched him for a second, then shook his head.

"He doesn't strike me as the type of guy who'd appreciate anybody poking into his business."

"I can't argue with you there," Randall had agreed.

But since then, Jake hadn't been able to get the man named Rivera out of his head, or Randall's comment about the possibility of him being a private security specialist. That sort of work appealed to Jake, or at least the idea of it did, anyway. He'd had training and experience that had enhanced his own natural skills to the point they were something not often needed in normal society. Not many people needed an ever-rougher man than usual standing ready to do violence on their behalf.

But when they did, it was often a matter of life and death, and Jake enjoyed pitting himself against high stakes like that. It was why he had never minded taking point on a mission, and that willingness to embrace danger probably was one big reason he had survived so many harrowing situations. He just wasn't the type to run scared.

He could see himself doing private security work. Some people would call him a mercenary, but he had never cared much what anybody thought about him.

If he dropped out of school, though, more than likely he would never see Natalie Burke again, and the thought of that bothered him more than it should have, he told himself.

He dragged his attention back to class for the last few minutes before it was over, then gathered up his stuff to leave. He needed to do some studying tonight . . . but that wasn't going to be easy when he would rather be thinking about those other options.

In fact, that was why he was distracted as he left the lecture hall and bumped right into another man hurrying along in the hall outside. Jake muttered, "Sorry," and started to step around the man with whom he had collided.

"Watch where you're going . . . Nazi."

Chapter 16

Jake knew he should just keep going and pretend he hadn't heard the man, but instead he stopped and half-turned to look back at him.

"What was that?" he asked as casually as if he hadn't understood the hateful words.

"I told you to watch where you going." The man wasn't content to leave it at that. He smirked and added, "And then I called you what you are: a Nazi."

He was about Jake's age, maybe a little younger, wearing a black T-shirt with *#resist* and *#fascism* printed across the chest. There was also the word *HISTORY* with an arrow underneath it. His dark hair was fairly long and swept up. Fashionable stubble adorned his cheeks and jaw.

Jake shook his head and said, "You've got me mixed up with somebody else. I'm not a Nazi."

"No? Who'd you vote for in the last election?"

"That's none of your business. They call it a secret ballot for a reason. People used to be able to vote for whoever they thought was the best candidate without being harassed for it."

"People need to own their bigotry. Everyone on

campus knows who you are. You've attacked women and people of color and gays. Don't try to deny it."

"I'm not denying anything," Jake said. "If you're talking about that riot the other night, when somebody in a black hood is trying to bust my head open, I don't stop to ask them what color they are or what parts they have or what they do with those parts. I just keep them from hurting me or anybody else."

A group was gathering in the hallway now. All of them glared at Jake. The man who had confronted him appeared to be right about one thing: everybody on campus knew who Jake was. And none of them liked him, either.

It was a good thing he didn't give a crap whether they liked him, he thought.

He didn't have anything else to say to the guy who'd confronted him, so he turned around and walked away. Students in the hallway stepped aside, although some of them with obvious reluctance.

"Hey! I wasn't done talking to you."

"But I'm done talking to you, snowflake," Jake said without turning around.

"You heard him insult me!" the guy yelped. "You're all recording this, aren't you?"

Smartphones, Jake thought. A wonderful invention, but the bane of modern life in many ways.

He heard rapid footsteps behind him.

"That's hate speech!" the guy said. "He attacked me with his words! I don't feel safe. None of us are safe as long as this racist, sexist, homophobic bigot is here at Kelton!"

Maybe he wouldn't be for much longer, Jake

thought. He was tired of this farce. The mood he was in right now, the only thing keeping him here was his determination not to give these lunatics the satisfaction of thinking they had run him off.

The guy ran up behind him and grabbed his left arm.

"We've had enough of your aggression—"

It was all Jake could do not to turn around quickly and pop the guy. He didn't figure it would take any more than one punch. In fact, that punch might well break his jaw. That would shut the annoying little bastard up, anyway.

And dozens of videos of the punch would be plastered all over social media in a matter of minutes, and by that evening Jake would probably be under arrest, and President Pelletier wouldn't hold back this time, no matter who Jake's grandfather was. Jake would be out of here.

Well, wasn't that what he wanted?

Yeah, he thought, but not this way. Not on the enemy's terms.

He kept walking.

The sudden alarm on the face of a young woman in front of him in the hall, facing in his direction, made him stop short and turn. He didn't seem to be rushing, but he got around in a hurry.

The man who had been mouthing off at him was about to hit him. Jake reached up. His reaction was almost too fast for the eye to follow. The guy's right fist smacked into the palm of Jake's left hand. The man grunted as his fist's forward motion was stopped instantly and utterly. A little off balance because of that, he leaned toward Jake.

Jake's fingers closed around the guy's fist and started to squeeze.

The man's eyes widened. His mouth opened. Some of the color drained from his face.

"Oh," he said. "Oh, balls." His voice was thin and breathless with pain.

"My name is Jake Rivers," Jake said, his voice loud and clear. "This man just attempted to strike me with his fist from behind, with no warning or provocation. I was attacked, and my action in response to that attack is entirely in self-defense. Any video you might see that makes this incident look or sound otherwise has been doctored to give that appearance. I don't know this man who has attacked me and am not at fault or in any way to blame for what he's done or for what I've done to defend myself. I'm going to let go of him now, and I won't take any further action against him as long as he doesn't attack me again."

Jake had spouted that speech off the top of his head, giving in to the whim that had come over him when he looked around and saw all the phones being held up by the other students as they recorded the confrontation. Most, if not all, of them were against him and might well try to edit what they were recording, but some might post it in its entirety. Jake wasn't really worried about what might happen to him. The speech wasn't a way of covering his ass. He just wanted the truth to get out there so people could see it and make up their own minds.

The left didn't want the truth getting out, though. To them, the liberal elite was smarter than anyone else, and so they ought to be the ones to tell people what to think and do. And liberals always included themselves in that elite, without it ever occurring to them that if the communists or the Islamist fanatics ever took over, they would be among the first lined up against a wall for the firing squads.

Jake looked at the guy whose fist he was holding. The man had another fist, and Jake hadn't done anything to stop him from using it. He could have tried to throw another punch and break free from Jake's grip at any time.

But instead he stood there, pale and trembling, clearly paralyzed by pain and fear. Jake had squeezed hard enough to make bones grind together in the guy's hand, but he hadn't broken anything.

A tear ran down the guy's cheek into his meticulously trimmed stubble.

Jake let go of him and stepped back.

The man's fist fell like it was a weight. He caught it with his other hand and cradled it against his chest as a sob escaped from him.

"You . . . you animal!" he gasped at Jake. "You barbarian!"

"You're the one who tried to sucker punch somebody," Jake said. "It backfired on you. Not my fault." He looked around at the phones recording him. "Self-defense, people. Remember it. It's a handy concept to master."

When he walked on this time, no one tried to stop him. He made it out of the building unmolested.

When he was on the steps, though, somebody called behind him, "Hey, Rivers, wait up."

Jake stopped and turned to look at a young black man coming toward him. He didn't seem like he was after a fight, so Jake just stood there and waited to see what was going to happen.

"I got that whole thing on my phone," the man said. "Give me your number and I'll send it to you. You might want a copy of the unedited footage."

"Why don't you just upload it yourself?" Jake asked.

"Oh, I intend to, but I thought you might like to have it, too. Experts would be able to prove it hasn't been doctored, if you ever needed it for legal reasons."

"Like in case of a lawsuit?"

The young man laughed.

"Idiots like that couldn't win a fight against you on their best day. He just let himself get carried away by his politics and the belief that being on the so-called right side of history makes you invulnerable." He paused. "It doesn't. Nobody's invulnerable."

"That's the truth. I appreciate the gesture . . . ?"

"Pierce," the man introduced himself.

"Really?" Jake said, then wished he hadn't.

The guy just laughed, though, and said, "Don't get racist on me when I'm trying to do you a favor, man."

"I didn't mean to," Jake said. "It's just that Pierce seems like kind of a trust-fund name, you know."

Pierce cocked an eyebrow.

"I happen to have a trust fund, you know."

"No, I'm afraid I didn't have a clue."

"My family has money," Pierce said without any self-consciousness about the admission, "just like nearly everybody else here at Kelton. It's not old money, mind you. My dad made it in the dot-com boom. But it spends just as well as if it were fourth or fifth generation." He lifted his phone. "Now, how about me sharing that video with you?"

"I appreciate that." Jake told him the number, and Pierce spent a minute tapping on his phone's display.

"There you go."

"Thanks. But I have to ask . . . why are you doing this? I mean—"

"Why's a black guy helping somebody accused of being a white supremacist?" Pierce shrugged. "For one thing, I was there and saw what happened the other night. There was nothing racial about it. Those guys mobbed you, and you had to fight back. Same thing here. You were trying to get away from that loudmouth without any trouble, and he wouldn't let you. I believe in fairness and sticking up for the underdog, whether I agree with his politics or not. Doesn't mean I have any use for Nazis or the KKK."

"Believe me, neither do I," Jake said. "A person can be a conservative without supporting either of those groups of loons."

"Maybe. I'll give anybody the benefit of the doubt . . . until they prove otherwise."

"Fair enough," Jake said with a nod. "Thanks again, man. I'll see you around."

"Yeah. So long."

Jake walked on, unsure what to make of this encounter. He wasn't going to overreact and decide that he had made an unexpected friend here on campus. There hadn't been nearly that level of warmth coming from Pierce. More of a willingness not to judge too prematurely or harshly.

Back in the army, Jake had run into a few guys who considered themselves to be what they called small-l liberals, or classical liberals. Guys who truly believed in free speech and individualism, rather than marching in lockstep and trusting the government to run everything from the top down. They didn't want to silence anyone who might have different ideas than they did. Their feelings weren't so fragile that they had to pitch a fit and retreat into a safe space every time anybody challenged one of their beliefs. They welcomed honest debate. Jake could respect guys like that, even when he believed that their policy ideas were all wrong.

Jake had heard many times that conservatives considered liberals wrong, while liberals considered conservatives evil. While few things were absolutes, including that, Jake had seen enough examples in real life to know that, by and large, that contrast was absolutely true. Guys like Pierce might be the exception, somebody who could disagree with somebody or something without resorting to demonizing. "Everybody I disagree with is literally Hitler," had been a popular saying on the right a few years earlier, and like all clichés, it contained more than a nugget of truth. That was the way the left truly thought.

The Cntrl-Left, Jake thought with a smile, remembering a term someone on the Internet had come up with to mock the lockstep progressives and their obsession with the so-called Alt-Right.

Because if there was any group in modern American society that truly wanted to control everyone and everything, it was the Left . . .

It was all politics, and all bull, and he wished it would just go away and leave him alone.

That wasn't too much to ask, was it?

Chapter 17

Evidently it was, because by the time he got back to Olmsted Hall and his room, he found an email waiting for him from President Pelletier's secretary, telling him—not asking him—to be at Pelletier's office at nine o'clock the next morning. The email didn't specify why the college president wanted to see him, but Jake was willing to bet it had something to do with this latest incident.

It wasn't difficult to see how Pelletier might have heard about it already, because when he checked social media, he saw that the video had been posted already, numerous different versions shot from angles all around him, in fact. One was titled *Neo-Nazi Rant*, and another emblazoned the words *Far-Right Extremist Goes on Rampage.* One was simply called *Bigot.*

Somewhat surprisingly, most of the videos didn't appear to have been edited much, if at all. It was like the posters were so sure of their fundamental infallibility that they hadn't even bothered. They knew that if they pointed at something and cried, "Bigot!" their followers would believe them unquestioningly.

Who you gonna believe, me . . . or your lyin' eyes?

The answer to that was simple and near-universal. If a liberal said it, other liberals would believe it, regardless of what the facts showed.

Actually, watching the various versions of the video, Jake saw that most of them had caught him when he turned around and saw the guy swinging at him, and he had to admit that he had a pretty intense look on his face. Not evil or deranged or anything like that, but he'd clearly been ready for trouble.

Then they concentrated on the guy who had attacked him, and his face revealed beyond a shadow of a doubt that he was in quite a bit of pain. Jake had spoken in a quiet, reasonable voice, but the close-up of the guy grimacing automatically cast doubt on what he was saying. After all, he was hurting somebody who didn't really look the least bit threatening. He had to be some kind of monster to do that, right? Actions speak louder than words.

Then Jake saw a video posted by Pierce Conners and knew that had to be the guy who had sent the fresh footage to him. Jake clicked on that, waited a second for it to load, and as it played, he saw that the shot was framed so he and the other guy were both completely visible. Not only that, but it started before the guy rushed up and took the swing at him, so it was clear that Jake was trying to walk away and avoid trouble. With both of them in the video, Jake came off as a lot more rational. There was even a faint twinkle of amusement in his eyes during the legalistic spiel he had improvised.

"Good job, Pierce," he muttered. He was glad the young man had posted this, even though most people wouldn't see it . . . and it probably wouldn't change their opinion of him even if they did.

Someone knocked on the door. He closed the laptop and stood up.

The way his luck had been running, he expected this visitor to be an unwelcome one. However, when he opened the door the sight that greeted his eyes was pleasant and most welcome. Dr. Natalie Burke stood there wearing a simple green dress that she managed to make look elegant.

"I saw the latest video," she said, "and thought you might want some sympathetic company."

Jake frowned. His reaction made her look puzzled and then a little bit offended.

"If you don't want me here—" she began.

"It's not that," he broke in. "Your company is pretty much the only thing I like about this place anymore. But you have to realized that you're risking your career by getting involved with me."

"Are we *involved,* Jake?"

"I don't know. It seems like we might be getting there."

She moved closer to him and rested the fingers of her right hand on his left forearm as she said, "I think so, too."

"You know how the administration feels about me. You don't want that stain rubbing off on you. You don't have tenure, do you?"

She shook her head.

"No, not yet."

"So Pelletier can fire you any time he wants to, and there's nothing you can do about it."

Natalie shrugged and said, "You always run that risk when you haven't been teaching all that long."

"Why make it worse by associating with me?"

She smiled up at him.

"Maybe I think you're worth associating with."

"I don't know why you think that. Everybody else around here hates me, except for maybe Chief McRainey. And I think he's starting to get pretty fed up with having trouble swirling around me all the time."

"None of that trouble has been your fault," Natalie pointed out.

"Maybe not, but I still seem to be a magnet for it. Remove me from the equation, and the trouble goes away."

She shook her head.

"No, the professionally outraged will just find something else to be offended and upset about. You know that, Jake. The way they move the goalposts, nobody can ever win with them."

"You're probably right about that," he admitted.

"So why worry about it?" She linked her arm with his and smiled. "Come on, let's go get something to eat. You haven't had dinner yet, have you?"

"No, it's barely past the time when the old people go to eat."

"Well, I'm older than you, remember?"

He laughed and said, "All right, you win. Where do you want to go?"

"There's a good steakhouse called Hickory Grove out on the edge of town."

"I think I've seen it," Jake said with a nod. "Let

me put on a nicer shirt, and we'll check it out. I'll meet you in front of the dorm in five minutes."

"I could stay here while you change," she suggested.

"Not unless we both sign releases," he said, smiling to show her that he was joking . . . mostly.

They took his pickup, with Natalie giving him directions to the steakhouse. Not that he really needed them. He knew he could have relied on his innate sense of direction to find the place. But he had never been one of those guys who resented it when he had to rely on someone else's directions. Some men got bent out of shape by that, especially when it was a woman telling them where to go . . . so to speak. Jake, however, seldom got lost, so it had never really been an issue.

Actually, he wasn't sure he had *ever* been lost, at least in the sense of having no idea where he was and not a glimmering of how to get where he wanted to go. That natural ability had come in handy many times during his military service. The units to which he was assigned had learned quickly to rely on him as a scout.

Hickory Grove was an old-fashioned steakhouse, with subdued lighting, lots of dark-wood paneling, booths and tables made of thick beams, and several sets of longhorns mounted on the walls, along with paintings of range life, some originals and some prints of classic scenes by artists such as Frederic Remington and Charles M. Russell. Jake liked the place as soon as he walked in.

He liked it even better when he had the first bite of the steak he ordered, which was cooked to perfection. The baked potato was excellent as well, as was the beer he drank to wash down the food.

"I figured you were a meat-and-potatoes sort of guy," Natalie said, smiling from the other side of the table in the booth.

"Well, I *did* get called a barbarian earlier today," Jake pointed out with a smile of his own.

"By an idiot."

Jake shrugged as if to indicate that that went without saying.

"No, it's just that people mistake having simple tastes for having no taste," Natalie went on. "They don't understand that there's always a reason certain things are always popular, like a good steak and baked potato. When they're prepared properly, they're always good. In an uncertain world, dependability means a lot."

"Some people think dependable is just another word for boring."

"Well, they're wrong. You strike me as being very dependable, Jake . . . and you're far from boring."

He laughed and said, "I'll take that as a compliment."

"That's the way it was intended."

The meal was so enjoyable that Jake didn't want it to end. He realized that was a cliché, but in this case, it was true. He could have sat there in Hickory Grove all evening, talking to Natalie Burke.

The management would have frowned on that, though, so eventually Jake paid for the meal—over Natalie's objections, since technically she was the one who had invited him out, but she couldn't overcome his old-fashioned stubbornness. And to tell the truth, she didn't seem to mind that much. Away from the college campus, with its toxic, persistent, victimhood-seeking feminism, Natalie was clearly okay with some gender-stereotypical impulses on Jake's part.

Like when he took her hand as they walked back out to his pickup in the early evening. She didn't object. She even squeezed back.

"The weather's nice," he said, acting on another of those impulses. "Why don't we drive out to the state park?"

"I'd like that," Natalie said. "Maybe we could walk around a little. That meal was delicious, but it *was* a little on the heavy side."

Jake couldn't argue with that. It would feel good to move around some.

The state park was a few miles south of Greenleaf and included a small lake, along with hiking trails and several picnic areas. It wasn't a big place, but it was popular with both the college kids and the townies. Its relative isolation made it a good spot for couples to go, but it was also a location where drug deals sometimes took place, as Natalie mentioned to Jake as he drove toward it.

"Yeah, I've heard that," he said. "I'm not particularly worried about it."

"Because you can handle trouble."

"Well, yeah. But also, it's pretty early. The sun hasn't been down long. I think it's going to be a while before any drug dealers are out and about."

"We can hope so."

Jake also wasn't worried because he had that little

Smith & Wesson revolver in his jacket pocket and a knife in his jeans pocket. Most people he knew who went armed fervently hoped that it would never be necessary to use the weapons . . . but they preferred to be able to do so if the need arose. There was a lot of truth to the old saying about how when life and death was a matter of seconds, the cops were only minutes away.

There was still a small, reddish-gold arch in the western sky when he brought the pickup to a stop in the parking area by the lake, where the hiking trails that ran all the way around started and ended. He saw a couple of people on bikes, and a family was just packing up from a picnic supper at one of the concrete tables overlooking the lake. It was a tranquil, domestic scene the likes of which Jake had experienced much too seldom in the past half-dozen years.

"Let's walk up the trail a ways," he suggested.

"Okay. I know a spot where there's a pretty good view of the whole lake."

This time she was the one who took hold of his hand, instead of the other way around. Jake didn't mind at all. They went to the right along the hiking trail, following it around the lake to the west. There was still enough light that they didn't have any trouble seeing where they were going.

A smaller, unpaved path branched off from the main trail and led up a rise to an elevated point with several large slabs of rock on it. Those rocks could be used to sit on and doubtless had been more times than anyone could count. Jake and

Natalie sat on one of them and gazed out over the mostly tree-bordered lake in the fading light. The array of colors lingering in the heavens was spectacularly beautiful.

But not any more beautiful than Natalie was in that golden light, Jake thought. He leaned over and kissed her. It seemed like the most natural thing in the world to do.

She returned the kiss with obvious pleasure. One hand came up and rested softly on his chest as she turned toward him. Jake slipped his arms around her.

When the kiss ended, as it finally had to, Jake said quietly, "I'm sorry I didn't ask your permission to do that."

"Don't be," she replied without hesitation. "Look, let's forget about all those ridiculous, politically correct guidelines. There comes a time between a man and a woman when none of that garbage matters."

He started to say something about how she was being awfully heterocentric there, with her comment about a man and a woman, but then he realized she was right. He shoved everything else out of his mind and let human instinct guide him as he kissed her again.

There were some things bureaucracies just couldn't make rules against, and what he was feeling now was one of them. Let the petty little tyrants try to regulate human emotions all they wanted to. In the end, they would fail. The human spirit wouldn't be broken.

If it ever was, that was a world Jake wouldn't want to live in.

Later, when they walked back to Jake's pickup,

Natalie asked, "What's your schedule tomorrow morning?"

"I don't have a class until eleven. I usually spend the morning studying." Then Jake remembered and grimaced. "But I'm supposed to be in President Pelletier's office at nine. He probably wants to chew me out again for defending myself."

"Maybe that won't take very long. Meet me in the library when you're done. I have some work to do, but I can do it there just as well as I can in my office. You can study. But we can be together while we're doing those things."

"Sure," he said, nodding. "If they haven't expelled me and gotten a restraining order against me to keep me off the campus. The library sounds good to me. A library date. I didn't know people still did such things in this day and age."

"Why not? Some things don't go out of style, do they?"

"Not as far as I'm concerned." He grinned. "Hell, I'd take you to the malt shop if there was one anywhere around."

"I kind of wish there was," Natalie said with a wistful note in her voice. "You don't know how much I'd like that . . ."

CHAPTER 18

Charlie Hodges was the head groundskeeper at Kelton College, bossing a crew of five guys. The four of them, plus Hodges, took care of everything outside the buildings. A separate maintenance and custodial crew handled the upkeep inside the buildings. If pressed, Hodges would admit that there was a certain rivalry between the two groups, but he liked to think that they were all professionals and cared more about doing their jobs than anything else.

It just so happened that Hodges liked to get to work first, before the maintenance guys, so the sun wasn't up yet when he parked his pickup next to the old, barn-like building at the edge of campus where his office was and where all the groundskeeping equipment was stored. Some people called it The Shed, but it was a lot larger and sturdier than an actual shed.

The building had a big roll-up door so the crew could get the mowers in and out, with a smaller door to the left leading to Hodges' office. He was headed for that door when a jeep pulled up next to his pickup and stopped. Rick Overman got out.

Overman was a wiry young guy who was new on the groundskeeping crew this year, but so far he had proven to be a friendly, efficient, hard worker. Hodges liked him. He lifted a hand in greeting and said, "Mornin', Rick."

"Morning, Mr. Hodges," Overman replied.

"Ready for a big day?"

The question caused a frown to appear on Overman's face.

"A big day? What's special about today?"

"Oh, nothing," Hodges said with a casual wave. He unlocked the office door. "Every day's a big day if you approach it right, isn't it?"

Overman nodded slowly and said, "That's a very good way of looking at life, sir. I'm going to believe that this will be a very big day."

Hodges grinned and clapped a hand on the young guy's shoulder.

"That's the spirit. Wait here. I'll go in and unlock the big door."

However, instead of waiting outside as Hodges had told him to do, Overman followed him into the office. Hodges flicked on the light and asked, "Something you wanted to talk about?"

"Actually, boss, there is," Overman said as he closed the door behind him.

Hodges turned toward the table at one side of the room where a coffeemaker sat, along with cups, sugar, and creamer.

"Let me get some coffee going—"

He heard Overman moving up behind him but didn't have time to turn around before Overman's arm looped around his neck and jerked back. Overman's forearm pressed against Hodges' throat with ferocious strength. Hodges was a fairly big guy and had worked outside all his life, so he was no weakling. But even though he tried to fight back, he couldn't even begin to budge that terrible, choking grip. His head started to spin as he flailed around.

"I'm sorry about this, Charlie, I truly am," Overman whispered in his ear. "You're a good guy and you don't deserve it. But I *do* deserve what I'm going to get today, and I can't let you stand in the way of that."

Hodges was able to force a strangled gasp from his tortured throat, and then a second later Overman's muscles bunched and twisted and Hodges heard a sharp crack that resonated through his brain.

He had just enough time to realize it was the sound of his neck breaking before he knew nothing at all.

Matthias Foster lowered the groundskeeper's body to the floor, then grasped Hodges under the arms and dragged him behind the desk. He had to pull the corpse's legs around and sort of fold Hodges double to make sure he couldn't be seen by anybody who came into the office, at least not right away.

Then he took the ring of keys off Hodges' belt and clipped it to his own. He stepped into the garage area and flipped the lights on. He didn't think he'd have long to wait, and sure enough, he didn't.

The office door opened, and Sam Torres, a stocky, middle-aged member of the crew, came in with a puzzled look on his face. By this time, Foster had a hip propped casually on a front corner of the desk.

"Hey, kid," Torres said. "How come the big door's not open yet? Charlie always has it rolled up by the time the rest of us get here."

"Some sort of problem with one of the mowers," Foster replied. "He's in there working on it now."

Torres scoffed.

"I know the engines on those mowers better than he does. He should have waited and let me take a look at it." He headed for the open door between the office and the garage. "Hope he hasn't messed it—"

That was when the heavy wrench in Overman's hand came down hard on the back of Torres's head and cracked his skull. He pitched forward onto his face. Foster leaned over him and hit him a couple more times to make sure he was dead. Then he rolled Torres onto his back and began stripping the coveralls worn by the groundskeeping crew from the dead man. That would get some blood and brain matter on the concrete floor, but it already had so much grease and dirt on it, Foster didn't think anybody would notice right away.

Anyway, he didn't intend to give anybody a chance to notice that something was wrong this morning. He went into the office, stuffed the coveralls in a desk drawer, and returned to the garage to drag Torres's body into the storeroom in the back where the trimmers, leaf blowers, and other smaller tools of the trade were kept. As he stepped out into the garage again, he heard voices from the office.

The other three members of the groundskeeping crew had arrived.

Foster put a friendly smile on his face as he walked into the office. The expression wasn't completely feigned. He liked these guys and had enjoyed working with them the past couple of months. If it hadn't been such a cliché, he would have thought of them as the salt of the earth: Jerry Brenner, Evan Underhill, and Walt Thompson.

"Hey, Overman," Thompson greeted him, using the false name Foster had adopted for this job. "Where's Charlie and Torres? I saw their vehicles out there."

"In the garage," Foster said, inclining his head toward the door, "having trouble with one of the mowers." The story had worked just fine once. No reason it wouldn't work again. They had to work on the zero-turn mowers often enough that the lie was completely believable.

Like most guys who worked with their hands, once these three heard there was some sort of mechanical problem going on, they couldn't resist going to take a look and offer their advice, just as Foster had known they would. They trooped into the garage just as obediently as if he had ordered them to, walking right through the small amount of brains and blood that had leaked out of Sam

Torres's head without ever noticing what they were doing.

Brenner looked around and said, "Where are they? I don't see them."

Foster took a small, flat, semi-automatic 9mm pistol from a pocket on his coveralls and pointed it at them.

"Don't move, boys. I don't want to hurt any of you, but I will if I have to."

They looked more surprised than angry at first, but that didn't last long. Then, glaring at Foster, Brenner said, "What the hell is this?"

"Take it easy," Foster said, keeping his voice calm and steadying. "I just need you guys to help me with something, and if you cooperate, nothing bad will happen to you."

"You're crazy," Underhill said. He was the youngest of the two, a grad student here at Kelton who was working to help pay his tuition. Since they were the closest in age, Foster had gotten to be friends with Underhill and knew his story. Underhill's parents were fairly well-to-do but not nearly as rich as the families of most of the students here. That was why he needed to work, since tuition was sky-high.

Underhill went on, "Rick, you need to put that gun away. You shouldn't even *have* a gun here on campus. You know they're prohibited. Hell, we put up the signs that say they're prohibited!"

"If you're planning on robbing us," Brenner snapped, "you're gonna be disappointed, you little punk. I've got like seventeen bucks on me, and

I'll bet these other guys don't have much more than that."

"I don't have that much," Walt Thompson said with a sigh.

Foster shook his head and said, "I don't want your money. You can keep it. All I want is your coveralls."

Now they looked confused again.

"Our coveralls?" Underhill said.

"Yeah. Take 'em off."

The three men exchanged puzzled, wary glances. Underhill said, "Why don't you tell us what's going on here?"

"Sorry," Foster replied. "I can't do that." He gestured with the 9mm. "Get out of the coveralls. Now."

With obvious great reluctance, the three men began stripping off the work clothes. Foster used his free hand to point at a wheelbarrow and ordered, "Just pile them in that."

They did so, and then, wearing just their underwear, socks, and shoes, they stood and stared angrily at Foster, whose gun had never wavered from them.

Nor did it now when he used his left hand to slip a cell phone out of his pocket. Without looking at it, he thumbed it on and placed a call. When Hank answered on the other end, Foster said, "All right, we're good."

"Be there in thirty seconds," Hank replied.

It was actually less than that when Hank, Jimmy, Carlos, and another member of the group named Royce came through the office and into the garage.

When the three groundskeepers saw the new arrivals, the outraged expressions on their faces began to fade into looks of fear.

"What the hell *is* this?" Brenner said again. "I don't like this, Overman."

"Trust me, it'll be all right," Foster said reassuringly. "We've got what we wanted. All you have to do now is turn around and get down on your knees. I'm sorry, I know that concrete floor is rough, but it won't take long. We're just going to tie you up and gag you so you can't cause a commotion. Somebody will find you after a while." He motioned with the gun. "Go on, do what I said."

Slowly, the men turned their backs. They knelt on the floor near the mowers. Three of Foster's followers moved up behind them.

Suddenly, Underhill's nerve broke. He yelled, "No!" and tried to lunge to his feet. Jimmy was too fast for him, pouncing and getting his left arm around Underhill's neck. His weight bore the grad student back to the floor.

Royce and Carlos moved in fast on the other two, grabbing them in similar choke holds. They brought up knives in their right hands and plunged the blades into the men's bodies, aiming just off center to the left between the shoulder blades so the tip would penetrate the heart and kill almost instantly. Brenner and Thompson died without a struggle. Jimmy had a little more trouble with Underhill, since he'd been trying to get to his feet, but he died only seconds after the other two.

"Leave the knives in place for a minute, until the

heart's stopped pumping," Foster said. "No point in getting more blood on the floor than necessary, although by the time anybody gets around to looking in here, it won't matter."

The others waited, as ordered, then withdrew the blades and stepped back. Foster nodded in satisfaction.

"Drag them into the storeroom and then get those coveralls on," he said. "We have a lot of work to do."

CHAPTER 19

Pierce Conners broke into a trot as he cut across Nafziger Plaza toward the Burr Memorial Library. He was supposed to meet his political science study group there at eight-thirty, and he was late. Not that it really mattered—they were just planning to go over some notes—but the group's self-appointed leader, Moammar Fareed, usually got mad if anybody was late.

Pierce had already been bitched at enough the night before. He didn't want Fareed on his case this morning, too.

"How could you post that video like that?" his girlfriend Dominique had demanded. "You made that racist skinhead look like he didn't do anything wrong!"

"Well, as far as I could see, he didn't," Pierce had tried to explain. "The other guy tried to hit him from behind. Rivers just stopped him, that's all. He didn't even really hurt the guy. Besides, I don't think he's a skinhead. He just keeps his hair cut short because he was in the military."

Dominique had not been convinced.

"He caused the whole thing just by being here,"

she insisted. "Hell, Pierce, the guy's a walking, talking, breathing symbol of white oppression! You saw how he got in a fight with members of the resistance."

"After a whole mob of them came at him with clubs and bike chains." A frown had creased Pierce's forehead as he sat next to Dominique on a padded bench in the student union building. "Besides, I don't like the way they wear hoods. Black hoods, white hoods, I don't see the difference."

"Well, then, you're blind. Freedom fighters have always had to hide their identities to protect themselves. You know good and well those damn white supremacists are settin' up death camps in Utah and Wyoming and are planning to send all the black folks there, just as soon as they steal enough elections to control the government completely."

The previous semester, Pierce had written a paper on voter fraud, and he knew from his research into the subject that in virtually all of the provable cases, the fraud had favored the candidate representing the Democratic Party. People on the left liked to argue that the Republicans engaged in voter suppression, which was also a form of fraud, but Pierce hadn't found any actual evidence of that. On the contrary, the only instances of voter suppression and intimidation he'd been able to find were cases where Antifa, Black Lives Matter, and other progressive groups had prevented conservatives from voting, sometimes by violence. As someone who had always considered himself very leftward-leaning, politically, but who was also devoted to the concepts of fairness and equal rights, those discoveries had been rather troubling for Pierce.

Not troubling enough to make him believe that his core values were wrong, however.

Pierce was off the concrete path and cut through the plaza to the library. The groundskeepers didn't like it when people cut through and trampled on the grass, and Pierce could understand why they would feel that way. He would rather risk their wrath than Fareed's, though.

Besides, he had seen what appeared to be all the members of the grounds crew over by Colohan Hall just a few minutes earlier, digging several holes in the turf along the building's front wall. He wasn't sure why they would be doing that, but as long as they were busy with something else, they wouldn't be worried or upset about him taking a shortcut through the trees in the plaza.

He reached the edge of the big, park-like area, hurried across the broad walkway that bordered it, and went up the steps to the columned porch that ran along the front of the library.

Once inside, he went down the escalator to the vast lower level, which contained not only "the stacks," shelf upon shelf of bound periodicals and older, noncirculating books with narrow aisles between them, but also a large area of tables, chairs, and conversation pits where study groups could gather. Small study carrels lined the walls. Sets of shelves containing current books and periodicals zigzagged among the conversation pits and created at least an illusion of privacy as well as muffling voices so one group was less likely to disturb the others.

Pierce saw the other four members of his political science study group in the area where they usually gathered, where there were two love seats and two armchairs with a low table sitting in the middle. Fareed was on his feet, stalking around the table and talking animatedly, as usual. He was a wiry young man who shaved his head but kept a layer of dark beard stubble on his face. As he spotted Pierce approaching, he stopped waving his hands and glared angrily at the newcomer instead.

Chunky, purple-haired Margery Dorne didn't look happy to see Pierce, either. Margery was never happy, though, so Pierce wasn't surprised. She was one of the most perpetually outraged people he had ever met . . . and that was saying a lot since Pierce's father saw racism everywhere he looked.

The other two members of the group just looked like they wanted to get on with it. Jenny Trumbull had been a cheerleader in high school, but a couple of years at Kelton had changed her. Now she wore her blond hair in dreadlocks, seldom washed it, and wouldn't be caught dead in makeup. Clark Mitchell was short, pudgy, round-faced, and wore glasses, the stereotypical nerd, but he was highly intelligent and fiercely devoted to Jenny, although she never paid him anything more than perfunctory attention.

"Well, here's the traitor now," Fareed greeted Pierce. "What have you done this morning to empower the oppressors of your people and mine?"

Pierce had worried about Fareed being annoyed

with him for being late. He should have known that Fareed would have seen the video he'd posted and had the same reaction to it that Dominique had had. For a second, he wanted to just turn around and walk out. He didn't need this grief from his study group after he'd already endured the griping from his girlfriend.

But he ought to give them the benefit of the doubt, he told himself. They weren't exactly his friends, but he felt a certain bond with them since they had been studying together for a couple of months.

"I didn't empower anybody," he said patiently. "I just posted something that was true. I can't deny the evidence of my own eyes, and neither can any of you."

Fareed let out a contemptuous snort and said, "Your own eyes. Like so many, you look, but you fail to see the truth. Evil men such as Jake Rivers must be opposed and stopped, no matter what it takes."

"He wasn't *doing* anything," Pierce said stubbornly.

Jenny said, "He attacked one of our brothers in the struggle against the white, capitalist patriarchy."

That was rich, Pierce thought, since Jenny was about as white as anybody could get, and capitalism had served her family quite well, considering that her father owned car dealerships, department stores, and was a partner in both an NFL and an NBA franchise. He was worth close to a billion dollars, which was why he could afford to send his daughter to a high-priced institution like Kelton College and never miss the money.

"You're right, Jenny," Clark said dutifully. "That

guy's just the worst, attacking one of our brothers like that."

Pierce said, "You're talking about the guy Rivers bumped into. That wasn't an attack. It was just an accident, the kind of thing that happens dozens of times a day in the halls. He just went after Rivers because he recognized him. I was there, dudes. I saw the whole thing."

Fareed shook his head.

"None of that matters. *Nothing can be allowed to distract from the narrative!* You know that. Jake Rivers is evil and must be driven from our midst."

"Yeah, well, why don't we just lynch him, then?"

They all stared at him. Margery gasped and said, "How dare you be so insensitive!"

"I'm the black guy, remember? I've got more right to say it than any of you. But I'm not going to let my race, or my political beliefs, blind me to the facts. Rivers hasn't done anything to deserve all this hate that's being laid on him. That's the way I see it."

"You should hate him just because he's white," Jenny insisted.

"Yeah," Clark added, glancing at her to see if she liked him agreeing with her that way.

"You two are white," Pierce pointed out.

Jenny sniffed.

"I identify as post-racial."

Clark nodded.

"Me, too."

Pierce knew he was wasting his time. Their opinions were set in stone, and nothing would ever change them. He said, "Let's just get on with studying, okay? We've got that test coming up Friday, and I'd like to do well on it."

"Tests are aggressions," Margery said under her breath. "Just another way for the patriarchy to keep oppressing us."

"The system keeps us in its iron grip," Fareed said, holding up a hand and clenching it into a fist to demonstrate. "But one day all the oppressed people of the world will join together and explode." He opened his fist emphatically. "Then there will come a reckoning for the sinful Western society and all its ills."

"Yeah," Clark said, venturing to express an opinion without waiting for Jenny so he could follow her lead. "The revolution! What a glorious day that will be. And we'll all be fighting to liberate the world together, won't we, Moammar?"

"Of course, my friend," Fareed said with a cold smile that didn't possess a shred of sincerity as far as Pierce could see. When the day came, if Fareed had his way, a soft little blob like Clark would be slaughtered with the rest of the infidels. Jenny, for sure, and maybe even Margery, would be raped to death for the glory of Allah. Pierce knew that a lot of black people had fallen for the Muslim line, but he never had. There was such a thing as taking "the enemy of my enemy is my friend" too far.

No, if Fareed and the guys like him ever captured any real power, Pierce wanted to be as far away as possible when that happened.

"All right," Fareed said as Pierce sat down, "we were talking about the unholy alliance between the corrupt American government and the equally corrupt capitalist business and industrial cartel and the imperialistic military establishment and how it is the sacred duty of all free, peace-loving peoples of the world to destroy this hegemony of evil and greed . . ."

Pierce wondered if this was going to be on the test.

CHAPTER 20

Cal Granderson felt a bit of satisfaction as he tucked the parking ticket under the windshield wiper of the SUV sitting there in a No Parking zone in front of the Language Arts building. The driver deserved it, not just because he believed he could defy the college's parking regulations but also because he drove a gas-guzzler like that. Didn't he know what his greed was doing to the planet? He had just turned away to continue on down the sidewalk when somebody called, "Hey! Hey, man, no! You can't do that."

Granderson turned his head to look and saw a fat white guy with shaggy hair and a mustache hurrying toward him. The guy waved a hand at the SUV and went on, "I just went in there for a minute to make a delivery."

"This ain't the delivery entrance, pal," Granderson said. He pointed at the No Parking sign. "And this part of the street is clearly marked. You don't see anybody else breaking the law along here, do you?"

"It's not the law," the guy blustered. "It's just some bullcrap rule you campus rent-a-cops have."

Granderson jutted his chin out and moved up on the guy in a hurry. He rested his hand on the stun gun holstered at his belt as he said through clenched teeth, "Are you creating a disturbance, mister?"

"Wait. What?" The guy started to back off. "No, no, I'm not lookin' for trouble, I just don't think you should've given me a ticket. I was just in there for a minute."

"I don't care if it was just ten seconds. It's still a violation."

"Yeah, I guess so, if you want to get technical about it—"

"It's not a technicality," Granderson said, making an effort not to snarl. "The law is the law."

"Fine, fine." The guy raised his hands, palms out, and patted at the air in a placating gesture. "I'll pay the damn fine—"

The stun gun came out of the holster as Granderson's eyes widened and he started to breathe harder.

"Lower your hands!" he screamed. "You're assaulting an officer of the law! I'll take you down, you son of a bitch!"

"What?" The guy backpedaled faster. "No, no! I'm not assaulting anybody—"

"On the ground, on the ground! Get down now, you scumbag!" Granderson's thumb trembled as it poised above the stun gun's trigger. He wanted to press it so bad . . .

"Cal!"

The shout startled him and almost made him

fire the weapon anyway. The deliveryman shrieked like a girl and threw his arms up over his face. He must have seen the nearly out-of-control rage in Granderson's eyes.

Granderson managed to hold off on pressing the trigger. With his chest heaving from the effort that restraint required, he looked over his shoulder to see who had called his name. Frank McRainey trotted toward him, a little red-faced because he was hurrying and wasn't as young and fit as he'd once been.

Granderson believed, in fact, that the job of chief had passed McRainey by. It needed a younger, more vital and energetic and dedicated man.

A man much like Granderson himself. In moments when he allowed himself to dream, he saw himself in the chief's uniform, leading the campus police force to be the fine representatives of law and order that they should be . . . instead of freakin' meter maids.

He shoved such thoughts out of his head for the moment and snapped, "Shut up," at the delivery guy, who had stopped shrieking but was sniveling now, a truly disgusting display for somebody as big as him. Didn't he have any self-respect?

McRainey pounded up and stopped, panting a little as he asked, "What's . . . going on . . . here?"

"This guy thinks he can just park anywhere," Granderson said as he waved his free hand at the man. "And when I gave him a ticket for it, he came after me, yelling and threatening to assault me."

"That . . . that's not true," the guy said. "Yeah,

maybe I yelled a little when I first came out of the building and saw him giving me a ticket, but I calmed down right away, and I never threatened him."

"He raised his hands to me and made aggressive gestures," Granderson insisted.

"What? I did this."

The guy did those placating pats again. As he did, Granderson jerked the stun gun back up and yelled, "Stand down! I told you to get on the ground!"

"Cal!" McRainey moved to get between Granderson and the delivery guy. "Cal, for God's sake, stop it! That's not an aggressive gesture. He's not threatening you or trying to assault you. He just doesn't want you to use that stun gun on him."

"Then he should cooperate with law enforcement and do as he's told," Granderson said, tight-jawed again.

McRainey scrubbed a hand over his florid face and muttered something under his breath that Granderson couldn't quite make out. He thought for a second that McRainey had said, "Asshole," but that was impossible. The chief would never say that about his most loyal, dedicated officer.

McRainey turned to look at the man and said sharply, "Get that ticket, get in your vehicle, and get out of here."

"Sure, sure, Chief," the man said as he hurried around the front of the SUV. "I never meant to cause any trouble—"

"You can pay the fine for that citation online, and I'd advise you to do so," McRainey interrupted him. "It's just a parking violation, so it won't be reported to your insurance company, and your rates won't go up. But if you ignore it, it'll cause more trouble for you in the long run."

"I won't ignore it. I'll pay it, I swear."

The guy climbed into the SUV, slammed the door, and drove off.

"The speed limit on this street is twenty-five," Granderson said. "I think he's going faster than that."

"Don't worry about it, Cal," McRainey told him. "He'll be off-campus in a minute, and he won't be our problem anymore." He pointed at the stun gun still in Granderson's hand. "Put that away. You shouldn't have drawn it to start with."

Granderson frowned and said stubbornly, "I didn't have any choice, Chief. He was aggressive, I tell you."

"Well, he's gone now, so let's just forget about it."

"I should have given him the ticket, shouldn't I? You can't be saying that I should have just ignored a parking violation."

"No, I'm not saying that at all. You just . . . Sometimes you get . . ." McRainey stopped whatever it was he was trying to say and shook his head. "Why don't you just go on over to the library and stay on duty there this morning?"

"Library duty?" Granderson snorted. "Nothing ever happens on library duty."

"That's the way I like it. It's a good thing when nothing happens."

Granderson supposed that from a law-enforcement standpoint, that was true. He sighed and nodded with obvious reluctance.

"All right, Chief. But if you need me, my walkie will be on."

"Of course it will," McRainey said.

"You just give me a call." Granderson slipped the stun gun back into the holster clipped to his belt. "I'll be ready."

He turned and headed for the library, careful to stay on the concrete walks that led around the buildings.

As he moved through the campus, students crowded onto the walks, and Granderson knew without checking the time that the eight o'clock classes were over. They stayed out of his way as he weaved through them, and he understood why. He was a symbol of the oppressive system they hated. His grandmother, who had been right in the thick of things at the University of Texas in Austin during the sixties, would have called him The Man, if she'd still been around. She had pretty much raised him, especially after his mom had disappeared, just walked off and never came back, following one of her failed stays in rehab. He had grown up hearing about fighting the establishment and speaking truth to power and what a great day it would be when the revolution finally came and the workers were in charge instead of the fat cats of the military-industrial complex, and he had soaked it all in.

Then he had gone and betrayed that heritage by trying to become a cop, a pig. All he'd managed to do so far was hire on with the campus force. Like most kids, he supposed, he had reached a point when he wanted to rebel against authority, and where his grandma was concerned, that meant joining forces with the authority she had rejected.

He had waited until after she'd passed away before he did that, though. There was no need to hurt her unnecessarily.

Since then, he had often felt like he was two people: cop on the outside, devoted to the rule of law; free spirit on the inside, wishing for that brighter day when all people would live together in peace and harmony like his grandmother had dreamed of.

For that to ever happen, the fascists on the right of the political divide had to be brought under control, or even gotten rid of, permanently. That would be just fine with Cal Granderson. There was no place for such relics of oppression in the new world that was coming. Round 'em up and ship 'em out, and if that didn't work, there were plenty of other ways to accomplish the goal. The ends justified the means, after all. Everybody from Alinsky on down taught that.

It could happen, too, once everybody understood and accepted that the only people in this world who ought to have guns were the police and the military. The Second Amendment had to be done away with and all the firearms in private hands confiscated. It would be a different world then, when he and the people who thought like he did were the only ones with guns. He would have a Glock or a Sig on his hip instead of some stupid stun gun. And when anybody tried to cause trouble, like that Jake Rivers, they'd be sorry. They'd be real sorry.

Granderson went up the steps, between the white columns, across the porch, and into the library.

He saw the sidelong glances the students gave him. They just didn't understand, he told himself. He might be a townie, but he was really *one of them*, somebody who believed in all the progressive ideals and wanted to put down the racist, sexist, homophobic fascists. All they saw was the uniform he wore. They couldn't see what was in his heart.

He had gotten into an argument once with a guy who had called him a crazy, mixed-up son of a bitch, before Granderson beat the hell out of him.

Granderson just didn't see how anybody could feel that way about him.

Chapter 21

Jake knew he probably ought to be worried about the summons to President Pelletier's office, but he couldn't bring himself to even think much about it as he waited in the administrator's outer office that morning. Pelletier let him cool his heels a while this time, and the only reason that bothered Jake was that it meant he would have less time to spend with Natalie at the library before he had to go to class. Assuming he still had a class to go to. It was entirely possible Pelletier might tell him to haul his butt off campus and never darken any of Kelton College's doorways again. That wouldn't be fair, of course—Jake hadn't done anything wrong, and the video Pierce Conners had shot and uploaded proved that—but "fair" wouldn't stop Pelletier from doing whatever he wanted to do. Jake knew he would have some legal recourse if he were expelled. His grandfather would be willing to help him fight the expulsion in court, he was sure of that. But he was no longer sure that he wanted to. He was tired of the whole damned thing.

He would have walked away from Kelton College without any regrets . . . other than one.

That would mean walking away from Natalie Burke, too.

"You can go in now," the president's secretary told Jake, breaking into his thoughts of Natalie.

He nodded and got to his feet, then hesitated. Go on into Pelletier's office, or say to hell with it, turn, and walk out?

Might as well see what the guy had to say, Jake told himself. He went to the door of the inner office, turned the knob, and went in, but his steps were a bit on the heavy side as he did so.

"Sit down, Mr. Rivers," Pelletier snapped from behind the desk. "I'm sure you know why I asked you to come here this morning."

Pelletier hadn't exactly asked, Jake thought. It was more like an order. He said, "I suppose it has something to do with what happened in the biology building yesterday afternoon."

"You clashed with another student again. It was a violent encounter."

Jake thought about some of the fights he'd been in during the past six years and said, "No offense, sir, but that wasn't violence. That guy might as well have been trying to play patty-cake with me."

Pelletier frowned across the desk.

"Don't make light of this, Mr. Rivers. I've already spent more time on your, ah, adventures recently than I like to think about. I have the real work of running this college to take care of, you know."

"And it would be a lot easier if I wasn't around, wouldn't it?"

Pelletier's lips thinned.

"I consulted with the college's legal counsel this morning. We watched several different videos uploaded by students. They paint a very vivid picture of what happened."

Jake slipped his phone from his pocket and held it out to the president as he asked, "Did you watch the one I have on here? One of those students who witnessed the whole thing gave it to me. It shows everything from start to finish and makes it clear that I didn't start the trouble. All I did was—"

Pelletier surprised him by slamming a hand down on the desk. That was unusual vehemence from the aging college president. His hand made a loud crack when it struck the wood.

"All you did was defend yourself," he said, his voice rising in anger. "My God, don't you think I've heard that enough from you, Rivers? It's your excuse every time you brutalize one of my students."

"I'm one of your students, too," Jake pointed out tightly. He was mad, too.

"For one of the few times in my academic career, I wish that were not the case," Pelletier said. "I wish you had never decided to attend this institution, or that you hadn't been granted admittance."

"But that was never going to happen because my grandfather donates too much money to Kelton, doesn't he? And that's not all he does. He helps fund-raise from other sources, too. A lot of the personal and corporate donations the college gets are because he did some persuading . . . or arm-twisting."

Pelletier made a sour face.

"Fund-raising is a necessary evil, I'm afraid. But there's a limit to how much I'll tolerate because of financial considerations, young man. I have to look out for the college community as a whole, and your presence here is a serious disruption to the learning environment."

"Why? Because I'm a conservative? In an institution of higher learning, especially, shouldn't there be room for all different kinds of viewpoints?"

"Not the ones devoted to hate," Pelletier said as his lip curled in a sneer.

"I don't hate anybody. Look around at the rest of the country, sir. The stock market's up, unemployment is down, the economy is growing at a nice rate. Around the world, other countries respect us again."

"You mean they fear what that lunatic in the White House might do."

"A little fear can be a healthy thing," Jake said with a smile. "And as time goes on and things keep on getting better, the only ones who think the guy's a lunatic are people like you who live in your little echo chambers and never hear what normal people think. You wouldn't believe it if you did."

Pelletier stood up, leaned forward, rested his hands on the desk, and snarled, "Get out, you impudent little . . ."

Words failed him, and he couldn't go on.

Jake stood up, still grinning, and asked, "Out of your office, or out of this college?" He shrugged. "Right now, I don't much care which it is."

Pelletier was so mad he was breathing hard.

"Out of my office," he said. "I have no grounds for expulsion right at this moment—"

"Ah, so you *have* seen the unedited video," Jake couldn't resist saying.

"But if you so much as get a parking ticket on this campus, you'll be gone, mister. I'll be speaking to all of your professors and to your faculty advisor, as well, to make sure they understand all the academic requirements to which you have to adhere in order to maintain your status as a student in good standing."

Jake shook his head and said, "My grades are fine. You won't be able to cook up something and claim that I flunked out. Not without falsifying a lot of records and getting a bunch of people to go along with you."

"Don't be so sure I couldn't do that," Pelletier warned.

He probably could, Jake thought. After all, the left specialized in banding together and spinning false narratives. The mainstream media had been doing it for decades. They took pride in being able to tell the public what to think, whether the so-called news they peddled bore any real resemblance to the truth or not. They had claimed that Hillary Clinton was the most qualified candidate for president in the history of the country, hadn't they?

"Do what you have to do," Jake said quietly, then turned to leave Pelletier's office. He didn't ask if Pelletier was through with him.

He was through with Pelletier.

He did pause in the doorway, though, to look back at the red-faced older man and said, "When you talk to my faculty advisor, say hello to Dr. Mtumbo for me."

"Get out," Pelletier snarled.

On his way out of the office, Jake told the secretary, "Sorry. He's gonna be a bear the rest of the day."

She just pressed her lips together and didn't say anything. Her expression was a mask, and Jake couldn't tell if she sympathized with him or shared her boss's dislike of him.

All he really cared about at the moment was that the meeting was over, it was only nine-thirty, and he still had some time to spend with Natalie before he had to get to class.

He wasn't really sure where things stood with Natalie. He knew he liked her, and he believed she liked him. But getting involved in a romance with a professor wasn't something he had even thought about when he came to Kelton College. If anyone had asked him about the possibility, he would have said that it was pretty damned unlikely, given that Kelton was mostly a liberal arts school, and he was about as far from the liberal arts type as anybody could get.

But he couldn't deny the fact that he was drawn to her. She had to have some political beliefs, probably even some strong ones, given that she taught criminal justice and was bound to have been exposed to a lot of what Jake considered sociological claptrap. She didn't put politics front and center of everything else in her life, though, as so many of the students, faculty, and administration at Kelton seemed to. Jake had heard many times that politics had replaced religion for the left, and he firmly believed that was true. Most of the progressives he had encountered were as fervent, fanatical, and evangelical in their politics as Bible-thumping holy rollers were in their spiritual beliefs.

The problem with trying to develop a real relationship with Natalie was that Jake didn't know how long he would be around here. His days on campus might well be numbered, and if he wasn't enrolled at Kelton anymore, no way was he going to hang around Greenleaf. Maybe he would see if he could get some contact info for that guy Rivera, the one he had seen out at the gun range, and let him know that if he had any intriguing and exciting assignments in the works, Jake would be interested in signing on. The idea of potential danger didn't bother him in the slightest.

With all those thoughts running through his mind, it wasn't difficult to ignore the students he passed or met on the sidewalk. Many of them knew who he was—he was big enough that it was hard to mistake him for anyone else—and he was vaguely aware of the hostile stares they directed at him. But the unfriendly looks just bounced off him. He didn't give a damn what any of those snowflakes thought about him.

As he reached the library steps and was about to start up them, he recognized a balding, gangling figure coming the other way on the sidewalk, seemingly bent on the same destination. Jake smiled and said, "Morning, Dr. Mtumbo."

Montambault frowned slightly, as if wondering whether Jake was making fun of him . . . which, of course, he sort of was. But the biology professor nodded and said, "Good morning, Mr. Rivers."

Jake leaned his head toward the big, imposing building and asked, "Headed to the library?"

"That's right."

"Me, too." Still smiling, Jake turned to walk up the steps. Montambault hesitated, but only for a second, and then fell in step beside him.

Jake went on, "You're probably surprised to see that I'm still here."

"Why would I be surprised? As your faculty advisor, I get email updates on your grades. You appear to be doing excellent work in all your classes, including mine."

"Thanks. But nobody can say the same about how I fit in, in any other way."

"That's true. You've acquired a certain, ah, reputation as . . . as . . ."

"A troublemaker?"

"You said that, Mr. Rivers, not me," Montambault responded. "I don't wish bad luck on any student."

"You haven't been cheerleading with President Pelletier to boot me out of here?"

"I most certainly have not." Montambault sounded almost offended that Jake would suggest such a thing. Jake didn't know whether to believe him or not, but the professor seemed sincere.

"All right. I'm glad to hear it. I don't guess I could go so far as to say that you're on my side—"

"You could not," Montambault said stiffly.

"But I'll take just not working against me. That

puts you ahead of just about everybody else on campus."

They had gone through the entrance doors and were inside the library's cavernous first floor. Montambault paused and asked, "Was there anything you needed to talk to me about?"

"Nope," Jake said with a shake of his head. "Running into you this morning was just an accident."

"I'll get on about my business, then," Montambault said. "Good day."

Jake nodded and turned in the opposite direction from the professor. Natalie was supposed to meet him downstairs, so he headed for the escalators.

On the way, he passed a couple of guys who were decked out in the green coveralls of the college's groundskeeping crew and wondered idly what they were doing in the library. It wasn't unusual to see members of the maintenance crew around, anywhere on campus, but the groundskeepers did all their work outside.

Then he forgot all about it as he stepped on the escalator and started down, because Natalie happened to be passing by at the bottom and stopped to smile up at him as he descended.

CHAPTER 22

Frank McRainey was still angry as he walked back toward the campus police station. Seething, in fact, and he didn't like that. Getting so upset wasn't good for his health, and he knew it. The last time he'd been in for a checkup, the doc had given him the usual "lose weight and exercise more" spiel, but he had also mentioned that it would be a good idea for Frank to manage his stress better and try to stay on an even keel emotionally.

That was easier said than done, especially when you had guys like Cal Granderson working for you. Granderson was particularly frustrating, because he wasn't *always* an aggressive, over-eager idiot. Sometimes he actually listened to what Frank had to say and had the makings of a good cop. Frank could tell that he *wanted* to be a good cop. Problem was, you never could tell when the idiot side of him would crop up with no warning, like it had this morning with that deliveryman in front of the Language Arts Building.

McRainey had witnessed that confrontation, although from a distance at first. But even though his ticker might be getting suspect, there was nothing wrong with his eyes, and he had seen that the man hadn't done anything to cause Granderson to threaten him and practically foam at the mouth that way. McRainey didn't know what had set Granderson off. It was entirely possible that Granderson himself didn't know.

But rather than speculate on that and maybe get even more upset, it might be a good idea not to go back to the station after all, McRainey decided. He would go over to the groundskeepers' shed and have a cup of coffee with his friend Charlie Hodges instead. For some reason, the brew from the coffeemaker in Charlie's office always tasted better than the coffee various members of the force, McRainey included, made at the station.

He knew the most efficient way to get anywhere on campus, so it didn't take him long to reach the shed. The big door was down, and no light showed through the office's single window. Indeed, the place looked dark and deserted, which was unusual for this time of day. Like McRainey, Charlie Hodges wasn't as young as he used to be and tended to hang around the shed most of the day, sending the younger guys on the crew out to do whatever was necessary. That was why McRainey usually dropped by here at least once a day to shoot the breeze and bum a cup of that coffee.

McRainey tried the door. Locked. Again, unusual. The crew was working today, McRainey knew that. He had seen several of them while he was on his way over here. They had been digging holes near one of the buildings, although he couldn't recall which. He wasn't sure what they were doing, either. Maybe planting some new shrubs.

After rapping his knuckles on the door a few times without getting any response, McRainey went over to the window. He leaned close to it and cupped his hands around his eyes to shut out the light while he peered through the glass. He didn't believe anybody was in there. Otherwise, there would have been a light on, the door would have been unlocked, or at the very least somebody would have answered his knock. But his curiosity was great enough to make him take a look.

The office was empty, all right. McRainey could see that much even though the room was gloomy with shadows. He started to straighten up, thinking that he ought to call Charlie's cell phone and find out what was going on. Maybe the head groundskeeper was sick.

Then, abruptly, McRainey stared through the window again. He had spotted something on the floor behind the desk, right at the back corner. He couldn't be sure, but he thought it looked like . . . the heel of a shoe . . .

McRainey jerked upright and two fast steps carried him to the door. He grasped the knob tightly, lifted on it, and rammed his shoulder against the door. That hurt like hell. McRainey knew there was a good chance his bursitis would flare up because of it.

He couldn't worry about that now. As far as he knew, Charlie Hodges wasn't having any major health issues, but he was at the age when an unexpected heart attack or stroke couldn't be ruled out.

When the door gave a little but didn't open, McRainey hit it again. This time it flew inward with a sound of splintering wood as the jamb gave way. McRainey stumbled a little as his balance tried to desert him. He was a couple of steps inside the room before he caught himself.

That brought him far enough so he could see part of the area behind the desk. A coverall-clad figure was lying there, curled up in an awkward ball. The heel of one work boot was the only thing sticking out far enough to be seen from outside, and most people never would have noticed it or realized what it was.

McRainey turned and reached out to flip on the light. It seemed harsher than usual as it spilled down over the room and reached behind the desk to illuminate the contorted face of Charlie Hodges. Charlie's eyes were open but staring sightlessly. McRainey moaned, "Oh, hell," as he stood there motionless and looked at his friend's body.

It must have been a heart attack or stroke, he thought again. His cop's mind put the sequence of events together. Charlie had been about to leave the shed. He had locked the office door and turned off the light because he was planning to open the big roll-up door and go out that way, probably on one of the mowers. Then whatever it was had hit him and he had staggered back over to the desk. Maybe he had been thinking that he would call for help. But it was too late. He'd collapsed and died there on the floor.

This wasn't the first time Frank McRainey had seen sudden, unexpected death. Actually, during his career in law enforcement he had seen lots of things worse than this. Hodges hadn't died peacefully, the expression on his face was proof of that, but in all likelihood, he hadn't suffered for long.

McRainey started to go to his friend so he could move Charlie out of there and then call for EMTs and an ambulance. He was certain that Charlie was dead, but like everything else in life, there were protocols to be followed . . .

He stopped short before he reached the body. Then a frown appeared on his face as he leaned forward and studied the scene more closely.

Every cop's instinct in his body had started clamoring that something was wrong.

For one thing, it was unlikely that somebody dying from a stroke would wind up in such a tight, drawn-up ball. Possible, of course, but McRainey just didn't think it would happen that way. There was a better chance someone suffering a heart attack would curl up around their pain like that. Even that didn't sound right to McRainey.

Then there was the matter of how Charlie Hodges' head was lying at an unnatural angle to his shoulders. McRainey's eyes widened and his own heart began to slug heavily in his chest as he realized that his old friend's neck was broken.

This was no death from natural causes or even an accident.

Charlie Hodges had been murdered.

McRainey was reaching for the walkie-talkie clipped to his belt to sound the alarm when he heard a sudden rush of footsteps behind him. He barely had time to turn his head before somebody tackled him and drove him into a crashing impact with the wall.

The glimpse McRainey had gotten of his attacker showed him a tall, well-built young man with a fringe of sandy beard. Then the side of the chief's head banged hard against the wall and he blacked out, like somebody had switched off a light.

Only for a second, though. He was still sliding down the wall toward the floor when awareness returned to him. He blinked rapidly, saw a flash of something coming at him, and flung a hand up to stop it. He screamed as the keen edge of a knife cut deep into his palm, but he closed his hand around the blade anyway, knowing that if he didn't, he would be dead a second later.

Acting mostly on instinct, he kicked out and felt the bottom of his foot slam into something. The would-be killer yelled and toppled forward onto him. McRainey couldn't hold on to the knife anymore, but as it slipped out of his blood-slick grasp, he brought his other hand up and hammered a punch at the guy's face. It landed with a satisfying smack.

McRainey planted his bleeding left hand against the man's chest and shoved. That got him a little room to maneuver. He tried to squirm farther away. The knife darted at him again. McRainey caught the wrist of the hand wielding it this time and forced it to the floor. The blade scraped over the tiles but didn't come loose from the man's grip.

McRainey's left hand was a mass of pain and didn't want to work now. He got that forearm under the guy's bearded chin and tried to force it back.

He could feel his strength deserting him, though. His age and the blood he had lost already were working against him. He knew that nine times out of ten, an older guy, no matter what shape he was in, couldn't match up with a fit younger man. And this was not that tenth time.

So he couldn't win a fair fight, but maybe he could win a dirty one.

He kept his hold on the guy's wrist and tried to ram a knee into his groin. The man twisted aside. Their legs tangled up. McRainey got a scissors grip on one and heaved. The man yelled in pain, more than the move seemed to deserve. McRainey wondered wildly if that kick he'd landed had broken the bastard's shin.

They flailed and writhed together on the floor, which was smeared thickly with blood by now. This was no carefully choreographed movie fight, where the moves were all graceful and the audience could tell what was going on. If there had been an audience in this office, they would have seen a bloody, awkward, desperate mess as the two men battled with life and death as the stakes.

McRainey hung on to his opponent's wrist to keep the knife away from him while trying to use his other elbow to break the guy's ribs. He lifted that arm and slammed it down into the man's torso again and again.

At the same time, the man punched at the chief's head with his left fist. McRainey's brain was already a little addled from hitting the wall and blacking out. The world spun crazily around him, as if it had tilted off its axis and gone flying off into space. He had to shrink the universe down to two primal items: keeping that knife away from him, and hitting the guy with his elbow.

The attacker stopped pummeling him and grabbed him by the throat instead. Purely by bad luck, the move caught McRainey between breaths, so he had barely any air in his lungs. Not enough to last more than a few seconds before he stood a good chance of passing out again. He had to force his badly slashed hand to work. It flopped like a dead fish as he managed to slap it across the man's face. He clawed at the man's eyes.

That made him jerk away and loosened his grip on McRainey's throat. McRainey heaved up and tried to knee the bastard again. This time the blow slipped between the man's knees and crunched home.

The guy screamed into McRainey's mangled palm.

McRainey hit him again, letting his own pain and desperation fuel the vicious blow as he tried to drive the guy's balls all the way up into his throat. The man spasmed in agony. The knife slipped from his fingers and clattered about six inches along the bloody floor.

McRainey grabbed it, brought it up and then down. The blade penetrated the man's chest, ripping through muscle and scraping on bone and finally coming to rest with its entire length buried. The man bucked up from the floor again, then his head fell back and with a distinct rattle, air gusted from his throat through his open, gaping mouth.

McRainey knew the man was dead.

The chief slumped forward as the last of his strength deserted him. He kept his good hand wrapped around the knife handle, but it didn't matter now. The fight was over.

McRainey's chest hurt, but not as bad as his wounded hand. His head throbbed, too. He was in bad shape, no doubt about that, but he was better off than the son of a bitch who'd jumped him, and he took a savage satisfaction in that.

The man must have killed Charlie Hodges, McRainey thought as the primitive self-preservation instinct that had gripped him during the battle began to recede and his brain started to function better again. Then the guy had hung around somewhere nearby and kept an eye on the shed to see if his crime was going to be discovered. When McRainey broke in here and found the groundskeeper's body, he had targeted himself for death.

That left the question of *why* the man had murdered Charlie, and he was beyond answering that now. His eyes were just as sightless as Charlie's as they stared toward the ceiling, McRainey realized as he pushed himself up off the corpse.

He rolled to the side so that he wound up half-sitting, half-lying with his shoulder propped against the desk. Blood still welled from the deep cut on his left palm. He used his right hand to fumble out a handkerchief from his pocket and wrapped it around the injured hand, pulling it as tight as he could and then closing the fingers around it.

Gritting his teeth against the pain, he tried to find his walkie-talkie. It wasn't on his belt anymore, having gotten knocked off during the fight. McRainey bit back a groan of despair. His sight was blurry as he peered around, but he spotted the walkie lying just under the corner of the desk, within reach. He took hold of it and lifted it with a trembling hand.

Maybe he could figure out later who the guy was and why he'd killed Charlie Hodges. That was his job, after all. But he couldn't do that if he sat here and bled to death. He thumbed the talk button on the walkie and said, "This . . . this is Chief McRainey . . . I need help . . . at the . . . groundskeeper's shed . . ."

Chapter 23

"Were you waiting right here for me to show up?" Jake asked Natalie as he stepped off the escalator at the bottom.

She laughed.

"Get over yourself, big man! You think I have nothing better to do than wait for you? No, it was just a coincidence that I was walking by here and happened to look up and see you. Once I did, I thought I might as well wait for you so you wouldn't have to look for me."

"That's a good story," Jake said with a grin. "I'll reserve judgment on whether I believe it or not."

"You just go right ahead and do that. Come on. I have my work spread out on one of the tables over here."

She led him into the study area. Jake was tall enough that he could see over some of the low sets of shelves dividing that part of the library's lower floor. He spotted a familiar face and recognized the kid who had given him the unedited video, Pierce Conners. Pierce was sitting with a group of students, one of whom was a young Middle Eastern guy.

Jake knew a lot of people would say it was racist

of him, but whenever he saw somebody like that, he always felt himself tense up inside for a second. Too many people who looked like that guy had shot at him or tried to blow him up. Once you'd lived with something like that for months, it took a long time for the instincts developed during such an experience to fade.

Natalie's laptop was sitting open on one of the tables with a number of papers and some thick books sitting around it. Jake gestured at the books and said, "I figured you'd be completely paperless. Aren't old-fashioned books supposed to be bad for the environment?"

"Old-fashioned is right. Most of these books were written eighty, ninety, or even a hundred years ago. Some of them even more. Nearly all of the old texts and statute books and legal histories haven't been digitized yet. Maybe they will be someday, but for now I have to use what exists."

"That makes sense." Jake started to pull her chair out for her, then stopped and said, "Wait a minute. I'm not supposed to do anything polite like that, am I?"

"Holding a woman's chair for her *is* a patriarchal microaggression . . . but I'll let it slide. This time." Natalie's smile and the twinkle in her eyes took any sting out of the words.

As she sat down and Jake walked around to the other side of the table, her expression grew solemn and she went on, "How did the meeting with President Pelletier go?"

"Well, he didn't have security remove me from the campus, so that's one thing to be grateful for, I suppose. I'm not sure I know what I want anymore. He got plenty upset with me, though. The spit was flying."

Natalie laughed, then immediately looked contrite.

"I'm sorry. I shouldn't do that. It's not funny, the things that have happened to you recently, Jake. It's just that I can see the poor old man. I'll bet his face got really red."

"It did," Jake said. "I got out of there before he could have a stroke."

"Well, I'm glad. That would have been terrible."

"Yeah. I don't have anything against the guy personally. We just don't see eye to eye. No surprise. My politics don't seem to agree with anyone's here at Kelton. I'll bet there are a few conservatives besides me, though. They just haven't owned up to it yet, and I can't say as I blame them." He looked intently at Natalie. "You and I have never actually talked politics, you know."

"I know," she said. "And I'd just as soon keep it that way."

"That's all right. I don't mind liberals, as long as they're fair and honest. I just haven't run into many who fit that description."

"I never said I was a liberal . . . or a conservative."

Her voice had a bit of a sharp edge to it now, so Jake held up his hands and said, "All right, point taken. And you're right. The last thing I want to do is turn into one of those people who filter everything though an ideological lens. I say we concentrate on the things we know we agree on and not worry about anything else."

"And what is it we agree on?"

"Well, that kiss was pretty nice . . ."

"Yes, it was," Natalie said, and Jake was both surprised and gratified to see that she was blushing a little. It was an unexpected reaction these days, but a charming one.

She looked down at the laptop, then said, "All right, I have work to do. This wasn't a date. You said you usually study at this time of day."

"Yep." Jake took out his phone. "I actually uploaded some notes on here so I can go over them."

He opened the app and started reading. Natalie flipped through documents and books and from time to time scribbled something on a piece of paper or typed something into the laptop. The silence between them stretched out, but it was a companionable one and Jake found himself enjoying it.

If you had to study, he thought, you might as well do it sitting across a table from a beautiful redhead.

Matthias Foster came out of the men's room on the first floor of the administration building in jeans, a pullover shirt, and a light jacket instead of the groundskeeper's coveralls he had been wearing earlier in his pose as Rick Overman. The civilian clothes had been in a taped-up cardboard carton he had carried into the building as if he were delivering something.

No one had glanced twice at him.

After changing, he had stuffed the coveralls in the trash can in the bathroom. By the time anyone discovered them there, it would be too late to make any difference.

In several different locations across campus, his men who had pretended to be part of the grounds-keeping crew were carrying out similar actions. When they left the buildings where they had changed clothes, they would drift toward the Burr Memorial Library, the way Foster was doing now.

He had been working at Kelton College for a couple of months, so it was possible that some of the students and faculty members he passed on the way thought he looked familiar, but he hadn't made any real friends on the campus and no one paid any attention to him as he walked toward the library. They probably took him for a student. He was young enough to pass for one, although he was older than most of the student body. But there were always older students at a college, sometimes a lot older than him.

And he actually had been a student at Kelton, not all that long ago. He had earned an academic scholarship, a full ride. He'd arrived on campus full of ambition and anticipation, ready to not only further his education but to make a difference in the world as well. Kelton was populated by those who shared his progressive ideals, his zeal to change the world for the better, his loathing for everything old and reactionary.

It hadn't taken him long, however, to realize that they loathed *him,* too, because he was poor. Their commitment to diversity and equality didn't extend to boys from squalid little oil-field towns like the one Foster came from, no matter how smart they were.

With his passion for learning and disdain for sports and hard work and his "liberal notions," he had never fit in, back in his hometown. It should have been different at Kelton, but although the reasons were different, most of the people there seemed to despise him, as well. He had joined all the right groups, said all the right things, and firmly believed what he was saying, but none of it seemed to make any difference.

The world was filled with assholes, no matter where you went, and there were only two things that really made any difference to them: money and power. For the most part, those two things went hand in hand. If you had enough money, you had power. Simple as that.

Matthias Foster was smart. Always had been. It didn't take him long to realize what he had to do.

He had almost reached the library when the burner phone in his shirt pocket chimed to let him know he had a message. He stopped and frowned. Everybody was supposed to be in position and at "radio silence" now, which included text messages. Foster took out the phone and checked the screen.

His heart jumped a little when he saw the message was from Curt Nevins, who he had left keeping an eye on the groundskeepers' shed, just in case anyone came poking around there. He opened the message and read: *Chief McRainey going into shed! Will stop him!*

"Oh, no," Foster said under his breath. He tapped into the phone: *Eliminate at all costs!*

Foster checked the time. Zero hour, if you could call it that, was less than fifteen minutes away. But there was still time enough for Frank McRainey to discover all those bodies in the shed and rouse the campus. Foster believed that he had allowed for enough contingencies that it shouldn't matter if McRainey did that, but it was better not to run the risk. Things could still go wrong, despite all of his planning.

Nevins didn't respond to the message, so Foster didn't know if he had gotten it or not. He would just have to trust to luck and hope that Nevins would take care of the threat. There was no time to do anything else.

Foster slipped the phone back into his pocket and went briskly up the steps, across the porch, and into the library.

The self-checkout stations were to his right as he went in the main entrance. Beyond them, a long reference desk where student assistants worked, something that hadn't changed in decades. One of his people was behind that desk, put in place at the first of the semester like a dozen others in various positions of trust and responsibility across the campus. At least two of Foster's followers were in all the main buildings, and like him, they were prepared to risk their lives to accomplish the objective.

He had an even larger number of allies here at the library. It was the centerpiece of the entire plan, with more students, faculty members, and staff on hand during a normal day than in any other single building at Kelton College. He was confident in the people he had in the administration building, the various classroom buildings, and the residence halls, but taking the library was the crux of everything.

How could it be anything else, since *he* was here? He was the mastermind of everything that was going to happen today.

He went into the first-floor men's room and locked the door behind him with a key provided by one of the maintenance crew who was part of his group. Nobody was at the urinals, but a student was coming out of one of the stalls. The guy didn't make eye contact with Foster, since men seldom acknowledged another man's presence in a restroom. He just went to one of the sinks to wash his hands, which made it easy for Foster to take him from behind, reaching around to lock an arm around the young man's throat so a twist and a heave snapped his neck. The young man sagged, deadweight now even though he was still alive. He wouldn't be for long, though, since his lungs no longer worked. He would die of suffocation within minutes.

Foster dragged him into one of the stalls, propped him up on the toilet, and left him there.

Then Foster pulled the trash can away from the wall at the end of the row of sinks and climbed up on it. He lifted one of the ceiling tiles and reached inside with his other hand, closing it around the canvas bag the same maintenance man had placed there last night. He pulled the bag out and jumped down to the floor again.

Inside the drawstring bag was a Glock 9mm pistol with a loaded magazine already in the butt, plus eight more loaded magazines. There were other ammunition caches scattered around the library if they became necessary. His people had been working on this for weeks. Planning and patience, those were the keys to an operation like this.

Somebody banged on the bathroom door and said, "What the hell?"

Foster tucked the Glock into his waistband at the small of his back, under the jacket, and stashed the loaded magazines in various pockets. Then he unlocked the door and said, "Sorry, man, we had a bad plumbing problem in here."

The guy was in a hurry and didn't seem to notice that Foster wasn't dressed like a maintenance man. He pushed past, heading for one of the stalls. Foster took out the Glock and slammed it on the back of his head, knocking him to his knees. Another hard, swift blow made the guy pitch forward, out cold.

Foster left him there, put the gun away, stepped out of the restroom, and locked the door behind him. The student would be unconscious for a little while, but stuck in the locked bathroom like that, he might actually be one of the lucky ones. Where he was, he stood a lot less chance of getting shot.

Of course, he might still get blown up . . .

With a pleasant half-smile on his face, Foster walked away from the restroom and toward the escalators. One of the campus cops was strutting around near them with an angry, arrogant expression on his face, a living symbol of the establishment oppression that Foster had once wanted to do away with, too, before he'd realized that what he really needed was something else entirely. The guy glanced at Foster but didn't really pay attention to him. Foster was used to that.

On the way to the escalator, he also passed a

couple of his guys. They made eye contact only for a fraction of a second, and the nods they gave him were so tiny and quick most people would have missed them, but they were enough to tell Foster that they had retrieved the weapons that had been hidden for them. He reached the escalator and started down to the lower floor.

Actually, there were more people down here than on the ground floor. This was the real hub of the library, where students came to study or work on projects or just hang out. When he was halfway down the escalator, Foster looked around and spotted the members of his inner circle spread out around the big room. Hank was to his left, over near the stacks. Jimmy to the right. Carlos straight ahead, sitting in an armchair pretending to be doing something on his phone.

And there was Lucy, sweet Lucy, right where she was supposed to be. She glanced up, and their eyes met across the intervening distance. Foster frowned slightly as he realized she didn't look as eager and ready to neutralize any threat as he had hoped she would be. It was way too late to be having any second thoughts or cold feet about the plan now. Foster knew that, and knew that no matter what Lucy's state of mind was, the rest of them had no choice but to carry on.

Because this was the time, he thought as he slipped his phone from his pocket with his left hand and checked the hour. He entered nine digits of a telephone number but not the tenth one that would complete the call. This had been checked out thoroughly. Cell service was actually pretty sketchy inside the library, but it was good enough for his purposes.

He held the phone in his left hand and reached behind him, under his jacket, with the right. As he stepped off the escalator at the bottom, he pulled the Glock free, pointed it at the ceiling, and triggered two shots. The gun-thunder was deafening in this confined space, but Foster had earplugs in to protect his hearing with their decibel-activated circuitry. They allowed him to still hear sounds at a nondamaging level, so he was able to hear the sudden, terrified screams that instantly followed the shots.

"Everyone do as you're told!" he shouted loud enough for his voice to carry across the entire lower floor. "Otherwise we're all going to die!"

Chapter 24

Cal Granderson was still muttering to himself as he walked around the first floor of the library. Chief McRainey was the boss, sure, but that didn't give him the right to banish Granderson here. That was what it felt like, for sure, banishment. The library was the dullest place on campus.

A student walked past Granderson on the way to the escalators. Granderson looked in that direction but was only vaguely aware of the guy. His brain was full of resentment over the way the chief had treated him, and in front of a civilian, too! That just made it worse.

Granderson had thought it over—he hadn't thought of much else since the incident—and he was still convinced that he had done the right thing. That deliveryman had broken the law and deserved the ticket, and once he started arguing with a duly appointed representative of the law, he deserved whatever happened to him. Simple as that. Couldn't have people being defiant to law enforcement. That way lay anarchy.

Except, of course, in cases where the law was just

being used as dupes by a fascist government. Then it was a true patriot's duty to resist, be it by hashtags or other, more direct methods.

Earlier, while he was taking a turn through the lower level, Granderson had spotted Jake Rivers sitting at a table with a good-looking red-haired woman, which was annoying enough to start with. Granderson thought the woman was one of the professors here, and that just made it worse. He didn't believe that students and teachers should be involved with each other like that, although there was a long history of such things happening on campuses everywhere. It was against the Kelton College code of conduct, though, which meant, in a way, that Rivers and the woman were lawbreakers. Granderson wished there was such a thing as giving a ticket for illegal fornicating. If there was, he would have slapped one down in front of Rivers and the woman in the blink of an eye.

It just wasn't fair that a guy could be such a racist, sexist, homophobic bigot and still get a woman who looked like that.

Granderson was brooding about that, as well as the deliveryman and Chief McRainey, when the walkie-talkie clipped to his belt just in front of the stun gun crackled to life. He unclipped it and lifted it in time to hear the strained tones of the chief's voice as he called for help at the groundskeepers' shed. Granderson's fingers tightened on the walkie as he picked up on the pain in McRainey's voice. Something was very wrong.

He whirled around and started for the main

entrance doors at a fast trot. He hadn't reached them when two guys suddenly got in front of him.

"Get out of the way!" Granderson yelled at them as he waved the hand holding the walkie-talkie. "Damn it, get out—"

Somewhere behind him, two shots blasted, so loud they seemed to shake the whole big building. Granderson stopped short, his feet skidding a little underneath him, and turned his head to stare in that direction. People were screaming down on the lower level, so it seemed pretty obvious that was where the shooting came from. Someone shouted, but Granderson couldn't make out the words.

He heard a man behind him say, "Nobody's going anywhere, cop."

That made him twist back toward the entrance. He was in time to see one of the men who had blocked his path a few seconds earlier lunging at him. The man had a gun in his hand. Granderson dropped the walkie-talkie and grabbed for his stun gun, but he had no chance to pull the weapon from its holster. The man crashed the pistol against his head and knocked him backward off his feet.

Granderson had been hit hard enough to knock the wind out of him and slid a few feet on the polished floor. Horrible pain filled his head. He was disoriented and for a few heartbeats couldn't have said where he was or what was going on. All he knew was that he was hurt and stunned.

Then a kick thudded into his ribs, bringing him even more pain but jolting him back to a sort of clarity at the same time. As he started to curl up around the agony in his side, he felt someone jerk the stun gun out of the holster. He was unarmed now, and in the shape he was in, utterly useless, too.

That knowledge was a bitter taste filling his mouth.

One of the men looming above him said, "Stay down, cop, if you know what's good for you."

Fury flooded through Granderson, for a moment overwhelming the pain and confusion he felt. Nobody could talk to him like that, especially one of those smart-ass college kids. He was as good as any of them, if only they would see that. Unarmed or not, he started trying to struggle to his feet.

"I told you, you stupid son of a bitch."

Granderson saw a hand holding a gun slashing toward his head again. He dived at a pair of legs in front of him. Shoulders rammed against knees, and that knocked the guy off balance enough that the gun smashed down on Granderson's back instead of his head. It still hurt like hell, but it didn't put him out. He grabbed hold of the legs and heaved.

With a startled yelp, the man went over backward. Granderson scrambled ahead and tried to get on top of him. He figured the other guy probably had a gun, too, but maybe he wouldn't risk using it for fear of hitting his friend. Granderson was fighting mostly on instinct, but he was thinking clearly enough to realize that much, anyway.

He got a hand on the gun and tried to tug it free. He didn't know what else might be going on in the library—trouble, no doubt about that—but he couldn't deal with anything else right now. He had his hands full wrestling with this one man, hoping to get the gun away so he would have a chance to deal with the other one.

That clout on the head had weakened him, though, and left him not operating at peak efficiency. The man he was grappling with lifted a knee into his belly, assuring that he couldn't get any air into his body to replace the air he'd lost when he hit the floor. Gasping, Granderson desperately clung to the gun with one hand and the man's wrist with the other. He tried to wrench the weapon free, tried so hard that he sobbed with the effort.

Then another terrific impact struck the back of his head. He didn't have time to wonder if he had been shot or merely pistol-whipped again. He didn't try to figure out what was going on here in the library or even venture a guess whether he was going to live or if he was already dead . . .

He just plummeted into blackness that seemed never-ending.

Pierce Conners bolted to his feet when he heard the shots. He was close enough to them that his ears rang from the thunderous reports. He jerked his head from side to side as he looked around, searching for the shooter.

He supposed that after all the horrible mass shootings of the past few years, anybody who spent time at a school or anywhere else large crowds gathered had to feel a little shiver of apprehension now and then. You couldn't help but wonder, at any moment, if somebody was drawing a bead on you. Would you even know what was going on, or would you just go on to . . . whatever was on the other side . . . without ever knowing what had happened?

Would everything just be over in less than the blink of an eye, like somebody turning off a switch?

Elsewhere on the library's lower level, people started to scream. A few ran here and there, aimlessly because they didn't know who they were running from or where they were running to. Most people hunkered down right where they were, though, hoping and praying that they wouldn't wind up as targets for whoever was doing the shooting.

Jenny was one of the screamers. Clark lunged toward her, wrapped his arms around her, and cried, "I'll protect you!"

She screamed again, started hitting at him, and yelled, "Get off of me!"

Margery dived to the floor and tried to crawl under the table between the chairs and sofas. It wasn't big enough to conceal all of her, but it would provide some cover, which was better than nothing, Pierce supposed.

Fareed was on his feet, too, looking around frantically like Pierce was. In the past, he had talked about how he wished he could strike back at the Great Satan, America, for the glory of Islam and the Prophet, but right now he just looked scared.

"Where is he?" Fareed asked.

Pierce knew he was talking about the shooter.

"There!" he said, pointing as he suddenly caught sight of a man standing at the foot of the escalators with a pistol in his hand, pointing toward the ceiling. The gunman was white, fairly young, and average-looking. Nothing about him shouted "mass shooter." Pierce was far enough away that he couldn't make out all the details, but this guy didn't seem to have the creepy vibe that a lot of spree killers put out.

No question but that he was the one doing the shooting, though. He proved that by sending another round into the ceiling and shouting, "Everyone down on the floor!"

Margery reached out from under the table and caught hold of Pierce's ankle.

"You heard him!" she said. "He'll shoot anybody standing up! Get down here!"

Over on one of the sofas, Jenny and Clark were still wrestling around. Jenny appeared to be panicking, but whether she was terrified of the shooter or of Clark, Pierce couldn't say. They slipped off the sofa, landed on the floor with a thud, and sprawled next to the table. At least they were out of the line of fire, if Clark could keep Jenny there.

Margery tugged at Pierce's ankle and urged, "Come on!"

Pierce looked over at Fareed, who glared defiantly and said, "I grovel to no American!"

"Do what you want, man," Pierce said. He dropped to his knees and then fell forward onto his belly. Instinctively, he raised his hands and clasped them over the back of his head . . . as if that would protect him from a bullet.

"Shut up and get down on the floor!"

That was a different voice, coming from a different direction. Pierce was curious enough that he lifted his head a little to look. He saw a tall, broad-shouldered black guy who also held a pistol. The man lashed out with it and hit a male student who tried to scurry away from him. The student cried out in pain and went down. The second gunman grabbed another guy by the shirt collar and slung him down, then shoved a girl off her feet. He swung the pistol back and forth, menacing everyone around him as he ordered again, "On the floor!"

More shouts from elsewhere in the library. There were several of the gunmen, Pierce realized. They had just been waiting for the signal to begin their attack. As scared as he was, it wasn't easy to think straight, but he forced his brain to work as he tried to figure out what was going on here.

Evidently, the gunmen's objective *wasn't* mass murder. If all they wanted to do was pile up bodies, they would have continued shooting once they started. That seemed obvious to Pierce.

They didn't mind killing, though, and that was demonstrated a moment later when a student rushed the man at the bottom of the escalator, yelling curses. The gunman leveled his pistol and pulled the trigger. The man charging at him stumbled, clapped a hand to his chest, and pitched forward. He didn't move again as Pierce watched, horrified at what he had just seen.

More people were screaming now. Several voices yelled for them to shut up. Pierce couldn't tell if those voices belonged to the gunmen issuing orders or frightened people begging for calm so they wouldn't get shot. Maybe both were true.

The only thing Pierce knew for sure as he looked down again at the floor only a couple of inches from his eyes was that this day, no matter how it had started, now stood a good chance of being the last day of his life.

Chapter 25

Old habits died hard. When Jake heard the shots, his first instinct was to hunt cover, the second to return fire.

But he didn't have anything to shoot back with, and in that split second when his brain began to process what was going on, he realized that he was more concerned with Natalie's safety than with his own.

He lunged across the table, slid on the papers, knocked books and laptop aside, and grabbed her. The impact toppled her chair over. She cried out in surprise. Jake twisted as they went down so that he hit the floor first and she landed on top of him, instead of the other way around. His weight falling on her might have seriously injured her.

As soon as they were down, though, he rolled so he was on top, on hands and knees, shielding her body with his own.

"Stay down," he told her through clenched teeth. "You'll be all right."

"Jake! What—"

"Shhh. Don't say anything." He didn't want her drawing attention to herself, or him, either. He wasn't sure what was going on here, but getting on the radar of a hostile with a gun was never a good thing.

Jake looked around as best he could without raising his head too much. His senses were working overtime right now, attuned to everything that was happening around him. He heard shouting and screaming from other parts of the library's lower floor and realized that the man who had come down the escalator and started shooting wasn't alone.

He was the only one Jake could see from where he was, though, as he peered past a table leg and through a gap in the furniture toward the shooter. The man was around Jake's age, maybe a little older, somewhere between twenty-five and thirty. Six-one, around one-seventy. Wiry. Brown hair. Good-looking in a cocky way. He seemed very self-composed, which was good, Jake thought. Wild-eyed panic would mean more shooting. This guy looked like he wouldn't pull the trigger unless he had a good reason.

One of the students gave him a good reason by yelling and charging him. The gunman calmly shot him down, accurately enough to put the guy on the floor with one round.

Jake's jaw tightened even more. That was a cold-blooded execution he had just witnessed. He had no doubt that the guy would kill him just as efficiently and ruthlessly if he tried anything stupid.

That meant when he made his move, it had to be a smart one, Jake told himself.

His only weapon was the folding knife in his

pocket. That wouldn't do him much good against three, maybe more, guns. He assumed that this guy's allies were armed at least as well as he was. The guy had a Glock 17 9mm, from the looks of it. He had fired three rounds. That meant he could still have fourteen or fifteen shots, depending on whether there had been one in the chamber when he loaded a full magazine. And Jake wouldn't be the least bit surprised if the guy had at least half a dozen loaded magazines in his pockets, just waiting for him to switch them out if he needed to.

So there was a lot of firepower in here, at least relatively speaking because Kelton College, like a lot of private colleges and universities, was a so-called Gun Free Zone. That whole concept was one of the stupidest things Jake had ever heard of, a glaring neon sign of an invitation for evil to march right in and have its way, unchecked, but that was the situation and wishing it was different was pointless. More than likely, nobody in the building was carrying. Even the campus cops who worked for Frank McRainey just carried stun guns, nothing lethal.

Which meant that if Jake was going to fight back successfully against these bastards, he needed to get his hands on one of *their* guns.

"Quiet down!" the gunman yelled. "Everybody just shut up!"

He had to repeat the order several times at the top of his lungs before the racket began to die away. The screaming gradually stopped, but when it did, Jake could still hear people sobbing and whimpering. Somewhere not too far away, somebody said an obscenity over and over again in a terrified whisper.

It grew quiet enough in the library for the gunman to be heard all over the big room as he said, "All right, now you all know that we mean business. We're not terrorists or fanatics, if that's what you're thinking. We didn't come here today to hurt anybody, but as you've seen, we'll do whatever is necessary in order to achieve our objective. Our group is large, spread out all over the campus, and committed to our cause. We're not only willing to kill in order to do what's right, we're also willing to die ourselves if that's what it takes to make America wake up."

Under his breath, Jake said to Natalie, "I thought he claimed he wasn't a terrorist or a fanatic. Sounds like it to me."

She didn't say anything. Her eyes were wide and she was breathing hard. He knew she must be scared out of her wits.

"I'm sure you're all wondering what it is we want," the gunman went on.

He was well-spoken, Jake thought. Probably smart and well-educated, too, although you couldn't really tell that by the way somebody talked. In the service, he had run across guys who sounded like they didn't have enough brain cells to rub together, yet who were actually some of the most intelligent people he had ever met. However, his instincts told him this man was no dummy . . . and that made him even more dangerous in the long run.

"It's really very simple. The only way anyone leaves this campus today without more bloodshed is if one hundred million dollars is transferred into an offshore bank account, the number of which I'll provide to the authorities in due time. That's a one with eight zeroes after it, for those of you who believe math is racist." The man chuckled, of all things. "And I know there are some of you in here right now who believe that. Trust me, I can see your point. Racism really *is* systemic in this country.

"Which brings me to my next point. We're not demanding that the government pay that hundred million dollars. No. It needs to come from the families of students here at Kelton College. There are approximately three thousand students enrolled here. That means—and again, I'll help out the math-challenged among you—that each of their families would have to come up with less than thirty-five thousand dollars."

He smirked, waved his free hand, and the gun in his other hand never wavered as he went on, "Most of the families you come from are one-percenters. Old money. *Dirty* money. Money made on the backs of the common people, wrung out of them along with their sweat and blood!" He didn't sound quite so self-controlled now as he heated up. "Seriously, are you going to try to tell me that your parents can't just sit down and write a check for that much and never miss it? You know I'm right!"

The guy might be a killer, but what he said was

true, Jake thought. A semester's tuition, housing, and other expenses could easily add up to that much or more. A lot of parents paid it, again and again, so their darling little snowflakes could get degrees in intersectional feminism or gender studies. Although this day and age, it would have to be gender-fluid studies.

"Now, I know what you're thinking," the gunman went on. "Some of your families can't afford that much. They really can't. You're here on scholarships or have managed some other way. And I believe you. I know there are students here at Kelton who don't fit in, who don't come from stereotypical filthy rich families. You've probably felt oppressed because of it, too."

In that moment, Jake had a ray of insight into the gunman's personality. He had to come from that sort of background. He was speaking from experience. Jake could hear it in his voice.

"So I'm not asking your families to pay. I don't want to ruin anyone."

It was *I* now, not *we*. That told Jake this guy really was the mastermind of the plan, not just a mouth-piece.

"And I'm sure there are some students who don't happen to be on campus right now. They'll know to stay away, too, because, hell, there have to be at least a dozen phones in here sending all this out to the rest of the world, right? It's breaking news across the country. That's fine. Nobody's going to shoot you because you're using a phone. We *want* the rest of the country, the rest of the world, to know what's going on here today!"

He had to pace back and forth a little. His emotions were high, his nerves were taut. Jake could tell that.

"Now, we all know that if somebody's kid was lucky enough to be somewhere else today, they're not going to come up with the money to save somebody *else's* kid, am I right? They don't care that all of *you* might die. They don't care about anybody but themselves and their families. They've proven that over and over again by supporting cuts in taxes and social programs that have ripped the safety net out from under countless people and let thousands die, just so they can pack a few bucks into their bank accounts! They're heartless bastards!" He jabbed the index finger of his free hand against the air in front of him, several times. "You know it's true! You know it!"

With a visible effort, he controlled himself and went on in a calmer tone, "So I'm not even going to ask those people to help save you. It wouldn't do any good. Just wasted effort to ask them to have a heart and help out those less fortunate than them. So what does that leave us?

"Well, if you subtract the families who truly can't afford it and the ones who are too uncaring to pitch in—because they never pitched in to pay their fair share of taxes, did they?—and the families who might have more than one kid attending here, can't forget them—I figure that leaves us with about two thousand families that need to come up with some cash. They only have to average fifty grand apiece, and I know there are a lot of them who can do more than that.

"So here's how it's going to work: the government will set up a special bank account—I don't care where, that doesn't matter—and your parents or guardians or what-have-you are going to transfer money into that account. And I want documentation of where every penny comes from, that's very important. No tax dollars ripped off from the middle class are going into this account. Only money from the oligarchs who have taken over this country. When the account reaches one hundred million dollars, which it has until five o'clock this afternoon to do, no later, that money will be transferred into the account I specify and the documentation showing where all the money came from will be delivered to my representatives as well. If everything checks out and nobody tries any tricks, we'll leave, and a short time later you'll all be free to go on about your business.

"How are we going to get away, you ask?"

Nobody had, but Jake was more than a little interested in that question himself.

"Nobody's going to try to stop us," the gunman went on. "We'll be taken to the airport in Austin where a jet will be waiting to fly us out of the country. When we've landed where we're going—and the flight shouldn't take much more than about three hours—it'll be all over and you'll be safe. But until then . . ." He cocked his head a little to the side and grinned. "Well, until then, we're all going to be in a little bit of danger. Because, you see, my friends and I have planted bombs all over this campus, and all it'll take is one signal from a detonator to blow Kelton College—and all of you—right off the freakin' map."

CHAPTER 26

McRainey must have passed out at some point from shock and loss of blood. He remembered calling for help over the walkie-talkie, and then the next thing he knew one of his guys was kneeling in front of him, cursing in surprise for a moment before saying, "Good Lord, Chief, what happened here?"

McRainey's wounded hand still hurt like fire, but the pain in his head and chest had receded to dull aches. He lifted his good hand and pointed.

"Charlie Hodges . . . dead behind the desk. Don't know where . . . the rest of his guys . . . are . . . They're probably . . . dead, too."

"I've called for an ambulance, Chief." The young officer's face was blurry and McRainey didn't recognize him at first. Then his vision cleared a little and he could make out enough of the guy's face to tell that he was Jeff Bagley, who had been working here at Kelton under McRainey for several years.

Bagley went on, "Who's this guy?"

McRainey realized he was talking about the dead man with the knife still sticking up out of his chest.

"He tried to . . . kill me. Guess he figured . . . I was a harmless old man."

Bagley blew out a breath and shook his head, said, "Not hardly. Did he kill Mr. Hodges?"

"Don't know. Must have . . . or had something to do with it, anyway."

McRainey wasn't breathing as hard now. He could tell that despite his injury and the infirmities of age, he was getting his body and his mind back under control again. Iron will and the habits of a lifetime had a lot to do with that. He wasn't going to let some punk get the best of him, and he sure as hell wasn't going to allow trash like that to put him under.

"I'll be all right, Jeff," he went on. "You'd better be careful. The bastard could have friends around here somewhere."

"Yeah, Chief, I think you must be right," Bagley said. He looked like he was worried about more than McRainey's condition now. "I heard reports on the walkie while I was running over here. We've got shots fired all over campus, sounds like."

McRainey bit back a groan. Hodges' murder wasn't a random killing, then. Kelton College was under some sort of coordinated attack by persons unknown. This was the sort of thing everybody in law enforcement had learned to dread over the past few decades of increasing political violence.

"Have there been . . . any explosions?"

Bagley shook his head.

"Not that I know of. You think it's terrorists, Chief?"

"Must be, if there's more than one or two of them."

"There have to be at least a dozen. From what I

could tell over the walkie-talkie, our officers were responding, but there aren't enough of us to cover the whole campus in a situation like this." Bagley swallowed hard. "Besides, we aren't equipped or trained to deal with terrorists."

And neither was the Greenleaf PD, McRainey thought. Some of those officers had probably had a little SWAT training, and they had some tactical gear, but up against a large force that wouldn't be enough.

"Call the DPS," McRainey said. "Tell them we need state troopers, Rangers, whatever they can send us. Better call the FBI, too. The Feds will want to get in on this." He closed his eyes for a second. "We'll have Homeland and ATF swarming all over."

"Better them than us, Chief, no offense. This is above our pay grade."

That rankled McRainey, and the irritation gave him more strength.

"Nothing that concerns the safety of this campus and its students is above my pay grade," he said as he sat up straighter. "Get out there and find out what's going on, then report back to me."

"But Chief, you're hurt—"

"And you've already called for help. The EMTs ought to be here soon—"

As if on cue, two men in the tan and brown uniforms of the local emergency medical service hurried into the office, both of them carrying bulky kits containing gear and equipment. McRainey recognized both of them.

"Chief McRainey!" one of the men exclaimed. "We didn't know you were the victim."

"I'm better off than that guy," McRainey said, nodding toward the man he had killed. "You don't need to waste any time on him."

"Yeah, I can see that." The EMT knelt beside McRainey and picked up his handkerchief-wrapped hand. "Do you have any other injuries?"

"I took a whack on the head, but I think I'm okay."

"Get the chief's vitals," the man said as he carefully unwound the blood-soaked handkerchief.

"And you get out there and find out what's happening!" McRainey told Bagley again.

"I can tell you some of that, Chief," the EMT said. "You have shots fired in multiple buildings, and there are reports of casualties as well."

McRainey couldn't hold in the groan this time. With his good hand, he motioned for Bagley to go on.

"You're gonna need a bunch of stitches here," the EMT said after he had uncovered the cut on McRainey's palm and taken a look at it. "We need to get you to the hospital. I'll bandage it better—"

"Can't you just, you know, glue it shut or something? You can do that, can't you?"

"Not a cut that's this deep and serious."

"Then just clean it up and bandage it the best you can and give me a shot of antibiotics or something. Because I'm not leaving the campus. Not with all hell breaking loose like this."

"Damn it, Chief, you're not going to be able to do anybody any good here. As much blood as you've lost, you're liable to pass out again at any time."

"Then give me a shot to bump me up enough

that won't happen. I'm not going to the hospital, I tell you."

"What I ought to do is give you a shot that'll knock you out, then we can do what needs to be done."

McRainey glared at the man and said, "You do that and I'll look you up when this is all over. You don't want that."

The two EMTs looked at each other. The one who had been taking the chief's pulse and blood pressure shrugged, as if to say that the decision was up to his partner.

Before they could make up their minds, Jeff Bagley ran back into the office. The young officer had his cell phone out.

"Chief, you need to see this," he said. "It's streaming live all over the place."

He dropped to a knee and held up the phone so McRainey could see the screen.

The shot was shaking a little, which told McRainey that the hand of whoever was shooting this was trembling, no doubt from fear. The angle was upward, because the person with the phone was on the floor. The shot showed a fairly young man, dressed casually like most of the students on campus, standing near the base of an escalator with what looked like a Glock 9mm in his hand. McRainey could see enough of the surrounding area to recognize the location: the lower left of the Burr Memorial Library, a few hundred yards from where they were right now.

The young man with the gun was talking. The audio quality wasn't great, but McRainey could make out most of what he was saying. It was the usual left-wing drivel about how the evil one-percenters were responsible for everything that was wrong with the world.

As it happened, McRainey actually did believe that there was too much income inequality in the country. For the most part, though, it wasn't the high earners who drove the economy and paid 95 percent of the taxes who were responsible for it.

In McRainey's opinion, the blame lay with the Democrats, and some politicians who called themselves Republicans, who had increased taxes again and again and again, who had loaded down the average working stiff with astronomically high health insurance costs, who had overregulated many small businesses to the brink of extinction. Those were the people who had done their best to grind the middle class out of existence, so that most of the population would be condemned to sucking on the government's teat forever and therefore would have no choice but to continue voting those politicians, and others of their stripe, into office in perpetuity.

Those were the vermin in human form who had created the income gap.

None of which had much bearing on the current disaster, so McRainey tamped those thoughts down as they flashed through his brain. He watched the man with the gun blather on, and his heart began to hammer harder when the guy mentioned bombs planted all over the campus.

McRainey didn't doubt the truth of that threat, not even for a moment. Anybody crazy enough to start shooting up a college campus was crazy enough to plant bombs, too.

Plant . . .

"That's it," McRainey said suddenly as he reached out and grabbed Bagley's arm with his good hand. "That's why they killed Charlie."

The second EMT had stood up and drifted off into the garage area of the groundskeepers' shed. He came back into the office now with all the color washed out of his face.

"It's not just Mr. Hodges, Chief," he said in a hollow voice. "There are some dead guys in the garage, too, and . . . and they're all stripped down to their underwear."

"It was the uniforms they wanted," McRainey said. "In those coveralls, everybody figured they were just the regular groundskeeping crew. That allowed them to spread out all over the campus and plant bombs."

"I saw some of them digging over by the Language Arts Building earlier," Bagley said. "You think—"

"Got to be."

Bagley jumped to his feet.

"We can find all the places they've been digging—"

"No!" McRainey said. "They probably have anti-tamper triggers on all those explosives. Stick a shovel down in that dirt and you're liable to blow yourself to kingdom come!"

Bagley stared at him and asked, "Then what are we going to do?"

"Get out there and warn everybody else on our force. Make sure any Greenleaf cops who show up know what's going on, too. And when the state cops get here, let them know. They'll be better equipped to deal with it than any of the locals."

Bagley nodded in understanding.

"How about you, Chief?"

"I'm fine, damn it," McRainey said as he gestured sharply again. "Now go on—"

He stopped as his head spun crazily. All that blood he'd lost was catching up to him again. He felt his eyes rolling up in their sockets. His head tipped back as he heard the EMT kneeling beside him exclaim, "Chief! Chief McRainey!"

Then consciousness was gone again, as McRainey descended into a nightmare vision of explosions spreading all across the campus of Kelton College, leaving a crimson sprawl of bloody death and destruction in their wake.

CHAPTER 27

Dr. Alfred Montambault pressed his back against the wall in the narrow gap between two sets of shelves and tried to will his heart to stop beating so hard. The pounding of his pulse inside his head was so loud he was certain the man with the gun had to be able to hear it, too.

The man with the gun was prowling around the Special Science Collection on the third floor of the library. Montambault had been in here by himself when chaos erupted below. He had no idea what was going on, but he had heard several muffled gunshots from one of the lower floors.

At least, he believed they were gunshots. He had never heard a gun go off in real life, only on television and in the movies, and he knew those were created by special effects departments and might not be what firearms sounded like when they were going off in real life.

He was pretty sure somebody was shooting, though, and the very idea of being around someone firing a gun was enough to make a cold ball of anxiety form in the pit of Montambault's stomach. His fingers trembled.

Then, as he stood up from the table where he had been working on his laptop and turned toward the open double doors at the entrance to the collection, he'd heard quick footsteps in the hallway outside.

Something, some primitive instinct Montambault didn't even like to think about, had made him duck back out of sight. Moving as quietly as he could, he had hurried around the bookshelves until he reached a spot where he couldn't see seen easily from the entrance. He could watch the open doors through a narrow gap between shelves, though.

Because of that, he had seen the stocky, young Hispanic man who had stalked into the room with a pistol of some sort in his hand.

Montambault knew at that moment that the man was there to kill him. Not him specifically, maybe, but anyone he found here. What other reason would anyone have for brandishing a gun like that?

The man turned right instead of left when he came through the door. That took him away from Montambault. After that, Montambault couldn't see him anymore, but he could hear him and could tell that the man was searching through the shelves on the other side of the room to see if anyone was there. When he was finished on that side, he could come over here, Montambault was sure of that.

And then he would kill Montambault.

The professor considered making a run for the door, but he didn't think he could do that quietly enough to escape detection. And even if he made it out of this room, that would put him in a corridor that led to the reception area for the Special Collections department, where there was an elevator leading down to the lower floors and up to the offices on the fourth floor. There was nowhere to hide in the corridor. Montambault would make a good target and would be gunned down before he could reach the reception area.

Instead, he thought about the storage closet in the back corner of this room. If he could reach it, maybe he could hide. It was unlikely the gunman wouldn't at least glance in there, but there was a stack of boxes in the closet containing books that had been culled from the shelves, Montambault recalled. Maybe he could arrange them so they looked like they filled up the space, and he could hide behind them.

An odd thought crossed his mind as he stole in that direction making as little sound as he could.

He wished Jake Rivers were here. Rivers was a crude, obnoxious, violent young man . . . but he probably had some idea how to handle a man with a gun. More than Alfred Montambault did, that was for sure.

He thought about his ancestors then, too. Ever since he had been old enough to understand the evils of imperialism, he had been ashamed of the role some of his forebears had played in colonizing Africa. They had been brutal rapists and exploiters and killers.

But if one of them had been able to come down

through the mists of time and stand between Montambault and that gunman right now, he would have welcomed the old reprobate with open arms.

That wasn't going to happen, of course. Montambault knew with a sickening certainty that he was on his own here.

He hadn't reached the storage closet yet when he heard a footstep not far away. The gunman had finished searching the other side of the room sooner than Montambault expected. He knew he couldn't make it to the closet in time to hide, so he drew back into the gap between two sets of shelves and tried to make himself as small as possible.

He had always been slender, and the shelves were deeper than most because they were built to hold oversized technical volumes. They stuck out from the wall perhaps eighteen inches. The gap was wide enough for Montambault to stand with his back against the wall, and he hoped that if he sucked in his stomach and kept his back and shoulders flat, he might be concealed well enough for the gunman to miss seeing him.

He held his breath as the footsteps echoed hollowly and came closer. If the gunman came along the aisle between the wall and the shelves, Montambault was doomed. If the man simply looked along the aisle and didn't see anybody, he had a chance . . .

The steps stopped. A long moment of silence dragged by. Then a man's voice said, "Yeah, this is Pete. The third floor is under control. We herded everybody who was up here into the reception area in the middle. We'll wait for your orders."

Montambault wanted to heave a sigh of relief but still didn't dare. The man hadn't seen him. Now there was at least a chance the man would leave this room without looking around anymore. Montambault could find a better place to hide and wait for someone to come and rescue him. The police had to have received reports of the trouble by now. They would be on their way, and they would deal with the threat. That was what they were paid for, after all.

Normally, Montambault thought of the police as racist, trigger-happy, power-mad bullies just looking for an excuse to shoot innocent black men. He was a fervent supporter of Black Lives Matter. But right now he couldn't wait for the cops to get here.

The footsteps receded. Montambault could tell from the sound of them that the gunman had left the room and was headed back to the reception area where his allies had gathered their prisoners. So they weren't here to just wantonly slaughter everyone they found, Montambault thought. Maybe he would have been better off letting himself be captured. They might be more likely to hurt him if they found him later and believed that he was trying to cause trouble for them. He supposed he could still surrender . . .

No, he was too nervous to risk that. He would hide, he decided. His first instinct had been the correct one.

Finally, desperate for air, he drew a deep breath. Steeling his nerves, he stepped out of the gap.

From the corner of his right eye, he saw the man standing at the end of the aisle in that direction. As pure reflex jerked him into a turn in that direction, the thought flashed through his mind that there must have been two of them, and somehow he had missed that fact. One of them had suspected someone might be hiding in here and had pretended to make a report to someone else, then sent the second man away so anyone who was in here would hear him leaving.

The ploy had worked. Thinking that he was alone and safe, Montambault had stepped out into the open, right into the sights of the gun that the man was pointing at him. Montambault stared in horror over the barrel of that pistol and saw the cold smile on the man's face.

The next instant, flame exploded from the gun muzzle.

Montambault was already moving when the shot erupted, though. He threw himself back into the small area where he had been hiding a moment earlier. As he did so, he thought he felt something brush against his left ear and heard a high-pitched whine like a mosquito.

That was the bullet passing by him, he realized. It had come that close to killing him. Panic gripped him as he heard rapid footsteps thudding closer to him and knew he had only seconds to live.

That panic somehow allowed him to find more strength than he ever would have dreamed that he possessed. He grabbed hold of the shelves beside him and heaved. They weren't attached to the wall, but fully loaded with books the way they were, he shouldn't have been able to budge them.

But with the power that his fear gave him, he tipped the shelves forward away from the wall, and once they were unbalanced, they went over with a huge crash, spilling books everywhere. Montambault heard a surprised cry from the gunman and knew that the man had been caught in the literary avalanche.

The falling shelves hit the ones across the aisle and stopped, leaving a small, book-littered, triangular space underneath them. The pistol came sliding out of that space, and as Montambault saw it, he knew the man must have lost his grip on the gun when the toppling shelves and books knocked him off his feet. Curses from underneath the shelves told Montambault the man might be trapped under there.

Montambault wasn't going to overlook such an unexpected gift. He bent down and picked up the gun, the first time he had ever held a firearm in his life. He hadn't even had any toy guns when he was a child. His parents would have been horrified at the idea.

But even though he had no clue what sort of weapon he held, he knew which end of the gun the bullets came out of and how to make them fire. At least he hoped the gun didn't have some kind of safety catch that was engaged. That seemed unlikely, considering that the man had fired it at him less than a minute earlier.

Montambault knelt, held the gun in both hands, and shoved it into the mouth of the opening formed by the fallen shelves. He pulled the trigger three times as fast as he could, crying out in involuntary shock at the deafening sounds and the way the weapon jumped in his hands.

He stood up and scrambled backward as he continued pointing the gun at the opening. He couldn't hear anything because of the gun-thunder that had filled the room. He wasn't sure he would ever be able to hear anything again except the throbbing roar of blood inside his own head.

As the gun's barrel wavered wildly in front of him, though, he realized that his hearing was coming back. He heard shouts from somewhere else on the Special Collections floor.

However, he didn't hear any more cursing from underneath the fallen shelves, which made him wonder if he had killed the gunman. Ordinarily that thought would have horrified him, as would the idea that since he now held the weapon, *he* was the gunman.

Right now, though, survival was the only thing in his mind. The man had friends close by. They would have heard the shots and the crash, and they would come to see what had happened.

Montambault couldn't be standing here in plain sight, gun in hand, when that happened.

He turned and fled toward the storage closet

that had been his goal before he was trapped and almost killed.

As he yanked the door open, another thought occurred to him. He looked up. The ceiling was acoustic tile to make it quieter inside the library. That extended into the closet. There were air-conditioning and heating ducts up there above the ceiling, and he recalled seeing movies and TV shows where people got into those ducts by lifting out ceiling tiles and climbing into the enclosed spaces.

That thought made a shiver go through him, but he knew he had only moments before the gunman's friends found his body and started searching for whoever killed him. Montambault set the gun aside on a box of books in the storage room and started moving some of the other boxes, building a pyramid he could climb.

He had never been one for physical labor. Where he found the strength to do such a thing so quickly, he didn't know. Human beings were capable of incredible feats when it was a matter of life and death, or so he had read.

When he had the boxes stacked high enough for him to be able to reach the ceiling, he pulled the closet door closed. Just enough light came under it for him to be able to see what he was doing as he picked up the gun and held it awkwardly while he climbed onto the boxes. Now he worried about shooting himself accidentally. But if he didn't get out of here, he would wind up being shot anyway, he was sure of that, and it wouldn't be any accident.

He reached up, working almost blindly, and lifted

one of the tiles. He moved it aside and then felt around. There had to be something sturdy enough up there to support his weight. After a few seconds that seemed much longer, his fingers brushed a board. He explored it by touch. It seemed strong, and it might be wide enough for him to lie on it.

He put the gun in his pocket. He didn't like that, but he didn't have any choice. He had to have both hands free to pull himself up.

Usually one thought of descending into darkness, but in this case, Montambault was climbing into darkness. The faint glow seeping under the closet door rose into the crawl space between floors but was swallowed up by the gloom almost immediately. The professor's eyes had adjusted enough for him to see the broad plank and the looming bulk of the air duct next to which it ran. The board was there for the convenience of repairmen who had to work on those ducts, he supposed.

His muscles trembled badly as he tried to lift himself. That brought back humiliating memories of being forced to attempt pull-ups in gym class when he was a boy. A bitter taste filled his mouth as that came back to him. That time was nearly forty years in the past. Why couldn't he forget about it?

A shout sounded somewhere not far away, muffled by the wall but clear enough for Montambault to hear it. The threat it represented was enough to galvanize his muscles yet again, but he sensed he was nearing the end of his strength and endurance. If he was going to escape, he had to do it *now.*

With a last surge, he hoisted himself high enough

to get a leg on the board. As he pulled himself higher, his head bumped painfully against something. One of the boards holding up the floor above, he imagined. He ignored the pain as he sprawled belly-down on the wide plank. His heart hammered, and he couldn't seem to get his breath.

But he was still in danger, and that awareness clamored in his brain. He had tried to stack the boxes of books so that they didn't look too much like a stepladder to the ceiling, but with that tile set aside, leaving a plain opening, it was obvious what had happened. Montambault tried to calm his breathing and started feeling around for the tile he had moved out of the way.

He found it, maneuvered it back into place, and pressed it down. As it dropped into position, the last of the light really was gone. Blackness closed in around him. Montambault shivered at its embrace.

But he was safe now, he told himself. That was the only thing that mattered.

After a moment, his brain began to race again. The gunman's friends would know that someone else had been in there. That had to be, since the man was dead or at least wounded. And they would know that their quarry had gone somewhere. They would search the room thoroughly.

They might even think to look in the ceiling.

He had to get away from this spot, Montambault told himself. Had to put some distance between himself and those who wanted to kill him. He would have gladly just laid here and tried to recover from the ordeal he had been through, but if he did that, everything he had done might turn out to be for nothing.

Whether he liked it or not, he had to move. He reached down to his pocket and carefully worked the pistol loose, being extra cautious to keep his finger away from the trigger and not let it catch on something else.

Then, holding the gun in front of him, he began to crawl forward into the impenetrable shadows that awaited him.

CHAPTER 28

Jake wasn't surprised to hear the bomb threat come out of the man's mouth. He knew enough about the radical left movement to know they had always been bombers, going all the way back to the fifties and sixties. That was just part of their methodology. Champion free speech by shutting up everybody who doesn't agree with you. Advocate for equal rights by taking other people's rights away from them. Protest violence by blowing up a bunch of people and stuff.

Cowards at heart, every damn one of them.

But some of them were committed enough to their so-called cause to risk blowing themselves up, too. Jake couldn't really wrap his brain around that idea. He had accepted the idea of possibly dying in battle when he signed up to be a soldier. It was part of the job description, after all.

He didn't think a willingness to die in an explosion excused the fact that you'd also be killing a bunch of innocent people, though. Martyr or not, you were still a freakin' murderer, as far as Jake was concerned.

Then he looked at the man with the gun standing near the escalator and thought, *This guy is no martyr.*

He wasn't sure what it was about the man, whose voice and face were perfectly sincere as he issued the threat. Most people would believe that he meant it, without a doubt. Something was off, though, and after a minute or so, Jake thought he knew what it was.

His mind went back to a hot, dusty, empty street in a city on the other side of the world, where he and some of his fellow grunts had been clearing the buildings as they came to them, slowly forcing the insurgents to retreat and killing as many of the bastards as they could along the way. The patrol had been passing an alley mouth when a faint sound had warned Jake and sent him spinning in that direction with his rifle up and ready.

Two insurgents stood there with rifles of their own, Russian-made weapons ready to spew death. Jake was maybe fifteen feet from them, plenty close enough to see their eyes.

One man just looked scared, like he wished he was anywhere else in the world other than this dirty alley, pointing a gun at an American soldier pointing a rifle at him.

The other guy, though . . . he was loving it. His life would never get better than this moment, standing there ready to deliver death to somebody he hated to the very depths of his being. Even if he died, it was still the best, most holy thing he could ever do. He was far beyond rational thought, so caught up in his primitive beliefs that it might as well have been the Middle Ages again and he was about to run screaming at the infidel with a curved saber in his hand instead of an automatic rifle.

Jake shot him first, giving the son of a bitch the death he wanted, although Jake figured whatever was waiting on the other side, it was going to come as a pretty terrible surprise to the guy.

Then he turned his attention to the second man, only to discover that he had dropped his rifle and was running away as fast as he could, arms swinging and knees pumping high as he tried to outrace a bullet.

Jake let him go. His CO had chewed him out for that later, but he still believed he had done the right thing.

And he had never forgotten the fires of fanaticism that burned in the eyes of the man he had killed. He had never stared into the abyss—and had it stare back at him—from that close before or since.

This guy holding court on the lower level of the Burr Memorial Library didn't have those same fires burning in his eyes. He would kill without compunction or even a second's thought, he had proven that, but he didn't want to die himself. He might rather die than be caught, but he wanted to get away. He figured he had something to live for.

The bomb threat was an empty one, Jake decided.

But that didn't mean the guy wasn't dangerous. He still had that gun, and he had allies who probably were just as willing to kill as he was, and there were a lot of innocent people on this campus who might die before this crisis was over. If Jake was going to succeed in stopping this somehow without a great loss of life, he would need to be very careful.

The idea of just standing by, doing nothing, and hoping for the best never occurred to him.

From elsewhere in the library came angry shouts as the leader's allies ordered people to get down on the floor. They seemed to be doing as they were told. Jake didn't hear any more shots. He tensed, getting ready to raise up high enough to get a good look around.

Natalie must have felt that in his muscles where he was pressed against her. She clutched at him and whispered, "Jake, no! Whatever it is you're thinking about doing, you'll just get yourself hurt."

"You don't think I should just lay here and let those guys keep hurting people, do you?"

"I don't want them to hurt *you.* Or me, for that matter. Let's just do what they say and see what happens, okay?"

The idea of that grated on Jake's nerves, but he could see that Natalie was very frightened. He couldn't blame her for that. She might teach criminal justice, but he didn't suppose she had ever had much real-life experience with all the bad things that can happen in the world. Not to the extent that he'd had, anyway.

He knew that evil could never be appeased. It just got worse and worse until everyone it touched was dead . . . unless someone took action to stop it.

But for now, he would do what Natalie begged

of him and wait. Maybe if he could play out the hand and get one of these guys alone . . .

Then he would have a gun and one less enemy, and things would be different.

Fareed still hadn't gotten down on the floor. As Pierce lifted his head again, just a little, he was shocked to see that not only had the Muslim student not followed orders, but as the gunman at the foot of the escalators finished his rant, Fareed started walking toward him. His hands were raised to about elbow level and held out slightly to his sides.

The man saw him coming and raised the pistol again. Fareed called out quickly, "Do not shoot, brother! You and I are on the same side."

The gunman looked more amused than angered by that bold statement.

"Is that so?" he asked. "How do you figure that . . . *brother*?"

"We both believe that this materialistic American society is the source of everything that is wrong in the world," Fareed declared. "We both would like to see it replaced."

"By a caliphate ruled by sharia law?"

Fareed shrugged.

"What would you prefer?" he asked. "A godless communist government? That argument is an endless one, and it can be resumed at another time. What is important now is that we both would like to see this country full of heathen capitalists and imperialists brought low, is that not true?"

"It is," the gunman admitted. "We agree on the

need for change. What form that change ultimately takes can be settled later, as you say. But what is it you want from me right now?"

"Let me join you in your righteous assault on this den of thieves and whoremongers," Fareed said. "Let me help you destroy this land of . . . of Kardashians! Give me a gun!"

The leader looked at him for a long moment, as if seriously considering the suggestion. Then he laughed abruptly.

"Oh, hell no! You're not getting a gun. What kind of idiot do you think I am? We may have some of the same enemies, but that doesn't mean I trust you." He pointed the pistol at Fareed, and his expression turned serious as he said, "Go back where you were and get down on the floor. I mean it."

Fareed swallowed hard and licked his lips. He began to back away.

"You are making a mistake," he said. "I will be a faithful ally to you and your cause."

"I have enough allies, here and in the other buildings and in the bombs we've planted all over campus."

The mention of the bombs made Pierce feel cold inside again. If that threat was real, several thousand people were in deadly danger right now. The idea of killing that many at once, right here on American soil, might have been outlandish once upon a time, but not now. Not anymore. It had happened before, and Pierce was confident that it could happen again.

Pierce lowered his head and pressed his forehead against the carpet. Much of the library floor was tile, but the areas on which the love seats and armchairs sat was carpeted.

That made lying here and waiting to die a little more comfortable, he supposed.

When Fareed had backed all the way to the conversation area, he got down on his hands and knees and then stretched out all the way on his stomach. He was about four feet from Pierce. He looked over and glared.

"Don't judge me," he whispered. "You should have been just as willing as I was to join forces with them. Your people are as oppressed as mine."

"My father owns two Fortune 500 companies," Pierce replied, keeping his voice equally low. He was a little angry now, on top of being scared. "He's as much a one-percenter as anybody else that guy was raving about. When you count my trust fund and everything else I'll inherit, I suppose I will be, too. So don't go thinking I'm opposed to the same things he is."

Fareed sneered.

"You are no true black man. If you were, you would embrace the Islamic faith and turn against your decadent Western culture. I always knew you were a fake!"

On the other side of the table and underneath it, Jenny, Clark, and Margery were looking at them. Margery stared at Pierce and said, "Uncle Tom."

"How do you even *know* about that?" Pierce asked as he struggled to control the irritation he felt.

"I've studied history. Evidently that's more than you can say."

"Yeah, you're just a . . . what is it?" Jenny said.

"Uncle Tom," Clark supplied. "It's from a book or something, I think. Means a black guy who sucks up to the white oppressors."

"I don't—" Pierce stopped short. This was a ridiculous conversation to be having in angry whispers, especially while madmen with guns were stalking around and threatening to blow everybody to hell—the ones they didn't shoot first, that is. He shook his head and didn't look at the others.

Probably they were every bit as scared as he was. Maybe they were just trying to distract themselves from that fear.

That made him wonder if there was anybody in here who *wasn't* scared. Maybe even somebody who was planning on fighting back against the terrorists, because that was the only thing it made sense to call them. The guy who had charged the gunman and gotten himself killed for it had just panicked, Pierce thought. He'd never had a chance. But somebody who knew what they were doing . . .

Were there any campus police in the library right now? There should have been, Pierce knew. Had they been taken prisoner, too? Had they been killed? And what could campus cops, who didn't even carry guns, accomplish against a bunch of well-armed fanatics, anyway? Who could even hope to stop them?

Then suddenly, for some reason, he thought about Jake Rivers.

Chapter 29

Cal Granderson heard somebody yelling, and his first thought was that his grandmother was trying to wake him up so he could go to school. He wanted to pull the covers tighter and put the pillow over his head in the hope that she would go away and let him sleep. Then he realized that it wasn't her voice, made raspy and screechy by decades of smoking weed, that he heard. It was some guy shouting, "Get down, get down!"

That sounded like something Grandma might have said, all right, but it wasn't her.

The other thing that made Granderson realize he wasn't back in his dingy bedroom was that his head hurt like hell. Way worse than a hangover. More like his head was *busted* somehow.

The left side of his face was pressed against something hard and cold. He forced his eyes open. The lids fluttered some, and even when he was able to hold them open, he couldn't see anything at first except a vague, grayish blur.

After a while—he couldn't tell how long, but the yelling was still going on, for whatever that was worth—his vision cleared some and he could tell what he was looking at, at such close range.

It was a floor tile.

Granderson knew a floor tile when he saw one. He had run a buffer over enough of them, during a stint working as a janitor a few years ago, before he'd decided to be a cop. There was something vaguely familiar about this one, and after a while he was able to force his thoughts through the pain that was clogging them up and recognize it as one of the tiles from the library floors.

That was enough to bring it all flooding back to him: the guys in groundskeeper's coveralls waving guns around, the fight, the blows to his head . . .

He hadn't been shot, after all. Just knocked cold. And now he was awake again.

The bastards would be sor—

Nope. He couldn't move. He wasn't going to be able to make anyone sorry they had crossed paths with Cal Granderson. Not yet.

He closed his eyes. The shouting wasn't far away, but it wasn't right over him. He was convinced the phony groundskeepers were the ones doing the yelling. Maybe they believed he was dead or at least still unconscious. There was no good reason to let them know otherwise. He could only hope they didn't have somebody watching him who had seen him open his eyes.

When nothing happened—when he didn't get hit again or kicked or anything like that—he knew nobody had noticed. He tried to keep his breathing steady and under control, too. That wasn't easy to do with his head hurting as badly as it did.

Think like a cop, he told himself. *Think like a cop.* What did the gunmen want? They weren't here to rob somebody, or they would have done that and gone already. They weren't spree killers, or surely they would have put some bullets in him. If they had been Middle Eastern, his first hunch would have been that they were terrorists—but then he felt ashamed of himself for allowing that thought to cross his mind now. He didn't want to be Islamophobic.

Yelling but not shooting . . . that probably meant they were taking prisoners and rounding them up. Hostages. So, not a simple robbery, Granderson told himself, but rather, robbery on a large scale. A truly epic scale. Take over a whole college campus. Demand an astronomical amount of ransom. Yeah, that made sense.

Granderson's right arm was stretched out in front of him. That was the way he had fallen when one of the bastards knocked him out. But his left arm was doubled underneath him, so they couldn't see that hand. He forced himself to try to move his fingers. He had to find out if his nerves and muscles still worked at all, or if he was paralyzed, perhaps permanently.

His teeth clenched as he made the effort but his fingers didn't move.

Sternly, he warned himself not to let his disappointment and anger show on his face. He kept his eyes closed and his expression blank, as it would be if he were still out cold. After a minute, he tried again. Tried so hard he felt a bead of sweat pop out on his forehead, despite the cold floor on which he was lying.

This time the little finger of his left hand twitched.

Now it was a challenge not to show his excitement at what he had just felt. He renewed his efforts and bent the little finger, then the others on the hand. As he flexed them, he felt sensation nibbling its way down his arm and into his hand. After a minute, he was able to tighten the muscles all the way up into his shoulder.

That was more like it. It might take a while, but he was confident that he would be able to get up and fight again. He had to be patient, though, and not try to rush things. If he made his move before he was ready, he might wind up just getting himself killed.

Luckily, from the sound of things and what he had been able to figure out about what was going on, he thought he had some time before all hell broke loose. The gunmen who had taken over the library—and maybe more of the campus, too, for all he knew—would have to make their demands known and wait for an official response from the authorities.

All those on the outside—Chief McRainey, the Greenleaf cops who had been too good to hire him, the state police, probably even the FBI—they would all be freaking out about now. What they didn't know was that they had a secret weapon on the inside, a secret weapon named Cal Granderson.

He had to smile a little at the thought, but not so much that anybody would notice.

* * *

McRainey woke up in the back of an ambulance. Somebody said, "All right, let's get him to the hospital."

"Wait just a damned minute!" McRainey tried to sit up but found that he couldn't. He lifted his head enough to look down and see that he had been strapped down on a gurney. "Let me off this thing!"

One of the EMTs who had been tending to him earlier was sitting beside him on a bench. He put a hand on McRainey's shoulder and said, "Take it easy, Chief. You passed out again, so we need to take you to the hospital and get you checked out thoroughly."

"I'm fine, blast it," McRainey insisted. "I just lost some blood and got banged around a little. And I'm old, damn it. I don't bounce back quite as fast as I used to. But I don't need to go to the hospital. We've got a crisis here on campus!"

"There are people here to deal with it—"

"That's my job!"

"And ours is to make sure you don't die," the EMT said. McRainey recognized the calm, reasonable tone the man was using. He had used it himself on irrational suspects, many times in the past.

So he had to let them know that he wasn't irrational. The other EMT was standing at the back of the ambulance, just outside the vehicle's open door. McRainey looked back and forth between the two men and said, "Listen, I know you've got a job to do. But you cleaned the wound on my hand and bandaged it, didn't you?"

"We did," the man beside him said.

"So I'm not in any danger of bleeding to death."

"You've already lost too much blood. You could be in shock."

"Do I *sound* like I'm in shock?"

"Well . . . no," the EMT admitted. He looked at the machines mounted above and behind McRainey, which were beeping away. McRainey realized he was attached to them, and he had an IV in, too, running fluid into him. "And your vitals are relatively stable. But you need stitches, and I'm sure the ER doc will start you on IV antibiotics, too."

"There's no reason all of that can't be done later, right? I'm in no danger of dropping dead?"

McRainey stared intently at the EMT until the man shrugged.

"No more than anybody else your age, I guess," he said with obvious reluctance. "But you really need an MRI and a CAT scan to make sure there aren't any hidden injuries."

"They can do that later, too." With a curt nod, McRainey indicated the strap across his chest. "Now unfasten that."

The two EMTs looked at each other again, as they had done in the groundskeepers' shed. Then the one next to McRainey said, "Hell with it," and reached for the strap's fasteners. "You'll make my life miserable if I don't, won't you, Chief?"

"Count on it," McRainey said.

"Assuming, of course, that you live."

"I will. I'm a stubborn old coot."

The strap fell free. McRainey sat up. His head spun for a few seconds, causing him to grab hold of the rail on the side of the gurney with one hand, but the feeling quickly passed.

"Don't worry, I'm not going to pass out again," he told the concerned-looking young man beside him.

"It's not my responsibility if you do. You're gonna have to sign some paperwork."

"Later," McRainey said. He swung his legs off the other side of the gurney and stood up. The machines had started beeping faster, but no alarms were going off. He held out the wrist where the IV was attached. "Unhook me."

A couple of minutes later, McRainey stepped out the back of the ambulance and saw that it was parked in front of the groundskeepers' shed, as he expected. The street was alive with flashing lights. In addition to the ambulance, two Greenleaf PD patrol cars were there, along with a fire truck and a state trooper's cruiser. Yellow crime scene tape was strung up all around the shed.

"Hey, Frank!"

McRainey looked around. A short, stocky man in the brown and tan uniform of the Greenleaf Police Department trotted toward him. McRainey recognized him as Steve Hartwell, the chief of the local department.

"I thought they were taking you to the hospital," Hartwell said a little breathlessly as he came up. Like McRainey, he was in late middle age. Mostly bald, he had a broad, friendly, freckled face that usually looked a little sunburned no matter what the season. Right now that face wore a look of grave concern.

"I'll be all right," McRainey said. He waved the bandaged hand in front of him. "Just a scratch."

"That's not the way I heard it, but I have to admit, I'm glad you're still here. You know this campus better than just about anybody."

"Damn right I do." McRainey looked around the street again. "Feds not here yet?"

"They're on their way from Dallas. They've probably flown into Bergstrom by now and are driving out here in SUVs. The governor has requested assistance from Homeland Security, too, but I haven't heard when they'll get here."

"What's the situation on campus?"

Hartwell looked extremely weary now.

"Not good. We've had reports of shots fired in six different buildings: the library, the administration building, the student union, and three instructional buildings."

"None of the dorms?"

Hartwell shook his head and said, "No, I suppose they figured there wouldn't be enough students in the dorms in the middle of the day. They hit the places where they could corral the greatest number of hostages."

"That's the way it sounds to me, too," McRainey said. "Have you blocked off access to those six buildings?"

"I know my job, Frank," Hartwell replied, a little testily now. "Perimeters have been established around all of them. That meant spreading my department pretty thin, but we managed, at least so far. That's not all. Your man Bagley told me you were worried about bombs being planted around the campus by phony groundskeepers."

"Yeah, that's why they killed poor Charlie Hodges and all his crew." McRainey inclined his head toward the shed as he spoke. "That's the only explanation that makes sense."

"Well, when I heard that, I sent officers scattering all over campus to look for places that had been dug up recently." Hartwell's face was haggard as he went on, "We found more than a dozen of them. I put guards on all of the locations, just in case. Had to use some of your men to do it. I hope you don't mind me taking command like that."

"No, I'm glad you did," McRainey said. "Who's in charge right now doesn't really matter, I guess. As soon as the FBI gets here, they'll take over. They always do."

"Yeah. Anyway, we don't have any bomb detection equipment, but the Austin PD does, and so do the Texas Rangers. Austin's sending a couple of bomb squad officers. They ought to be here soon, and so should the Rangers. This whole thing's really about to blow up, Frank." Hartwell grimaced. "That was a bad choice of words, wasn't it?"

"There's nothing good to say about something like this. What about the media?"

"I've been keeping them back, but it's not easy. They're like a bunch of rabid vultures."

McRainey wasn't sure if vultures could get rabies,

but he knew what Hartwell meant, and he couldn't disagree.

"Are you in contact with the leader of this bunch?"

"Not yet," Hartwell said. "You think he's going to want to talk to us? He already gave his demands in that little speech he made in the library, the one that's all over the Internet."

"He'll be in touch," McRainey said. "Guys like that are always full of themselves. He'll want to put on a show. He's playing to the whole world, and he knows it." McRainey rubbed his chin and frowned in thought. "That might be as important to him as the money. You never know with these lunatics."

Hartwell drew in a deep breath and asked, "What do you think the Feds will do? Will they give him the money and let him go?"

"There are several thousand lives at stake. The students and faculty and staff inside those buildings, and probably a bunch of us out here if bombs start going off. Do you see any way to stop them?"

Hartwell's freckles stood out even more than usual because his face was drained of color. He shook his head and said, "Seems to me like the only way is if some of those hostages are able to get the upper hand. But even if they do that, there's still a chance that madman will set off the bombs."

"Unless somebody stops him," McRainey said.

He wondered suddenly where Jake Rivers was right now.

Chapter 30

Even though Natalie had asked him to keep his head down and not draw attention to himself, Jake had managed to sneak enough looks around over the past half hour to have a pretty good idea how many gunmen there were on the lower level and where they were located.

For one thing, the leader had left his position by the escalators and swaggered around arrogantly, checking with his lackeys. With the hostages terrified into being quiet, it wasn't hard to track the movements of the gunmen. Jake heard the leader having conversations with several of them, although he couldn't make out the words.

There were three men down here in addition to the leader, Jake decided: one by the elevator that was there for handicapped accessibility, in the back of the big room; one by the reference desk at the front of the room; and one by the little break area where there were vending machines with soft drinks and snacks. Students weren't allowed to take food or drinks out into the main room, but there were several tables and chairs in the alcove with the machines where they could sit and get away from their work for a while.

These four, including the leader roaming around, could cover the entire lower level of the library. This was where most of the students currently in the building would have been when the gunmen took over. There probably hadn't been many people at all on the third and fourth floors. Two, or at most three, terrorists would have been necessary to control those floors. And then, if the leader was smart, he would have all the hostages brought down here and gathered in one place.

So that meant ten or twelve of the bastards here in the library. Jake had no idea how many other buildings had been targeted, or how many members of the gang had been assigned to each building. How many total were on campus? Forty? Fifty?

Enough to spill a lot of innocent blood, that was for sure, even if the bomb threat was actually a bluff, as Jake suspected. Even armed with pistols, if shooting broke out they could kill dozens, even scores before they were stopped.

That raised the issue of communications. Jake assumed they were using cell phones, maybe walkie-talkies. If somebody on the outside was smart enough, they might think of shutting down all the cell towers around the campus. They might even be able to block walkie-talkie signals. That would leave the gunmen unable to communicate from building to building, and if the bombs were on cell phone triggers, assuming there were any bombs, that would prevent them from detonating.

Jake just hoped that whoever Frank McRainey called on for help had some experience with massive hostage situations.

* * *

Jeff Bagley hurried up to McRainey and stopped to stare at his boss in surprise.

"I thought they were taking you to the hospital, Chief," Bagley said.

"Change in plans," McRainey said. "I'm staying here until this is over, one way or another."

Bagley gestured over his shoulder with a thumb and said, "The FBI is here. They just pulled up at the command post Chief Hartwell established at the edge of campus."

The two police chiefs looked at each other and nodded.

"Let's go talk to the Feds," Hartwell said.

Not surprisingly, three black SUVs were parked in the blocked-off street that ran along the western edge of the campus. The federal agents liked their sinister-looking vehicles.

One man turned to greet McRainey with an outstretched hand, though. With his burly shape, chocolate skin, and close-cropped gray hair, he looked like somebody's affable black grandpa.

"Chief McRainey?" he asked in a deep voice.

"That's right."

"I'm Special Agent Walt Graham," the man said as he gripped McRainey's hand. "And you'd be Chief Hartwell, I'm betting," he went on to the boss of the Greenleaf PD.

"Yeah." Hartwell shook hands with Graham, too. "Are you running this operation for the FBI?"

"I am," Graham said with a brisk nod. "I've dealt with a few of these messes before."

"Not like this one, I'll bet," McRainey said.

Graham smiled thinly and said, "You'd be surprised."

An Austin Police Department van pulled in behind the SUVs that had brought Graham and the other FBI agents to the scene. Several officers in tactical gear piled out. One of them had a dog with him, a good-sized German shepherd.

"Bomb-sniffing dog?" McRainey asked.

"Sometimes the simplest methods are the best," Graham said. "We also have a robot equipped with sensors that will detect explosives. If one of you could show the Austin officers and my men the locations where you suspect bombs might be planted . . . ?"

Hartwell said, "I can do that."

"I'll need an overview of the situation and the layout of the campus, as well," Graham went on.

McRainey nodded and said, "I have a map in my office. I'll show you everything I can."

They turned toward the campus police department while Hartwell hurried off to join forces with the bomb-squad officers from Austin. McRainey and Graham had taken only a couple of steps, though, when a dark-colored sedan joined the other vehicles parked in the street and a woman in a midnight-blue dress got out. Her long brown hair was pulled back into a ponytail that hung halfway down her back. She was about forty years old, McRainey estimated, and striking in her appearance without being classically beautiful.

"Agent Graham," she said as she strode up to the two men.

"Agent Vega," Graham said.

From the sound of their voices, neither had much liking for the other, despite the obvious fact that they were acquainted.

The woman turned to McRainey and went on, "I'm Theresa Vega from Homeland Security. "And you are . . . ?"

"Frank McRainey, chief of the campus police," he introduced himself. He saw the abrupt lack of interest in Theresa Vega's eyes and knew that she had dismissed him out of hand as being unimportant in this crisis.

He didn't suppose he could blame her for feeling that way. He was just a campus rent-a-cop, after all.

She turned back to Graham and asked, "What do we have here?"

"I'm sure you've seen the video that streamed out of the library."

"Of course. The man's name is Matthias Foster. He was a student here several years ago."

Graham nodded and said, "I know."

"Wait just a minute," McRainey said. "You know the identity of the guy who's behind this, and you didn't tell me?"

"There hadn't been a chance to yet," Graham said. "I was going to fill you in while we looked at that map in your office."

McRainey supposed that was reasonable enough, but he still felt a little irritated. He knew that federal agents were notorious for keeping local law enforcement out of the loop. There were a couple of reasons for that. If there was any glory attached to a case, the Feds wanted it to land at their feet. And many of them genuinely regarded local cops as being incompetent at best, corrupt and stupid at worst.

McRainey hadn't really detected that sort of arrogance from Walt Graham so far, but it fairly oozed from Theresa Vega.

"If we're going to debrief Mr. McRainey before we start planning our next move, we should get on with it," she snapped.

"That's Chief McRainey," he said. It probably wouldn't do any good, but he was going to stick up for himself anyway.

Vega made a slight face but didn't say anything. After a moment, McRainey went on, "My office is this way," and pointed toward the campus police department.

As the three of them walked along, Graham said, "I heard that you killed one of the terrorists and were injured in the fight."

That appeared to make Vega's interest perk up a little.

McRainey told them about the desperate battle in the groundskeepers' shed after his discovery of Charlie Hodges' body. He held up his bandaged hand and said, "I got a pretty good cut on my hand and a knock on the head."

"Maybe you should be in the hospital getting checked out," Vega suggested.

"That'll wait. I'm responsible for the safety of this campus and everyone on it."

"Well, you haven't done a very good job of it so

far, have you? How many fatalities so far? At least five confirmed, including the man you killed?"

McRainey stopped on the sidewalk. Anger hardened his face.

"I had no warning of any of this," he said. "Isn't it the job of the FBI and Homeland Security to sniff out terrorist plots and stop them before they can get started? Was this guy Foster already on your radar?" He looked back and forth between the two federal agents. "Is that how come you know his name already?"

"You have no need to know that—" Vega began.

Graham interrupted her by saying, "Foster's name surfaced in an investigation we've been carrying out involving some illegal gun sales. That's all I can tell you, Chief, other than we've had reason in recent days to grow more concerned. It's likely we would have brought him in for questioning in the next few days." The burly special agent grunted. "He acted sooner than we expected, though."

Vega glared at Graham and said, "You shouldn't have told him that. It's none of his business."

"This is his campus that's being threatened. I think that makes it his business."

McRainey didn't know if there had been bad blood between the two federal agents before now, but there would be in the future, it seemed.

He didn't care about that. He said, "What do you know about Foster?"

"Let's talk about it on the way to your office, why don't we?"

McRainey was all right with that. The three of them started along the sidewalk again.

"Foster was enrolled here for three semesters," Graham continued. "I doubt if you remember him. He didn't get into any trouble while he was here, as far as we've been able to uncover."

McRainey shook his head and said, "The name's not familiar to me at all. Kelton's a small school, but there are still way too many kids who go here for me to remember all of them."

"Foster was what used to be called a radical. Went to some protests and helped organize a few of them. Posted a lot of Hashtag Resist and pro-Antifa stuff on social media. He strayed close to advocating the violent overthrow of the government but never was blatant enough about it to draw any real interest, at least from us. His name was in our database, but most of what I just mentioned was dug up in a hurry today after we were called in on this. After Foster dropped out of school here, he dropped out of sight, as well. Obviously, though, he's been hanging around and putting this plan together at least part of the time since then." Graham shrugged. "If Homeland knows any more than that about him, Agent Vega will have to tell you."

Vega's expression made it clear that she wasn't going to tell McRainey anything.

He didn't really care. It didn't matter to him who Matthias Foster was or what his motivation might be, unless that information would help to end this hostage situation somehow, with as little loss of life as possible. McRainey didn't think that was likely.

When they reached the station, an air of tense

urgency gripped the place. The dispatcher came out from behind the counter where she worked and hurried over to meet McRainey.

"Chief, we heard you were injured," she said. "Everybody's been so worried about you."

"I'll be all right, Doris," he told her. "Just need some stitches in my hand and some antibiotics when this is over. No need to fret over me. Has anything new come in?"

Doris shook her head and said, "We're all just waiting to see what's going to happen."

She looked at Graham and Vega and seemed to be waiting for McRainey to tell her who the two strangers were, but he didn't. Instead, he said, "We'll be in my office if you need me." Then he led the two federal agents down the short hall and through the door into the office.

The big, framed map of the campus took up most of one wall. McRainey pointed out the various landmarks situated around Nafziger Plaza, including the library, the administration building, the student union, and the other three buildings that according to reports were under the control of armed terrorists. He tapped a finger against the library and said, "That's where Foster was when that video streamed, and he must still be there since Chief Hartwell set up perimeters around all those buildings. The library and the student union will be the places where the most hostages are."

"Any way to get SWAT teams in there?" Graham asked.

"Sure," McRainey said with a shrug. "You can breach all these buildings without too much trouble.

They weren't designed for defense, after all, and I doubt if there are enough terrorists to cover every point of entry. But if Foster can set off bombs all over the campus with one push of a button, a direct assault probably isn't a very good idea."

Vega said, "He's bluffing about the bombs."

"We don't know that," Graham said, "and it's too big a risk to run until we do have confirmation one way or the other."

"What are you going to do? Negotiate with him?"

"I wouldn't call it negotiating as much as I would playing for time."

McRainey said, "Between the dog and the robot, will you be able to tell for sure whether there are actually any explosives planted in those places Foster's men dug up this morning?"

"We should have a pretty good idea—" Graham began.

He didn't get any further before a blast somewhere not far away shook the floor under their feet.

CHAPTER 31

"All right, let's move," the tall black man with a gun said as he approached Jake and Natalie where they still lay on the floor. The left sleeve of his shirt had something bulky under it, Jake noticed, as if that arm were bandaged. If the man was injured, though, he didn't seem to let it bother him.

"Where are we going?" Jake asked as he pushed himself up. "Disneyworld?"

"Don't give me any trouble," the gunman said as his lips drew back from his teeth in a grimace. "I'd just as soon shoot you, you son of a bitch."

That sounded personal, Jake thought. He wondered if the guy had a real reason to hate him, or if his skin color and political views were enough to justify that hatred. As far as Jake recalled, he had never seen this man before.

Of course, in recent days he had clashed with plenty of guys whose faces he'd never seen, because they were concealed under black hoods . . .

That opened up an interesting chain of thought, but Jake didn't really have time to follow it right now. He didn't want the gunman going unhinged while

Natalie was right there in danger, so he climbed carefully to his feet and said in a calm voice, "No trouble. Just tell us what you want us to do."

Being so cooperative went against the grain for him, but there were innocent lives to think of.

Natalie was pale and looked scared, but she appeared to be calm and had her emotions under control, too. The same couldn't be said of most of the other people who had been taken prisoner. Some were sniffling, some were outright crying, and everybody looked scared as the three gunmen who had been positioned around the edges of the room began herding the hostages toward the center of the lower level. There was an open area there, near the escalators, that was large enough for all of them to huddle together. It would be easier to guard them that way, Jake knew.

And once he was surrounded by innocents, there was no way he could make a move without endangering all of them. Even though he had said that he wouldn't cause any trouble—even though he was worried about Natalie—he had to go back on that promise if he was going to have any chance to fight back against these guys.

A glance to his left showed him that Pierce Conners and the people he was with were being marched toward the middle of the lower level, too. Jake caught Pierce's eye. He had no idea if he could count on the young man for anything, but instinct told him that if he had any allies in here, Pierce was the most likely to be one of them. Maybe the quick look Jake flashed toward him would be enough to tip him off that something was about to happen.

Jake stopped short and said in a loud voice, "Wait just a damned minute. They're bluffing."

That drew the leader's attention. As he swung around to look at Jake, for a second his face was contorted by naked fury before the look of cold, smooth menace came over his features again. He smiled thinly and said, "Bluffing? Do you really think so?"

"You're not crazy enough to blow yourself up along with everybody else," Jake said. "I can tell that by looking at you. You're no martyr. You don't believe there are ninety-nine virgins waiting in heaven for you."

The Middle Eastern–looking guy standing with Pierce glared at Jake when he said that. Jake ignored him.

"Keep talking," the leader said. "You're smart. I want to hear your thoughts."

"No, you probably don't."

"Do you honestly believe we didn't plant bombs all over this campus? Is that what you mean by bluffing?"

"That's right," Jake said. "You just want everybody to believe you did, so they'll be too scared to make a move against you."

The leader took a cell phone out of his pocket and held it up.

"So I won't push a button on this phone and send out the detonation signal?"

"Won't do you any good if you do. By now all

the cell phone towers in the area have been taken offline." Jake turned to address the crowd. "Check your phones. You won't have any service."

As far as he could tell, nobody did what he said. They were too afraid—with good reason—of the guns pointed at them.

But the leader, smiling with a self-satisfaction that Jake found worrisome, turned his phone so he could look at its display and said, "Well, what do you know? No service, just like you predicted." He put the phone back in his shirt pocket and reached for his pants pocket instead. "It's a good thing the triggers on those bombs are linked to sat phones instead."

The phone he pulled out of his pants pocket was bulkier than the slim little cell. As Jake tensed, the leader thumbed numbers into the satellite phone, held it to his ear, and smiled.

The boom was muffled by distance and building walls, but it was clearly an explosion. Many of the hostages screamed and grabbed at each other, thinking that the end had come.

But as seconds ticked by and the library didn't erupt in a holocaust of flame and destruction, they began to calm down a little, although there was still a lot of sniffling going on.

"Still think I'm bluffing?" the leader called out in a ringing voice. "That was one bomb. Call it a demonstration. I can set them off one at a time, or I can call a number that will detonate all of them at once. If I do that, this whole campus will be blown off the face of the earth. Is that what you want?" His mouth twisted in a snarl as he went on, "Is it?"

He was staring right at Jake as he asked the question, so Jake responded, "Take it easy. Nobody wants you blowing things up."

So the business with the bombs wasn't a complete bluff. He'd been wrong about that, Jake supposed. But he still didn't believe that this man intended to die today. The leader wasn't doing this to make a point. He was doing it because he wanted that ransom money.

But that didn't mean he wouldn't slaughter dozens, maybe even hundreds, of people to get his hands on it.

In fact, the guy's eyes did look a little more crazed now as he stalked toward Jake and waved the pistol in his hand.

"Nobody wants to be blown up," he said. "Nobody wants to die. So you'd better all hope the authorities cooperate with me, hadn't you? You'd better hope all those rich bastards on the outside whose kids go to school here come up with that hundred million! Otherwise—and I don't care if you believe me or not—nobody leaves here alive today!"

In that moment, Jake actually did believe him. He saw that he had misjudged this man. The leader had no cause other than his own, but he wanted that money so badly he was prepared to die if he couldn't have it. Jake had faced people who were dangerously fanatical when it came to their religion or the political beliefs—and for many on the left, their politics *were* their religion—but he had never run into anyone whose lust for money could rival this man's. That might make him even more dangerous.

But the leader's anger, as he got caught up in his own ranting, had led him to make a mistake. He had stalked forward, gesturing with the gun in his hand, until he was only about ten feet from Jake now.

And that was too close.

Cops had what was called the 21-Foot Rule, developed from a training drill that had a "suspect" charge an officer from inside that distance. That was close enough that in many cases the officer was unable to draw, aim accurately, and discharge his sidearm before the attacker reached him.

The leader's pistol wasn't holstered, but he had flung his arms out while he was yelling, so the Glock wasn't pointed at Jake. The distance between them was only half of the distance involved in the 21-Foot Rule, as well. In that split second, Jake realized all that and allowed his instincts to take over. If he could get hold of the leader and take that gun away from him, then he'd have a hostage of his own. He didn't know if that would make the others back off, but the guy seemed charismatic enough it was worth a try.

Jake lunged forward.

The guy saw him and tried to swing the gun toward him again, but Jake had already left his feet in a diving tackle.

Jake crashed into him. He was considerably bigger and heavier than the leader, so the impact drove the man off his feet and toppled him over backward. He landed hard, with Jake slamming down on top of him. Jake hoped it broke every one of the bastard's ribs.

He made a grab for the wrist of the leader's gun hand and closed his fingers around it. As Jake bore that hand toward the floor, he reached across his body and clamped his other hand on the 9mm's slide so the man couldn't fire it. Problem was, that meant both of Jake's hands were occupied, so he couldn't throw a punch. He drove his right elbow at the guy's jaw, though, and connected solidly.

Unfortunately, it wasn't enough to knock him out, and even though Jake was bigger, the leader was wiry and strong. He brought a knee up sharply, aimed at Jake's groin, but it caught him in the abdomen instead. Hurt like hell and knocked some of the wind out of him, but it didn't incapacitate him as it might have if it had landed on its target.

Jake wrenched at the gun. The leader's grip on it seemed to slip a little, but he didn't let go of it. He tried to wriggle out from under as Jake attempted to plant a knee in his belly and pin him down.

Jake was vaguely aware that a lot of shouting was going on around him, but no guns had gone off—yet. He heard one man yell for somebody to stay back, and another cried, "Don't shoot! Hold your fire!"

That was what he wanted to hear. They weren't going to blaze away at him for fear of hitting their boss. If he could just get that gun loose and hold it to the guy's head . . .

The leader's grip slipped again, and this time Jake was able to rip the gun away from him. Because of that, Jake didn't have to hang on to the guy's wrist anymore. He balled his left hand into a fist and brought it over in a short but powerful blow that rocked the man's head to the side. Jake shifted his hold on the Glock and grabbed hold of the leader's shirtfront with his other hand. He surged to his feet and dragged the guy up with him. He swung the man in front of him and rammed the pistol's muzzle against his head, just above the right ear. At the same time, Jake's left arm went around the man's neck and tightened to hold him in place.

He caught a glimpse of movement from the corner of his left eye and glanced in that direction to see that Natalie had moved up beside him. The unexpected sight of her made alarm go through him.

"Natalie, get back," he snapped. "Find some cover and get down!"

He turned swiftly, hauling the stunned leader around with him so the man's body was between him and the other gunmen. Would they drop their weapons, or would they shoot through the man who had planned this operation and brought them here today?

Jake never had a chance to find out what the other gunmen would have done, because at that moment he felt something hard and round press against the left side of his body. He recognized it as a gun barrel, and as he looked over, shock went through him to his core. Natalie was crowded close beside him with an intense expression on her face the likes of which he had never seen from her before. He could tell from the way the gun dug into his side that she was the one holding it.

"Stop it, Jake," she said. "Let him go and drop that gun. I don't want to kill you."

The leader was regaining his senses after that punch from Jake. He turned his head enough so that Jake could see the triumphant grin on his face as he said, "Good work, Lucy."

Chapter 32

Jake had never been shocked speechless in his life . . . until now. However, despite his surprise he didn't let go of the leader or drop the gun as Natalie had ordered. Natalie . . . or Lucy, as the man had called her. All along, she had been deceiving him, Jake thought. Everything that had been between them was a lie.

Everything . . .

"Please, Jake," she said in a half-whisper. "I really don't want to hurt you."

"Too late for that," he said, finding his voice again. Once he had spoken, it was easier to go on. "That's not a very big gun you've got there."

"A .32," she said, "and it's aimed right at your heart. You'll die in seconds if I pull the trigger."

"That's plenty of time for me to splatter this bastard's brains all over the floor."

"Please," the guy said in a mocking tone, "if you're going to threaten me, you might as well use my name. It's Foster. Matthias Foster."

He was pretty cool-nerved for somebody with a gun to his head, Jake had to give him that much. He couldn't *admire* the guy, of course. But Foster seemed to have ice water in his veins, and Jake acknowledged that.

"Jake . . ." Natalie said warningly.

"Just tell me one thing: are you really Natalie Burke, or is your name Lucy?"

"I'm Dr. Natalie Burke," she said. "And I really am a professor of criminal justice. Lucy is just . . ."

Her voice trailed off, as evidently she was at a loss to explain herself.

Not Matthias Foster, though. He said, "Lucy is what we call her. You know, like Carlos the Jackal back in the old days. And like Carlos, she'll kill you if you don't do what she says, Rivers."

"You know who *I* am?" Jake grated.

"Of course. We've been worried about you all along, my man. Why do you think we kept testing you to find out just how dangerous you really are?"

That explained some of the attacks on him and why no one on campus seemed to know about them. The black-hooded figures hadn't been Antifa at all. They had been part of Foster's cell or gang or whatever you wanted to call it.

"And that's why we decided it would be a good idea to get somebody close to you," Foster went on in his smug, mocking tone. "Our little Lucy did a good job, didn't she? You never suspected that she was one of us."

Jake's gaze cut over to Natalie again. She was pale and clearly upset, but the line of her jaw was resolute. So was the look in her eyes.

"I'm warning you, Jake—" she began.

"Yeah, I know," he said, not bothering to try to

conceal the harsh note of anger in his voice. "You don't want to shoot me, but you will."

"I won't have any choice."

"We've always got choices," he said. "How long are the rest of you going to carry on with this madness if Foster here is dead?"

"We've all gone too far to back out now," she said.

He believed her. And even though he had absolutely no fear of dying, he believed that the best chance they all had of coming out of this alive was if he was still breathing and able to seize another opportunity to turn things around. It made him a little sick to his stomach to do so, but he took the gun away from Matthias Foster's head.

"That's more like it," Foster said. "I'm glad you listened to reason, Jake. There's no reason anybody else has to die, anywhere on this campus. We're not about bloodshed. We just want to make a statement about the cesspool that this country has turned into."

"And that so-called statement is going to result in you putting a hundred million dollars in your pocket."

"Well," Foster said, still grinning, "that'll help average out the income inequality a little, won't it?"

"You're just a crook on a grand scale."

Before Foster could respond to that, Natalie said, "Go ahead and put that gun on the floor, Jake."

He had already made the decision not to push things right now when he lowered the gun from Foster's head. If he tried to raise it again now, he had no doubt that Natalie would pull the trigger.

He felt a bitter hollowness inside him at her betrayal, but one thing he had learned in combat was that emotions had no effect on facts. The time for them was after the danger was over.

He leaned to the side just enough to let the Glock slip from his fingers and fall a short distance to the floor. As soon as it had thudded onto the tile, one of Foster's gun-toting flunkies rushed forward to scoop it up, then backed off quickly while still covering Jake.

"Now let go of Matthias," Natalie ordered.

"How come you don't have an alias for the revolution, Foster?" Jake asked.

"Don't need one," the man replied. "I'd rather operate out in the open."

"More stroking for your ego that way, right?"

Natalie said, "Just let him go."

"Sure," Jake said. He released his hold on Foster's neck and stepped back.

No sooner had he done that than all the lights in the Burr Memorial Library went out.

The explosion somewhere on campus made a mixture of fear and anger boil up inside Frank McRainey. Not fear for himself, but for the students, faculty, and staff who might have been killed in that blast. He was charged with protecting their safety, and that he had failed to do so was what made him mad.

He started toward the door, but Walt Graham said, "Wait a minute, Chief. We'll be better off staying here and waiting for reports on what just happened."

"This is my campus," McRainey responded. "I'm not going to just stand here and do nothing—"

Before he could do or say anything else, the office door opened and Doris said, "I'm sorry to interrupt, Chief, but Jeff just called on his radio."

"Don't worry about interrupting," McRainey snapped. "What did he say?"

"The explosion was just outside Oliver Hall. It blew a hole in one wall and set the building on fire. The Greenleaf fire department is trying to put out the blaze."

"Casualties?" McRainey asked tersely.

"No fatalities, Jeff says. Some injuries to the Greenleaf officers who were posted nearby, but he doesn't know how bad. The building isn't one that was taken over by the terrorists, so it had been evacuated and was empty as far as Jeff knows."

Relief washed through McRainey. He was worried about the Greenleaf officers who had been hurt, but at least no one had been killed outright, at least as far as they knew now.

"That was a warning," Theresa Vega said. "Whoever is in charge of this group, he was telling us to take him seriously."

"There was no chance of us not doing that," Graham said. "We need to establish a line of communication into the library. I want to talk to that son of a bitch. But before we do that . . ." He turned to McRainey. "Can we kill the power to the individual buildings, or will we need to shut it down over the whole campus?"

"That's not in my department, but I imagine you'll have to shut it down all over. We have our own power plant with generators, in case the regular electricity goes out for a long time, but it can be taken off-line easy enough, I expect."

"Can you make those calls, Chief? I want them in the dark, literally. And since we've already had the cell service turned off, they'll be incommunicado except for the landline going into the library."

The FBI agent's request made McRainey feel a little like he was being shunted aside, but he knew Graham was right. The more they could inconvenience the terrorists, the better.

He nodded and said, "I'll take care of it."

"Right. I'm going out there and take a look around."

Vega said, "More bombs could go off. Perhaps we should evacuate this part of the campus as well and all of us pull back to a command center out of the danger zone."

"You go ahead. I want to get a feel for the situation, and I can do that better with my feet on the ground."

"And that way the FBI gets credit for anything good that happens, right? As well as most of the media coverage?"

"I'm too old and tired to give a damn about any of that," Graham said. "You do what you want, Agent Vega."

"I intend to. I'm coming with you."

Graham nodded and took a small radio from his pocket. He handed it to McRainey and said, "Stay in touch, Chief."

"I'll let you know when all the power is shut down," McRainey said. "Be careful. That bunch could have snipers posted that we don't know anything about."

Graham nodded and left the office. Vega followed him without a glance back at McRainey, who sank wearily into the chair behind his desk and pulled the phone toward him to make those calls.

The first one was to the campus power plant. He thought it might have been evacuated by the Greenleaf PD, but chief engineer Jonas Dietrich answered on the first ring.

"Yeah, once I heard what was going on, I told everybody else to get the hell out, Frank," Dietrich said once McRainey had identified himself and asked what the situation was there. "I figured I'd better stay, though, in case I was needed."

"You sure are. I'm going to have the electric company shut down the power to campus, and I don't want those generators kicking on when that happens."

"Don't worry, I'll take care of it," Dietrich assured him. He unconsciously echoed Walt Graham when he added, "Gonna leave those sons o' bitches in the dark, eh?"

"That's the idea," McRainey said. "Don't know if it'll do any good or not, but it can't hurt."

Another call quickly put him in touch with the manager of the local electric provider. Once McRainey had explained what he wanted, the man said, "Yes, we'll have to shut off the power to the entire campus. We could turn it off at each building, but I'd have to send crews out there to do that manually, and to be honest with you, Chief, I don't want to do that. My people deal with danger all the time when they're working on power lines, but this seems like an unnecessary risk."

"I agree with you," McRainey said. "I'd rather have you turn it off all over."

"Give me five or ten minutes."

With that done, McRainey hung up the phone, sat back, and blew out a breath. His wounded hand throbbed. Despite that, he wished he was out there on the front lines, so to speak, with Graham and Vega and Steve Hartwell.

Thinking about the FBI agent prompted him to pick up the handheld radio. He keyed the microphone and said, "Agent Graham?"

Only a couple of seconds went by before Graham's deep voice intoned, "I'm here, Chief."

"The power all over campus should be shut down any time now."

McRainey had just said that when the lights went out.

Chapter 33

It wasn't like the lower floor of the library was plunged into stygian darkness when the power went out. There were no windows, of course, since it was below ground level, but the opening where the escalators came down from the ground floor let in light from above. And since there were a lot of windows up there, it meant that a considerable amount of light slanted down to the lower level.

But the difference was so sudden, so unexpected, that for a couple of seconds everyone down there, including Jake, couldn't see much of anything. The shock made several people cry out in alarm. A gun blasted somewhere, deafeningly loud, and that caused more screams of terror.

Jake didn't have to see to do what he did. He twisted sharply and lashed out with his left arm. His forearm struck Natalie's arm and knocked it to the side. He hoped she wouldn't jerk the trigger and fire the .32, endangering the innocent hostages.

But he couldn't stay a prisoner himself and hope to do any good.

Natalie cried out, but the gun in her hand didn't

go off. Jake planted his hand against her shoulder and gave her a hard shove that sent her flying backward. In the next split second, he drove forward, hoping to grab Matthias Foster again and maybe get the upper hand once more.

Foster was already gone, though, darting away into the shadows. Jake's hurried gaze couldn't find him. More shots roared. Muzzle flame split the gloom. Shrieks of pain and fear ripped the air.

Somewhere, Foster shouted, "Kill Rivers! Kill him!"

Instinct sent Jake diving to the floor. A bullet whistled somewhere above him but didn't come close. He came up on hands and knees, scrambled behind one of the love seats, and heard a slug thud into it. Another lunge carried him into the stacks, those rows and rows of shelves full of old volumes and bound periodicals. The shadows really were thick in those narrow aisles. With each step he took, it grew darker around him.

He didn't mind that. Darkness was his friend right now.

As he ran, he trailed the fingers of his left hand along the shelves beside him. When he came to an opening, he ducked into it. It was a good thing he did, because a second later, Foster or one of his men reached the spot where Jake had disappeared into the stacks and emptied a magazine of 9mm rounds along that aisle.

By then, Jake was two aisles over, moving as silently as possible. He glided along that path for a moment, found another of the cross aisles, and slipped into it.

"Damn it!" Foster yelled. "Use your phone lights! Get in there and find him!"

Jake stayed on the move, weaving his way through the stacks toward the back of the lower level. The wheels of his brain turned over rapidly. He had already figured out that was the direction he needed to go. The stairwell was back there. If he could reach it, he could head up and lose himself somewhere on the other floors of the library. Foster didn't have enough people to hunt him down.

Once he had accomplished that, he could start planning his counterattack.

Counting Natalie, Foster had only four allies on this level. He couldn't send all of them after Jake, because the hostages might well panic and try to escape if they weren't being closely guarded. Jake looked back toward the front of the room and spotted two moving, flickering glows among the stacks. Those were the two men Foster had sent after him, using the lights on their phones to look for him.

Jake wanted to avoid them if possible, but he would take his chances against them if he had to. He liked the odds if he had to take them on one at a time, even though they had guns.

He didn't let himself think about Natalie and her stunning betrayal. Those thoughts tried to crowd into his mind, but he wouldn't allow them to do so. Later, what she had done would be painful to consider . . . assuming he was still alive to do so.

Assuming any of them made it through this alive.

His eyes had adjusted to the shadows. He knew he wasn't far from the stairwell.

Unfortunately, the same thought must have

occurred to Foster. The man shouted, "Get to the stairs! Don't let him get out that way! Keep him trapped in those shelves!"

So much for stealth, Jake thought. He broke into a run, his shoes pounding against the floor as he headed for the stairwell.

Normally an exit light burned over the heavy steel door with its push bar. Since the power was out, that light was dark now, but Jake was able to spot the door anyway as he emerged from the stacks. The stairwell was about twenty feet to his left, beyond a pair of water fountains. The doors to the men's and women's restrooms were back to his right.

As he turned toward the stairs, one of Foster's men emerged from an aisle beyond the metal door. The light from the phone in his left hand splashed over Jake, who slowed down, but only for a second, just long enough to grab a heavy book from the end of a shelf he was passing.

He flung the thick volume at the gunman as hard as he could.

The book struck the man's gun hand and knocked it aside just as he pulled the trigger. The bullet whined off one of the metal shelves in the stacks.

Jake had charged right behind the thrown book. His outstretched left hand clamped around the gunman's right wrist. Jake's right fist rocketed up and crashed into the man's jaw with enough force to slew his head far around to the side. He went limp.

Footsteps slapped the floor behind Jake, who

whirled around and pulled the stunned gunman with him. Flame spurted twice from the muzzle of the gun fired by the man who had just emerged from the stacks in front of the restrooms. Jake heard the bullets smack into the back of the first gunman and felt his body jerk. The pain jolted the man back to consciousness for a second as his eyes widened. Then they began to glaze over in death.

Jake plucked the dead man's gun from nerveless fingers, thrust his arm under the man's arm, and triggered twice as the pistol Jake had just liberated belched fire three times. The trio of swift shots spun the second gunman off his feet. His gun flew out of his hand.

Jake might have liked to have that second pistol, but it had landed somewhere in the stacks and he wasn't going to take the time to hunt for it. He did slap the pockets of the first man as he lowered the corpse to the floor and came up with three magazines. He hoped they were fully loaded but didn't take the time to check as he stuffed them in his pocket, then slapped open the stairwell door.

It was dark as pitch in there once the door swung closed behind Jake. He wished he had some way to wedge it closed so Foster's men couldn't pursue him, but there was nothing he could use for that. Instead he switched the gun to his left hand, since the stair railing was on his right, and started up as fast as he could, sliding his hand along the rail so he would know when he reached a landing.

Running upstairs in the dark was more of a challenge than he thought it would be. He stumbled several times and dropped to a knee once, banging it painfully on the stair riser. But he didn't waste any time getting to the next level, which was the ground floor.

He was able to make out lines of light coming through the tiny gap around the door on this level. It was a lot brighter here because of the large windows in the library's front wall.

Jake hesitated for a moment, uncertain whether to try leaving the stairwell here. There was at least a chance he'd be able to fight his way past Foster's men and reach the doors before they could stop him. Then he would be out.

But he wasn't sure he *wanted* to be out. Once he left the library, he wouldn't be able to do anything to stop Foster's plan. All the innocent people in here would be left to that madman's mercy.

A short time earlier, he would have included Natalie with those innocent people, he thought bitterly. Now that he knew the truth about her, he felt like he ought to hate her and believe that whatever happened to her, she had it coming.

Somehow, he just couldn't do that.

If he escaped from the library, eventually things would come down to a bloodbath. The authorities would breach the building sooner or later. There was no way of knowing how many would be slaughtered in that battle. Taking Foster down from the inside was still the best chance to minimize loss of life, Jake decided.

He started up the stairs to the second floor.

As he climbed, he thought that probably all the members of Foster's bunch were carrying satellite phones. Foster seemed to be pretty smart. He would have anticipated that the authorities would take the cell towers off-line and jam the walkie-talkie bands. It would be difficult to stop the sat phones from being able to communicate with each other, though. By now Foster would have warned his men on the other floors of the library about Jake being loose. All they had to do was guard the doors to the stairs and be ready to shoot him down if he poked his head out.

He might have escaped one trap by charging right into another, he mused. But under the circumstances, there was nothing else he could have done.

When he reached the second floor, he didn't stop. He didn't even slow down. The idea of going all the way to the roof had started to nibble around the edges of his brain. If he could get up there, he might be able to communicate somehow with whatever law enforcement agencies were on hand. He might even be able to help them work out a plan to storm the building without too much loss of life.

There was still the matter of those bombs, Jake reminded himself. He still believed there was a good chance Foster was running a bluff. Foster's men could have planted one or two actual bombs, just enough to make it seem like a possibility that he could blow up the entire campus.

Or maybe by the end of the day, what had been Kelton College would be just a huge, smoking crater in the ground. Jake didn't know. One thing was certain, though. Matthias Foster couldn't set off any bombs if he was dead.

Even though only a few minutes had passed, it was starting to seem to Jake like he had been climbing forever in the darkness. There was one landing between each floor, so he knew when he reached the third floor. He paused at the door this time and wondered why none of Foster's men had started down from above. They would have had him corralled in the stairwell with nowhere to go. He supposed they didn't want to risk a firefight in such cramped quarters. They might feel like they had a better chance by waiting him out.

He pressed his ear to the door and heard nothing from the other side. Well, that made sense, he told himself. If there were two of Foster's men on this level, one of them would be watching any hostages they had taken—probably not many, considering that this floor was devoted to Special Collections and not as many students utilized those—while the other would be hidden somewhere with a good view of the door to the stairwell, ready to fire if Jake emerged from it.

He thought about kicking the door open to draw the gunman's fire, then trying to pick him off. Every bit he could whittle down the odds against him made it more likely he would survive the final showdown.

He had just about discarded the idea, though, when he heard a sudden crash on the other side of the door. A man yelled, "What the hell?" at the same time as someone else let out a startled, incoherent cry.

Then guns started to roar, but Jake realized

quickly that none of the bullets were striking the door. Nobody was shooting at him.

That meant somebody else was in bad trouble in there, and Jake didn't hesitate once that thought went through his mind.

He bulled the door open with his shoulder and plunged out onto the third floor with the pistol gripped in both hands, ready to deal out death.

CHAPTER 34

Dr. Alfred Montambault was lost . . . and not just in the physical sense. He had no idea where he was, he had no idea what to do, and he had no idea what was going to happen next. All he knew was that he had been crawling around up here in the dark for what seemed like hours, and it was only a matter of time until he did something wrong and died because of it.

He was not cut out for this. Not at all.

And making it even worse . . . he kind of needed to pee.

He didn't allow himself to think about that. As long as he didn't acknowledge the need, maybe it wouldn't become urgent.

He stopped and drew in a deep breath. As he did, dust settled in his nose and throat and tickled maddeningly. He wanted to cough, but he stifled that impulse. One of the terrorists might be right below him, and if he coughed, the killer would hear him, realize that someone was in the crawl space, and open fire. Those flimsy ceiling tiles wouldn't stop any bullets. The thick plank on which Montambault was lying might shield him, but he didn't want to risk that. So it was best to be as quiet as possible while he continued his quest to find a way out of here.

He must have covered the entire area up here more than once, he told himself. If there was any sort of ladder or hatch that led out of the crawl space, he hadn't found it. If there was such a thing, it might just lead him into more trouble. His choices were limited, though. He could continue exploring, or he could just give up, lie here, and wait to see what happened.

Chances were, he would die no matter what he did.

With that bleak thought in his mind, he started crawling forward along the plank again. He hadn't gone more than a few feet when, without warning, he sneezed.

The dust he'd inhaled a few minutes earlier had caused that reaction, he knew, but knowing the cause didn't make things any better. His nose, which was on the prominent side, made sure that the noise it produced was loud and resonant.

A man's shout from below dashed his hope that the sneeze hadn't been heard.

Montambault started crawling faster as another man responded with a shout of his own. Even though he was hurrying, he still tried to be as quiet as he could, so maybe they wouldn't be able to track him by the sounds of his flight.

Whether they could hear him or not, they started shooting through the ceiling, just as he feared they might. The gunfire was thunderous and made him cry out involuntarily. The wild thought crossed his mind that maybe he should shoot back at them—he had a gun, after all—but he couldn't even see where he was going, let alone being able to aim at the men trying to kill him.

Something punched through a ceiling tile near him and thudded into a board, chewing splinters from the wood that stung Montambault's face. That bullet had almost hit him. He gasped in shock and crawled even faster.

Suddenly the plank wasn't beneath him anymore. It had come to an abrupt end. The air duct and the path alongside it must have turned, probably at a right angle. Thrown off balance with nothing to support him, Montambault sprawled forward. His outstretched hands struck one of the ceiling tiles.

The tiles and the metal latticework that held them up weren't meant to support any sort of weight. The tile broke under Montambault and fell out of its frame. He yelled as he plunged headfirst through the opening that hadn't been there a second earlier.

Montambault had always been clumsy and unathletic. It was pure luck that he didn't break his neck when he hit the floor. He had dropped the gun when he fell, but he was able to catch himself with both hands and roll over to take away some of the impact. Despite that, he landed hard enough on his back to take his breath away, rattle his teeth, and shake himself to his core.

Someone yelled, "What the hell?" The shout reminded Montambault that he was still in deadly danger. His brain screamed at his muscles to move, but they weren't quick to react.

He moved a lot faster when a shot blasted and a bullet whined off the tile less than a foot from his head. He jackknifed halfway up and tried to get to his feet as his instincts told him to run.

But run where? He glanced to his left and to his horror saw two men pointing pistols at him. There was nowhere to run, no place to hide.

Then he heard something from the other direction and a voice bellowed, "Doctor, get down!"

Montambault did what he was told. He dived, landing flat on his belly this time, and as he did, he lifted his head enough to look up and see Jake Rivers standing just outside the door to the stairs, with a gun clasped in both hands and thrust out in front of him.

That gun spat flame as four shots erupted from it, the reports rolling through the air so fast they sounded almost like one long roar. A tiny wisp of smoke curled from the muzzle as Rivers stopped shooting.

No more shots came from the other men, either. Montambault jerked his head around, twisting his neck so he could see them lying on the floor a few yards away. One man was motionless, but the other still writhed and spasmed as a little fountain of blood arched up from his ruined throat where a bullet from Rivers' gun had torn through it.

Then with a hideous gurgle, that man slumped down, too, and didn't move again. Montambault's brain was stunned, but enough of it still worked for him to realize that Rivers had killed those two men in not much more than the blink of an eye.

Now Rivers stalked toward him with the gun still

held ready. Montambault covered his head with his arms. Surely Rivers hadn't saved him only to kill him, but the young man hated him, Montambault was sure of that. There was no telling what a bloodthirsty barbarian like Rivers might do.

Something thumped against Montambault's side and made him jump. Rivers said, "Grab the gun, Doc, and get back on your feet. There might be more of them around here."

That was the pistol he had dropped when he fell through the ceiling, Montambault realized. Rivers must have slid it over to him with a foot. He wasn't going to kill him after all.

Rivers strode past the professor to check the two terrorists and make sure they were dead. While he was doing that, Montambault pushed himself into a sitting position and gingerly wrapped his hand around the butt of the pistol lying beside him. Rivers glanced over his shoulder, smiled faintly, and said, "You know how to use that, Doc?"

"I . . . I killed one of them a little while ago," Montambault said. His voice sounded hoarse and strange in his ears.

Rivers cocked an eyebrow in surprise and said, "Good for you. You'll probably get to do it again before the day's over."

Jake hadn't known what to expect when he stepped through the door, but the sight of Dr. Montambault lying on the floor while two of Foster's men tried to kill him wasn't it. He was pretty sure of that.

Actually, now that the two guys were down and out of the fight and Jake was leading the way up a corridor toward the center of the library's third floor, he hoped those two actually had been part of Foster's bunch. He didn't see how they could have been anything else, since they'd been trying to kill the professor, but you came right down to it, he didn't know any of Foster's followers by sight except the few he had already encountered.

Foster had boasted of having the entire building under his control, though, so anybody with a gun ought to be an enemy.

But Montambault had had a gun, Jake reminded himself. In fact, the professor had the weapon in his hand again, but only because Jake had prodded him to pick it up.

He paused and said quietly over his shoulder, "Do you know how many of them are on this floor?"

"N-no. All I know is that I shot one of them, while the others were trying to get all the prisoners together in the central part of the floor."

"How many prisoners are we talking about?"

"I have no idea," Montambault replied with a shake of his head. "I was the only one in the section where I was. Maybe a few people in each of the other sections, a couple of staff members . . ." He shrugged. "A dozen in all, perhaps."

"If that's all, Foster's men might have left just one person guarding them."

"Foster?" Montambault repeated, frowning in apparent confusion.

"Matthias Foster, or that's what he claims his name is, anyway. He's the guy behind all this."

"I never heard of him."

"Could be not many people did before today," Jake said. "Sometimes when guys pull big stunts like this, it's as much for the sake of their ego as for the money they hope to collect."

"I still don't know what you're talking about. I'm afraid I have no idea what's going on."

Quickly, Jake sketched in what he knew about the takeover of the campus. Montambault, already pale, blanched even more when Jake told him about the bombs.

"That madman is going to blow us all to kingdom come," the professor said.

"That's what he wants us to believe," Jake said. "That might not actually be the case, even though one explosion went off. That doesn't mean there actually are more bombs."

"But surely the authorities won't risk it—"

Jake held up a hand to stop Montambault as he heard somebody moving up ahead of them. This corridor didn't have any windows in it, so the light was dim here. The windows on the library's upper floors weren't as large and numerous as the ones on the ground floor, either, so not as much light filtered in from them.

Jake spotted a door ahead of them on the left. A quick step brought him to it. He grasped the knob, turned it, and opened the door to a supply closet.

"In here," he whispered to Montambault.

They crowded into the closet. Jake pulled the door in but didn't quite close it all the way. With Montambault behind him, he waited to see what was going to happen.

Slow, careful footsteps approached along the hall. Jake didn't breathe, and as he heard Montambault's nervous exhalations behind him, he moved his right elbow back until it prodded the professor's midsection. Montambault seemed to get the idea. Jake couldn't hear him breathing anymore.

He was still a little flabbergasted by finding Montambault the way he had. He knew from the broken ceiling tile that Montambault had gotten up there into the crawl space somehow, and he claimed to have taken one man's gun away from him and killed him. That seemed even more far-fetched to Jake than any book he had ever read about dragons or wizards or alien invaders. He would almost be more inclined to believe in those things than to accept the idea of Montambault performing such heroics.

But Montambault had the gun, so Jake supposed he had to believe him. He had his doubts, though, that the professor would be that lucky in any future gunfights.

Jake's eye was close to the narrow gap he had left between the door and the jamb. He saw a man's shape move past in the shadowy corridor. The guy had a gun, and he wasn't wearing any sort of uniform, which meant the odds were he was one of Foster's men. Jake wasn't going to shoot him from behind in cold blood without knowing for sure, though.

Instead, as the man eased along the corridor past the supply closet, Jake opened the door silently and stepped out behind him. The Glock rose and fell and came down hard on the back of the man's head. He grunted, pitched forward onto his knees, and dropped his own gun. Jake hit him again and drove him facedown on the floor.

He checked for a pulse and found one. The guy was just out cold, not dead. Jake knew he'd risked killing him by hitting him like that, but it was a chance he'd had to take.

Montambault whispered, "Is . . . is he . . ."

"He's alive," Jake said. "Come on out of there so I can drag him in."

He tore strips off the man's shirt and used them to tie his wrists and ankles, then crammed another piece of shirt into the guy's mouth and bound it in place. They left him in the closet. The cops could get him out later, assuming they hadn't all been blown sky-high.

A moment later, they reached the end of the corridor and the reception area for the Special Collections floor. Several desks sat behind a counter. On the floor around those desks were seven women and four men, lying facedown on the carpet.

For a bad couple of seconds, Jake figured they were all dead, executed by thc gunmen. But then he realized that he didn't see any blood. In fact, one of the older women, with graying brown hair, lifted her head enough to look around, and when she spotted Jake and Montambault, she cried out, "Oh, God! Don't kill us! We stayed right here where you—"

She stopped short, stared, and then exclaimed, "Doctor Montambault?"

The professor hurried past Jake and said, "Mrs. Taylor, are you all right?"

Some of the other people had lifted their heads and were looking around now. Jake told them, "You can get up now. Those guys who threatened you won't hurt anybody ever again." He added quickly, "Did they leave just one man to guard you?"

"That's right," one of the women said. She was young enough to be a student or maybe one of the library staff. All of them except the older woman fit that description. As she climbed to her feet, she went on, "When the other two didn't come back, and then there was all that shooting, he told us to lie down and not look up, or someone would kill us. Then I guess he went to look for the others."

Jake didn't take the time to explain that the last guard was now tied up in the supply closet. Instead he asked, "Is anybody hurt?"

He got head shakes all around.

"Just scared half to death," one of the young men said. "What's going on?"

"Doctor Montambault can tell you. Right now, is there any place you can hole up, a fairly small room with only one entrance?"

"The rare book room," the older woman said.

Jake nodded. It would have been good if he could have gotten these people completely out of the building. The cops probably had a perimeter set up outside. The hostages could have hurried behind that line to safety. But there was no way to reach the ground from the third floor without jumping, and that would likely result in some broken arms and legs, if not worse.

Of course, that was better than getting blown up,

but Jake still didn't believe the situation had gotten that desperate yet.

The gun Montambault held was also a 9mm. Jake took one of the loaded magazines from his pocket and extended it to the professor.

"Hang on to that," he said. "You may need it."

Montambault looked a little like Jake was trying to hand him a rattlesnake. But he took the magazine and asked, "Are you going to leave us here?"

"Trying to get out of the building right now would be too risky. Better to get to someplace you can defend if you have to." Jake looked at the others. "Does anybody else have any experience with firearms?"

Of course, they all just looked at him like he'd asked if they could flap their arms and fly to the moon. The typical Kelton College student not only had never fired a gun, the very idea would be abhorrent to them . . . at least until their lives were in danger.

"Looks like you're the only gunfighter around here, Doc," Jake said to Montambault.

That made the professor's eyes widen in horror. He started to stammer something, but Jake cut him off.

"I'm counting on you to keep these folks safe."

Montambault opened and closed his mouth a couple of times, swallowed hard, rubbed his free hand over his face, and said, "I . . . I'll do my best, Mr. Rivers."

Jake nodded, clapped a hand on the man's shoulder, and said, "I knew I could depend on you."

He didn't know that at all, but he didn't figure it

would hurt anything to say something positive to Montambault.

"What are you going to do?" the professor asked.

Jake smiled grimly.

"Still rats to clean out of this nest," he said.

Chapter 35

When the lights went out, the first instinct Pierce Conners felt was to stay right where he was, hunkered down on the floor, face pressed to the tiles. When the shooting and fighting started, he knew that was the right thing to do.

But then something began nagging at him, and it wouldn't let go.

He was supposed to be an activist, somebody who believed in working to bring about change and make the world a better place. Nobody ever changed anything by curling up in a ball and whimpering in fear.

All too often, he had listened to his fellow progressives complain about a situation, then conclude by saying, "Somebody needs to *do* something!"

When he was feeling in a particularly contrary mood, instead of simply agreeing with them, Pierce would ask, "Who?"

That always brought a blank stare and usually a question about what he meant.

"Who should do something?" he would press.

And the answer was always, "Why . . . the government, of course."

Pierce believed in government and the power

it could and should wield. But that didn't mean individuals shouldn't do their part, as well. Too many on his side were all talk, no action. Pierce didn't want to be that way.

With that thought prodding him, he started to crawl away from the other members of his study group. Fareed had finally gotten down on the floor with the others.

Margery reached out and clutched Pierce's arm as she whispered, "Where are you going?"

"I'm going to see if I can hide and get away from them." He pulled free of her hand. "Come with me."

"No! Are you crazy? They'll kill us."

"They've got their hands full right now." In the gloom, Pierce couldn't tell exactly what was going on, but he was willing to bet that Jake Rivers was right in the middle of that violent commotion. "This may be our only chance to get away!" He looked over at Jenny and Clark. "Come on, you guys."

Jenny shook her head in wordless terror, so of course Clark said, "We're not going anywhere, man. We're gonna stay right here and not get shot."

Stay right here and die, Pierce thought, but he knew it wouldn't do any good to say that. Instead he started crawling, staying as low to the floor as he could. He headed for the side of the room where the restrooms, the stairs, and the vending area were located. There might be somewhere over there he could hide.

The idea of maybe fighting back against the men who had taken over the library hadn't occurred to him when he started moving, but it did shortly thereafter. Problem was, he couldn't see any way of doing it.

There were enough prisoners here on the library's lower floor that if they all rose up at once and struck back at their captors, they would overwhelm the gunmen, no doubt about that. It was possible, even probable, that some of them would lose their lives, but that couldn't be helped. The alternative was to remain hostages, at the mercy of people who might well be ruthless enough to slaughter them all.

Pierce might have been willing to run that risk if he believed anyone would fight at his side. He suspected the only man here who would do that, however, was already battling the terrorists: Jake Rivers.

A voice behind him suddenly cut through his thoughts by shouting, "Stop him! He's trying to get away!"

Surprise froze Pierce for a second. He had hoped all the gunmen were distracted enough they wouldn't notice him crawling toward the stacks. Evidently, that was the case, because he recognized the voice of the man who had called out the warning.

Moammar Fareed.

The leader of his study group. A fellow student. Not really a friend, but a fairly close acquaintance and someone who claimed to share some of Pierce's progressive beliefs.

And yet he had betrayed Pierce without a moment's hesitation. He had already tried to suck up to the leader. This was just more of the same, Pierce realized as he sprang to his feet. That made him more of a target, but he could move a lot faster.

He had never sprinted faster during his high

school track team days than he did now as he ran toward the stacks.

"I'll stop him!"

Fareed again, on his feet and moving fast, too. He dived at Pierce from behind and tackled him around the knees. Pierce fell heavily. He tried to pull free from Fareed's grip and got his right leg loose.

He kicked out, felt the heel of his shoe slam against something. The impact was a satisfying one. Fareed grunted and let go of Pierce's other leg. He groaned and rolled onto his side, clutching at his jaw where Pierce had kicked him.

In the blink of an eye, Pierce was up and running again. He expected to hear rapid footsteps coming after him. His muscles were braced for the deadly impact of a bullet.

Neither of those things happened. Pierce reached the stacks and ducked in among the close-set shelves. He guessed the gunmen had their hands too full dealing with Jake to worry about him.

He hurried along the narrow aisle, wincing every time a shot rang out because he thought it was aimed at him. He reached the end of the aisle without being hit, though, and knew that the gunmen weren't aiming at him. If they had been, they couldn't have missed in such close quarters.

Then more shots blasted somewhere close by, close enough for Pierce to catch a whiff of the cordite tang. He pressed his back against the set of shelves to his left for a few moments, then risked a look around the end of them.

He was just in time to see Jake Rivers disappear into the stairwell. The big man had a gun in his hand, and since there were a couple of bloody bodies lying sprawled on the floor, Pierce had a pretty good idea where Jake had gotten the weapon.

Jake had escaped, which meant that the surviving terrorists would try now to regain control of the hostages on this level. Pierce had no doubt at all that Fareed would try to curry favor with their captors by ratting him out. If he stayed where he was, they would find him, probably sooner rather than later.

As soon as that realization hit him, he knew what he had to do. Wherever Jake Rivers was, there would be trouble . . . but that was better than here. Pierce might have at least a fighting chance to survive.

He took a deep breath, ran to the stairwell door, and shoved it open. The stairwell was dark, but Pierce didn't hesitate. He started up after Jake.

It hadn't taken as long as Dietrich estimated to get the power shut down. Frank McRainey spoke to Graham over the radio and confirmed that the electricity was out, then asked the FBI agent, "What do you want me to do now?"

"It might be a good idea for you and any of your department who are still there to go ahead and evacuate, Chief," Graham replied. "I lean toward thinking that the bomb threat is mostly a bluff, despite that explosion earlier, but there's no point in taking chances. Besides, you've been wounded and need more medical attention."

McRainey glanced at his bandaged hand. It hurt,

but he didn't see any blood seeping through the dressing.

"I'm fine," he said. "The safety of this campus is still my responsibility."

"Then join Chief Hartwell at the command post just off campus. My men will need to call on both of you for advice before this is over."

McRainey didn't like the idea of leaving the station. It seemed too much like running away. But Graham might be right: the command post might be where he could do the most good from here on out.

Anyway, Doris would probably refuse to evacuate the station until he left, too, and he didn't want anything happening to her. It would be partially on his head if it did.

"All right, Agent Graham," he said as he held down the microphone button. "If you need me, that's where I'll be."

"Thanks. I'm going to try to make landline contact with the suspects now."

The connection broke. McRainey sighed, stood up, and put the radio in his pocket. He was about to go out and tell Doris they were leaving when she appeared in the doorway. Frowning, she said, "Chief, there's a man here—"

A figure came up behind her and moved her aside without seeming to put any effort into it. His actions were gentle, though, not the least bit rough. He smiled at McRainey and said, "Chief, I need to talk to you."

McRainey had never seen the man before. He

was older, from the looks of his weathered face and the silver in his hair that had once been dark and still bore traces of that. He moved and carried himself like a younger man, though. McRainey had seen guys like that before, men who took such good care of themselves—and who were blessed with good genes, to boot—that it was difficult to tell if they were forty or seventy. This lean, medium-sized stranger fit right into that category.

He was dressed casually in boots, jeans, a faded blue work shirt, and a lightweight gray jacket. McRainey couldn't see any overt signs that the stranger was armed, but something about the man told him that he was. In fact, he seemed like the sort of man who would seldom if ever go anywhere *without* being armed.

McRainey said, "You shouldn't be here, Mister . . . ?" When the stranger ignored that hint for his name, McRainey went on, "The campus has been evacuated and is on lockdown. All civilians need to leave as quickly as possible. It's dangerous here."

"I've never worried that much about being in dangerous places," the stranger replied with a faint smile. "I suppose I wouldn't know what to do if I found myself somewhere that *wasn't* dangerous."

"What are you doing here on campus, anyway?" McRainey demanded. "Were you visiting somebody when the trouble broke out?"

"Actually, I wasn't here when the trouble broke out . . . but I got here as quickly as I could. There are a lot of rumors flying around all over the media, Chief. I need you to tell me what's actually going on."

McRainey was getting even more confused. He said, "That doesn't make any sense. The campus is closed off. You couldn't have gotten here once it went on lockdown."

The man just shrugged slightly and said, "I can usually get in wherever I need to be." He turned to smile at Doris and went on, "You really should leave, ma'am. Like the chief says, it isn't safe here."

She glared back at him defiantly.

"I'm not going anywhere until Chief McRainey does," she declared.

"Then you'd better tell me what I need to know, Chief." The stranger gestured toward the map on the wall. "Where's the library? That's where the ringleader has established his headquarters, isn't it?"

"Damn it!" McRainey burst out. This guy didn't exude even an ounce of arrogance or even smugness, but McRainey wasn't sure he had ever run into anybody with more self-confidence. "You're some sort of federal agent, aren't you? If you're FBI, I was just talking to your boss—"

"I'm not FBI," the man broke in. "Or Homeland Security, either. But I *have* done a few chores for the government in the past."

A chill went through McRainey. He had never met an actual spook before, at least that he knew of, but something told him that's what this man was. A killer, pure and simple, if he needed to be in order to get the job done.

"Who sent you here? Or is it a death sentence just to ask the question?"

The stranger shook his head and said, "You've got me all wrong, Chief. Nobody sent me. I've got a personal reason for being here. I just want to help."

"The situation is under control," McRainey said heavily. "The only way civilians can help is by staying out of the way."

"Well"—another faint smile and a shake of the head—"that's not going to happen, so you might as well go ahead and tell me what I want to know."

"There's the map," McRainey snapped. "If you're such a hotshot, read it yourself. You'll be able to figure out everything, I'm sure."

"All right."

The man stepped over to the map and gazed at it for a long moment while Doris stood just outside the office doorway and looked worriedly at McRainey. Then the stranger nodded as if satisfied and turned away from the map.

"Thanks, Chief. I really do think you should leave now. I don't believe that Foster really intends to blow up the entire campus, but in circumstances like this, accidents sometimes happen."

McRainey didn't question how the stranger knew Matthias Foster's name. He probably had some pretty highly placed sources in the government.

"Just what is it you intend to do?"

"Whatever I can to put a stop to this with as little loss of life as possible." The stranger paused, then added, "I'm sure you know the old saying about cutting off the head of a snake . . ."

With that, he turned and started toward the door.

"By God, at least have the decency to tell me your name!" McRainey exploded.

The stranger paused and looked back.

"It won't do you any good," he said, "but it's Barry. Barry Rivera. But you can call me Dog. Just Dog."

CHAPTER 36

Jake had taken the pistol being carried by the man he'd knocked out, as well as the extra loaded magazines in the man's pockets, so he was well armed as he headed up the darkened stairwell toward the fourth floor. It would have been nice to have an AR-15 or something like that in addition to the two 9mm semiautomatics, but a man worked with the tools he had.

The fourth floor was where all the library's offices were located. He didn't know how many people would be up there, normally, but he guessed not many. Which meant that Foster might have sent only a couple of men to round them up. If he could take care of those guys, it would open a path all the way to the roof . . . and that might be how the hostages could get out of here.

Foster's men had to have heard the shooting from the other parts of the building, though, so they would be alert for trouble. Jake might not be able to take them by surprise.

He would deal with that when he got there, which wouldn't be much longer now, he thought as he rounded the landing halfway between the third and fourth floors and continued upward.

When he reached the top of the stairs and the door to the fourth floor, he took hold of the metal bar and pressed it slowly and carefully until he heard the latch disengage. Then he pulled on it with just enough force to open the door an inch or so.

Unfortunately, it didn't budge. Jake pulled harder, then frowned as the door still didn't move.

It wasn't locked. He had heard the latch click. He wasn't sure the stairwell doors even *could* be locked, since the stairs served as the building's emergency exit. But it wasn't opening, that was for sure, which meant the gunmen on this floor had done something to keep anybody from coming up the stairs and taking them by surprise, which was exactly what Jake had intended to do.

He put his ear to the door and listened intently, but heard nothing from the other side. No voices, no one moving around. Someone had to be up here, though. The sabotaged door proved that.

Somewhere below him on the stairs, something thudded, followed immediately by a gasped "Damn it!" Then a swift shuffle of footsteps before total silence fell.

Jake pressed his back to the wall beside the door and aimed the pistol in his hand down the stairs. He stayed there for a long moment, silent and motionless. Someone was following him up the stairs. Judging by the sounds he had heard, whoever it was had tripped in the dark, probably had fallen and banged a knee on the stairs, and cursed at the pain. Then, realizing he might have given himself away, he had frozen and was standing down there somewhere, not moving.

The question was whether the man was a friend or an enemy, and since Jake didn't have any friends in this building right now, at least as far as he knew . . .

"Jake? Jake Rivers?"

The call floated up the stairwell in a strained half-whisper. Something about the voice was familiar to Jake, but he couldn't place it.

He didn't respond, just in case someone was aiming a gun at him right now, just waiting for him to say something in order to pinpoint his position in the thick gloom. He figured that if he was patient, whoever it was might say something else.

Several long, tense moments dragged by in silence. Then the same voice said, "Jake, if you're up there, this is Pierce Conners. You know, the guy who gave you that unedited video . . . If nobody's up there, then I guess I'm talking to myself and I feel really stupid. But if one of those guys with guns is there . . ." Pierce sighed. "I may be dead soon. I think I'd rather feel stupid. But one way or another, I'm not going to turn around and go back down there where everybody else has been taken prisoner. I'm coming on up, and I really, really hope I don't get shot."

Jake didn't respond, even though he could hear the fear in Pierce's voice and wished he could reassure the kid. But somebody could be listening right on the other side of that door, and he didn't want to confirm for them that somebody was in the stairwell. Without making any noise, he moved over to where he was standing beside the top of the stairs. He tucked the pistol behind his belt and waited.

He heard Pierce coming up the stairs and could tell that the young man was trying to be quiet. However, Pierce obviously didn't have much experience at being stealthy, because Jake was able to track his progress all the way up the stairs.

When Pierce reached the top and stepped onto the landing, Jake was ready. He looped an arm around Pierce's neck and jerked him back against him. Jake moved fast enough, and his grip was tight enough, that Pierce wasn't able to make a sound before he found himself caught.

He fought, though, flailing his arms and jerking his body around for a couple of seconds before Jake tightened his grip even more and growled in Pierce's ear, "Stop it."

Pierce went still. Air rasped in his throat as Jake loosened his arm enough for him to breathe. But only for a second before Jake clamped down again.

"Listen to me," he whispered. "This is Jake, like you thought. We're alone, and you're not in any danger right now, do you understand?"

He felt Pierce's head move and recognized it as a nod.

"If I let you go, you're not going to yell and you're not going to fight. Right?"

Again a nod from the young man. Jake eased off the pressure on Pierce's throat but didn't let him go completely. Instead he whispered in Pierce's ear, "Keep your voice down when you answer me. Are you all right?"

"Y-yeah," Pierce managed to say. He still sounded

pretty breathless. His chest rose and fell rapidly against Jake's arm as he tried to recover from being choked.

"I'm going to let go of you the rest of the way. Just stand there. Don't try to do anything."

"All right." Pierce's voice sounded a little stronger now.

Jake released his grip and stepped back a little. Pierce was still close enough for him to grab in a hurry if he needed to, but he didn't expect that to happen. Despite any disagreements they might have politically, right now he and Pierce definitely ought to be on the same side.

"What are you doing here, Pierce? You were down on the lower level the last time I saw you."

"I was able to sneak out of there right after you got loose from them. When you killed those two guys by the stairs, there was nobody right there to see me start up after you."

The conversation was conducted in whispers. Jake could tell that Pierce had turned to face him.

"Yeah, but why did you follow me? You're not a fighter."

Jake didn't mean any offense by that, just stating a fact as far as he was concerned, but Pierce sounded a little miffed as he said, "I can fight. I was an athlete in high school. I've been in a few fights in my life."

"Not like this one," Jake told him. "This is life and death. Foster and his flunkies don't care if they kill all of us. They just want that money they're demanding."

"I don't care what that guy says, he's not trying

to make a point about income inequality," Pierce said with an obvious note of bitterness in his voice. "He's just a crook."

"Yeah, I think you're right about that. Doesn't make him any less dangerous."

"I know, but I'm not scared. Well . . . I *am* scared, I'm not crazy, but somebody's got to stop these guys. I'm with you, Jake. What's your plan?"

Fate had given him some strange allies, Jake thought. A young black liberal and a middle-aged, snowflake professor. Not much of a fighting force. In a way, Jake would have preferred to be on his own, but he supposed Pierce and Montambault were better than nothing. Maybe.

"So far my only plan has been to kill as many of them as I can and not get killed while I'm doing it. But I've cleared the third floor and got the folks who were taken hostage there hiding until help arrives. If I can deal with the gunmen here on the fourth floor, that'll give us access to the roof. Maybe we can get in touch with the authorities and have them bring in a helicopter. If a chopper can land on the roof—and I don't know at this point if it can—then we can evacuate the freed hostages that way and get a SWAT team in here to finish clearing the building."

"What about the bombs?"

"I think that's mostly a bluff on Foster's part," Jake said. He shrugged in the darkness. "If it's not, I guess we may die a little sooner than we would have otherwise."

"I don't suppose it would be best just to wait and hope they get the ransom money they asked for . . . ?"

"Trying to buy off evil never works. It's entirely possible that Foster doesn't intend to leave any of us alive no matter what happens."

"So I guess we have to fight," Pierce said. "I never really believed in violence. Maybe we don't have a choice, though."

"You have a choice," Jake said. "Find a corner away from everybody and everything and stay there until it's over."

"And hope for the best? I don't know . . . My parents raised me to fight for things I believe in. They didn't mean it in terms of literal fighting, of course, but sometimes . . ."

"Sometimes there's no other way."

"You're right. I'll say it again, Jake: I'm with you. What do you want me to do?"

"That door won't open. It comes in toward us, not out, so blocking it wouldn't do any good. I think they must have tied a rope or something to the bar and then tied the other end around something that won't move. We have to get it open, though. There's nowhere else for us to go. So what I'm going to do is try to budge whatever it is holding the door closed. I'm a pretty big, strong guy. If I can get it open even an inch or so, you'll be able to look through the gap and see what's holding it. Think you can shoot a rope in two?"

"Do I think I can—Wait—What?"

"Hold out your hand," Jake said. "I'm going to give you a gun. *Don't* shoot me. Keep your finger off the trigger."

"Jake, I don't know about this—"

Jake reached out, found Pierce's hand in the darkness, and pressed one of the 9mm pistols into it.

"Careful," he warned. "Don't drop it. You've got it?"

"Yeah, I . . . I guess so. I've never fired a gun before. What do I have to do?"

First Montambault, now Pierce. How did people grow up without ever putting their hands on a gun, Jake wondered? He couldn't even begin to comprehend that. But now wasn't the time to ponder such things, he told himself.

"This is a semiautomatic, and there's a round in the chamber. That means all you have to do is point it and pull the trigger, and it'll fire every time you pull the trigger until it runs out of ammunition. Look at what you're shooting at and point the gun at it like you'd point a finger. There's not enough time to get any more sophisticated than that. Can you handle it?"

Jake couldn't see it, but Pierce swallowed so hard he could *hear* it. Pierce said, "Yeah, I'll do my best."

"Okay. You can see where the door is, because there's a little light around the edges. Stand on the side where it opens, just to the left there, and turn so you can see through the gap when I pull on it. You won't have much time, so be ready. If there's a rope, shoot at it. If it's a chain, that probably won't work and we'll have to think of something else. Got all that?"

"Yeah. I'm ready, Jake."

The latch had clicked back into place. Jake braced himself, got his feet set firmly on the floor, and pressed down the bar on this side of the door until he heard it unfasten again. Then he heaved with all his strength, putting so much into the effort that he grunted.

The door shifted toward him a little, just enough so that the latch wouldn't engage again. He relaxed for a split second, then threw his muscles into it again. Something scraped on the other side. They had tied the door to a desk or a set of shelves, he thought.

A narrow ray of light slanted through the gap Jake had created. In the glow from it, Jake saw Pierce standing there and gripping the gun with both hands as he aimed it. The young man pulled the trigger three times fast. In the narrow confines of the stairwell, the reports slammed painfully against Jake's eardrums.

But the door sprang open, the sudden release of tension throwing Jake backward. He caught himself before he tumbled down the stairs.

In old movies, guys shot through ropes all the time. In real life it wasn't so easy. But here at close range, Pierce had managed. Jake yelled, "Stay back!" at him as guns began to go off on the other side of the door. Jake used the door itself for cover and heard slugs thudding into it as he dropped to one knee, pulled the other pistol with his left hand, and fired around the edge of the barrier. He wasn't as good a shot with his left hand as he was with his right, but he was good enough to plant a couple of rounds in the body of a gunman standing about fifteen feet away behind a desk.

The man went over backward. His pistol flew

from his hand as he fell. Jake held his fire and waited, but no more shots sounded.

Instead, after a couple of minutes that seemed even longer, a woman's voice asked in a quavering, frightened tone, "Who . . . who's there? Are you the police? Is it safe?"

Jake didn't answer the question directly. Instead he said, "Was there only one of them, ma'am?"

"Yes, and he . . . he looks dead. There's blood all over . . ."

Jake could practically hear the shudder in the woman's voice as her words trailed off.

"Stay here," he told Pierce, keeping his voice down as he did so. "There might be a guy with a gun to her head, making her say that. Only one way to find out."

"And if . . . if I hear shots?"

"Then I'll count on you to have my back," Jake said. Without giving Pierce time to worry about that, he pulled the door open wider and stepped out onto the library's fourth floor.

Chapter 37

Things were going wrong, but Matthias Foster had always known there was a good chance that would happen. Good planning could eliminate a lot of unwanted possibilities, but it couldn't account for everything. There were always flukes in real life.

There were mistakes that could be made, too, and he wasn't egotistical enough to believe that he was perfect. Looking back on it now, he knew he should have had Lucy—Natalie, there was no need for code names now—kill Jake Rivers during one of the many times when she'd had the chance. Rivers had fallen for her; he never would have suspected anything until it was too late.

Foster had been confident that he and his men could handle Rivers, though, and besides . . .

He wasn't sure Natalie would have killed the big son of a bitch even if he had ordered her to. He was beginning to think that maybe he couldn't depend on Natalie as much as he had believed he could.

For the moment, though, he had no choice but to depend on her, because he had two men down and only Natalie and two other men to help him keep dozens of prisoners under control. She certainly seemed like she was trying to do her part, holding her gun steady and keeping a menacing scowl on her face as she helped herd all the hostages together.

When they had swept the entire floor and had everyone huddled together, trembling in fear, in the center of the big room, Foster took out his radio to check with the other floors. It still worked, although it was only a matter of time until the authorities jammed this frequency, too. He had heard what sounded like shots somewhere on the upper floors of the library, and he fervently hoped that meant Jake Rivers was dead.

"Jimmy," Foster said into the radio. "Report."

"The first floor is under control," Jimmy responded immediately, which made Foster feel a little better. "We've got a campus rent-a-cop here, but he's not giving us any trouble. What happened down there? We heard a lot of yelling and shooting. I wanted to come help you, but—"

"But you knew better than to abandon your post," Foster interrupted him. "That's good, Jimmy. I knew I could count on you. We had a few problems. Rivers managed to get away from us. He's loose somewhere in the building, so keep your eyes open."

"Rivers! Son of a—I knew that guy was gonna McClane us, Matthias. We should've killed him when we had the chance."

Natalie was close enough she had to hear what Jimmy said. Foster turned a little, not wanting to see her glaring defensively at him.

"We'll deal with it," he said calmly. "Just stay alert

and keep your prisoners under control. They're going to give us what we want, you know that."

"They had damned well better."

With that, Jimmy broke the connection.

Foster grimaced and used the radio to call the second floor, saying, "Chad, check in."

"We're here," a voice came back. "No problems so far. We have seventeen prisoners, and I'm pretty sure they're all accounted for."

"We need better than pretty sure," Foster snapped. "Sweep the floor until you're certain."

"We've done that. I'm certain now." Chad's voice showed the strain they were all under. "It was just a figure of speech, Matthias. You don't need to worry about us. I heard shooting up on the third floor a little while ago, though. Something happened up there, and it didn't sound good."

"I know," Foster said. Actually, he hadn't been able to narrow it down until now where the shots had come from, but he trusted Chad's report that the trouble had been on the third floor. "Is it still going on?"

"Nope. Quiet up there now. Should one of us go—"

"No!" Foster said. "You stay right where you are. We can't start running around all over the building. Things will get crazy if we do. We need to stick to the plan."

"Got it."

Foster broke the connection this time. He switched the radio to the band he had assigned to the men on the third floor and said, "Jeremy? You there?"

This time there was no answer.

Foster had sent three men to the third floor to round up everyone who was in the Special Collections rooms. That had seemed like enough. He had to think for a second to remember who had been with Jeremy. When he did, he said into the radio, "Seth? Darrell?"

Still no response except silence.

Foster lowered the radio. It might not be working, he told himself. It was still possible that everything was all right up there.

But not likely, he thought. Not likely at all. And there was only one way to find out whether it was or not.

He looked at Natalie and said, "I'm going up there."

"We can't afford to lose you, Matthias," she said as she shook her head. "Let me go. I . . . I owe it to you for letting things get out of hand earlier."

"You don't owe me anything," he told her. "You've done everything I've asked you to."

"I should have pulled the trigger as soon as I shoved this gun into Jake's side."

"He might have still been able to kill me if you had."

She couldn't argue with that, but she still said, "I want to go. I won't let you down."

It was true that, looking at the situation from a completely pragmatic viewpoint, he could afford to lose her more than any of the others. Even though she had trained for this mission as hard as anyone else, she wasn't as good at handling violence as the men were.

However, she had an advantage none of the rest of them did: Foster knew good and well that if she ran into Jake Rivers, he would hesitate before pulling the trigger on her. That hesitation, even if it was just a split second, might be enough to make all the difference.

"All right," he said. "Go ahead. But be careful. And if you see Rivers . . ."

"Don't worry. I know what to do."

He just hoped she could actually do it.

A middle-aged woman with graying brown hair rushed at Jake as soon as he stepped out of the stairwell. He had to restrain the impulse to point the pistol at her. It was like one of those drills where you moved through a fake village and cardboard cutouts popped up without warning, giving you only a second to decide if they were innocent civilians or legitimate targets.

He lifted the gun in both hands and pointed it toward the ceiling, giving the woman the chance to rush up to him and throw her arms around him.

"Oh, thank God, thank God!" she said. "I thought we were all going to die!" After hugging Jake tightly for a moment, she leaned back a little and went on, "Are you a policeman? A soldier?"

He smiled and said, "A grad student, ma'am."

She stared at him in amazement. His answer clearly seemed unbelievable to her. Finally she said, "You're not one of those . . . terrorists?"

"No, ma'am." He looked around, saw several more people peeking over desks. "Are any of you hurt?"

"N-no. When that man showed up, all of us cooperated with him. Maybe we shouldn't have—"

"No, you did the right thing," Jake told her. "You're not trained or equipped to deal with something like this."

"What's happened? We heard shots, and what sounded like an explosion . . ." She shuddered. "That terrible man said he and his friends were going to kill all of us if they didn't get what they wanted."

"That was the idea," Jake said, "but we all have something to say about that. The bad guys don't win unless we let them."

The woman frowned and commented, "I must say, that doesn't sound like what I usually hear the students here at Kelton talking about."

"I'm not the usual student." Jake motioned with his free hand to the other office workers who had been terrorized. "Come on, folks." He turned his head to look at the door to the stairs. "You, too, Pierce."

Pierce came out of the stairwell and asked, "What are we going to do now, Jake?"

Instead of answering him, Jake asked the older woman, "Is there a way to get to the roof from in here? Guys have to be able to get up there to work on the air-conditioning system and such."

She shook her head and said, "Not from in here, I'm afraid. Maintenance workers have to bring in one of those tall lifts if they need to work on anything on the roof. I've seen them do it many times."

Jake bit back a curse. He had been hoping that he could take all the hostages from the third and fourth floors up to the roof and signal for the authorities to evac them with a chopper. Evidently, though, that wasn't going to happen.

"All right, you'll all stay here. Find someplace to fort up. A small office, maybe, or just move those desks and filing cabinets around and make a shelter from them. Pierce, you'll be staying here, too."

"I thought I'd stick with you and help you," the young man objected.

"You've been a big help already," Jake told him. "I need somebody I can trust to leave here and look after these people."

"You trust me? We don't agree on much of anything, Jake."

"You talking about politics?" Jake waved his free hand dismissively. "You've heard the old saying about how there are no atheists in foxholes?"

"What's a foxhole?" Pierce asked with a puzzled frown.

Kids these days, Jake thought, ignoring for the moment the fact that he was only three or four years older than Pierce. There was a world of difference in their souls and backgrounds.

"Never mind. Just know that labels like liberal and conservative don't mean much when you're fighting for your life and the lives of innocent people. So yeah, I trust you. I've seen what you can do."

Pierce nodded. He glanced at the gun in his hand and still seemed to find it difficult to comprehend he was holding a weapon, but he said, "I won't let you down, Jake. But what are you going to do?"

"Nothing left for me to do except head back down. I'd hoped to get some of the hostages out of the building to safety, but I don't see any way of doing that now." He shrugged. "At least I've whittled down the odds quite a bit. Now's the time to go after Foster, while he's weakened."

"He's not alone, though," Pierce pointed out. "He's still got gunmen around him."

Jake nodded. He was all too aware of the truth of what Pierce was saying.

And one of those allies Foster still had on his side was Natalie Burke . . . or Lucy, as Foster had called her. Jake couldn't help but wonder how he had gotten her to fall for his line. Then he realized it didn't matter. No matter what had happened in the past, Natalie was the enemy now. He had no doubt that she would kill him without hesitating if she got the chance.

The question was, could he do the same?

He honestly didn't know the answer.

CHAPTER 38

Six men had taken over the administration building. Carlos was in charge of them. He was pleased that Matthias Foster had entrusted him with such an important job. Foster's political stances were what had drawn Carlos into the group in the first place, and then he had stayed for the irresistible crack at millions of dollars. But he still admired Foster and didn't want to let him down.

Carlos and his cohorts had taken over the lobby area first, then gone from office to office rounding up the men and women who worked in the admin building. The lobby stretched across nearly the entire front of the building, so there was plenty of room to gather the approximately thirty hostages there. Then Carlos set two men guarding them, while he and the other three spread out to the doors. There were more than four entrances, but a member of the maintenance crew was among the prisoners, and Carlos had been able to put a gun to his head and force him to lock all of them. He and his fellows guarded the ones where an attack was most likely to occur, in Carlos's judgment.

Carlos stood near the door at the west end of the

building, gun in hand, watching through its glass upper half to make sure no one was trying to sneak up on them. When he heard a footstep behind him, he didn't get in any hurry to turn and look, because he assumed it was one of the other men coming to ask him a question.

When he did turn his head, he caught just a glimpse of an old man in casual clothes standing there. Carlos didn't remember seeing him among the prisoners before, but he couldn't be anybody else. Anger flared inside Carlos because the guards had allowed this old man to wander off, but that lasted only a split second.

It was replaced by shock as the old man moved in a blur of speed, catching Carlos around the throat with one arm while yanking him back and pushing on the side of his head with the other hand. Nobody that age ought to be so fast and strong—

That was the last thing Carlos thought, because the next instant his spine snapped and he blacked out. He would die within seconds.

His killer lowered the body to the floor and turned away from it with Carlos's gun in his hand. He had his own weapons, of course, but might as well use the other guy's ammunition if you got the chance.

It had all happened so fast none of the other terrorists had noticed what was going on. But the man at the main entrance to the building saw the old guy striding toward him, gun in hand, and reacted quickly. He got his own gun halfway up before a pair of rounds shattered his skull, cored through his brain, and blew the back of his head off. He dropped in a loose sprawl.

Some of the prisoners were screaming now. The two men guarding them charged toward the center of the lobby. Their guns roared. The older man dropped to one knee and fired twice. Both were chest shots. The slugs exploded the hearts of his targets.

With four of the six gunmen down, that left just two. They were thrown for a loop by the sudden, unexpected violence that had cost the lives of their allies. They couldn't understand how the old man had even managed to get in here, let alone to kill Carlos and the other three in less time than it took to talk about it.

So they were scared, and that prompted each of them to grab one of the prisoners for use as a human shield. The one holding on to a terrified young woman pointed his weapon over her shoulder and yelled, "Drop that gun, you old bastard!"

The old bastard in question fired a single shot that sizzled past the hostage's right ear and into the open mouth of the gunman hanging on to her. The bullet shattered the man's spine and dropped him so fast he never had a chance to pull the trigger on his own gun.

The other prisoner being used as a human shield was a fat, middle-aged man who had probably not been in a fight for decades, if ever. But terror gave him strength and he twisted free, then rammed his shoulder into the chest of the man who had grabbed him. The gunman staggered back a step, and that gave the deadly stranger plenty of room and time to plant two rounds in the middle of his face.

In a little less than a minute, the terrorists in the administration building had been wiped out and the hostages were free.

Some of the former prisoners rushed toward the man, who waved them on and pointed toward the door at the west end of the building.

"Bust that down if you have to, and get out of here," he told them.

"We won't have to break it down," one of the men said. He wore the uniform of a maintenance worker and still had a ring of keys attached to his belt. The gunmen had failed to take it away from him, which was pretty careless on their part. The maintenance man quickly unlocked the door and flung it open. He looked back at the stranger and asked, "Who the hell are you, anyway?"

"Just call me Dog," the man said.

The maintenance worker and the others all rushed out of the building, only to find themselves suddenly surrounded by SWAT officers in tactical gear and body armor.

The man who had freed them faded away along a shadowy corridor in the administration building, returning to the back of the building where he had cut a hole in a window and gotten in without anybody seeing him. It was the one place on the entire building that none of the men surrounding it had a good view of.

Anyway, he was used to moving where he wanted to and getting into places without being seen. He had been doing it for a long, long time.

* * *

The radio clipped onto Walt Graham's belt crackled. He lifted it and said, "Graham."

Chief Hartwell of the Greenleaf PD said excitedly, "I'm getting reports that the hostages in the administration building have escaped! I'm on my way over there now."

"I'll meet you there," Graham said. He and Agent Vega of Homeland Security were studying the library building from a distance. They had to circle a block around the park-like plaza at the center of the campus to reach the administration building.

By the time they did, they found several dozen former hostages huddled together, surrounded by weapons-toting SWAT officers. Hartwell arrived at the same time and ordered, "Get these people well away from the building! They need to be taken safely beyond the perimeter and debriefed."

"Hold on a minute," Graham said. "What happened in there? How did you get away from those terrorists?"

"All the terrorists are dead," a man in the uniform of the college's maintenance department answered.

"You overpowered them?" Graham said, somewhat amazed by the idea.

"We didn't do anything," the man replied. "It was that other guy. The old guy."

"What old guy?"

"I don't know where he came from." The maintenance man looked around at the other hostages.

They shook their heads to indicate that they were just as baffled as he was. "He was just there, all of a sudden, shooting those terrorists. I never saw anybody handle a gun like that. When they were all down, he told us to get out, and believe you me, we weren't gonna argue with him."

"Who was this man you never saw before?" Vega asked.

"Just some old guy."

"He was an old man?" Graham's voice was sharp as he posed the question.

"Well, actually . . . come to think of it . . . it's hard to say." The maintenance man scratched his chin. "He had mostly gray hair and his face had this well-worn look to it, you know, like he'd been around for a long time, but dang, he moved like a twenty-two-year-old athlete. Even as scared as I was, I could tell that much."

Some of the others nodded in agreement, evidently equally impressed with their rescuer.

"Did he tell you his name?" Vega asked. Exasperation crept into her voice.

"That's another funny thing," the maintenance man replied. "I asked him about that. He said to call him Dog."

"Dog!" Vega repeated with a disgusted snort. "That's all? Just Dog?"

"Just Dog."

It was Graham's turn to repeat something, as he said softly, under his breath, "Just Dog."

"Wait a minute," Vega snapped. "That means something to you."

"A long time ago—and I'm talking about going back thirty years or more—when I was just starting out in the bureau, we used to hear rumors about a guy who went by the code name Dog. Nobody knew who he was or if he even really existed. But the stories about him said that he was some sort of freelance troubleshooter who answered only to the president. He had been a truck driver, so he roamed around the country in this specially outfitted truck, looking for . . . well, wrongs to right, corny as that sounds. Sometimes the government would point him in a certain direction and turn him loose, like a force of nature, but most of the time he found his own cases. And he did a lot of good for a while, before he dropped completely out of sight."

Vega stared at Graham for a long moment before she made another disgusted sound and said, "You believed that fairy tale? Some sort of superagent working for our side?"

"There was nothing super about him," Graham said. "He was a guy. A very dangerous guy, sure, but definitely human."

"What else would he be? This isn't some sort of fantasy world, Agent Graham."

"I know that. It's just curious, that's all. Nobody knows what became of Dog. Some said the mob or a terrorist organization had killed him. Others claimed he'd retired and was living somewhere deep in the woods, figuratively and literally, where he'd never been found again." Graham paused. "And some said he was still out there after all these years, working behind the scenes to bring down the bad guys. Doing the dirty jobs that nobody else can do because all the rules and regulations tie their hands."

"A government-sanctioned vigilante," Vega said flatly.

Graham shrugged.

"I'm just telling you what I've heard, that's all. I don't know if it's him or not. But somebody killed those terrorists and freed the hostages—"

One of the campus cops ran up, panting a little as he said, "Agent Graham! We've just gotten word that all the hostages in Olmstead Hall have been freed, and the gunmen who took over the building have been killed!"

Graham's eyebrows rose. He looked over at Vega and said, "I don't know who's doing it, Agent, but it seems like somebody is cleaning house."

Chapter 39

Before leaving the fourth floor, Jake told Pierce that he was going to stop one floor below and send Dr. Montambault and the other former hostages down there up to the fourth floor.

"You'll have a larger force that way," he explained, "and a second gun, too, if you need it."

Not that Montambault was any sort of fighter unless he was pressured and panicked into it, Jake thought—but that was better than nothing.

"I'll see if I can't get the folks on the second floor loose, too," he went on, "and if I do, I'll send them up here to join you. If you have to make a stand, this is as close to the high ground as you're going to find."

"Be careful, Jake," Pierce said. "You may have whittled down the odds, as you put it, but there are still a lot of guys with guns in this building who would like to see you dead."

"The feeling's mutual," Jake said. He lifted a hand in farewell and stepped into the stairwell.

He moved quietly and stopped to listen every few seconds, just in case more of Foster's followers were creeping up the stairs toward him. He didn't hear anything or run into anybody by the time he reached the third floor. He pulled back the door, but before he stepped out into the open, he called, "Dr. Montambault, it's me, Jake Rivers!" He didn't want Montambault getting trigger-happy and blasting away at the slightest movement.

"Mr. Rivers!" Montambault exclaimed, somewhere to Jake's right. "You're alive. We heard more shots from the fourth floor and weren't sure what to think."

Jake stepped out of the stairwell and grinned. He didn't feel much like smiling after everything that had happened—especially Natalie's betrayal—but it never hurt to keep your spirits up, and those of your allies, as well.

"C'mon, folks," he told Montambault and the other people here on the third floor. Pointing upward with a thumb, he went on, "I want you to head on up to four. There's a kid named Pierce Conners up there who's working with me, and he's forted up with the people who were working on that floor. You can join them."

"Will it be safer up there?" the professor asked.

"Well, I don't honestly know, but they say there's safety in numbers. There'll be more of you in case you have to put up a fight. Some of you guys, gather up guns and ammunition from the men I killed."

Nobody moved to accomplish that grisly chore. Jake glared at them and managed to hold in the caustic comments he wanted to make about snowflakes and pajama boys. The stern look was enough to make a couple of the men budge.

"Head on up when you've got that done," Jake told Montambault.

"I . . . I'm just not cut out for this."

"You're doing fine, Professor."

"You don't understand," Montambault said. "I don't *want* to do fine. I don't like knowing that I'm actually capable of such . . . such savagery."

"Those guys who are willing to kill hundreds of innocent people to get what they want, they're the savages, Doc, not us. Just remember that."

Jake started on down the stairs, hoping Montambault wouldn't pass out if he found himself facing trouble again . . . or worse, try to reason with Foster's bunch. You couldn't reason with thieves and killers.

He was moving faster now as his anticipation grew. He had slipped a fresh, fully loaded magazine into the Glock. Once he reached the second floor, he would probably need it, he told himself. No way were any of those bastards giving up their shot at a share of a hundred million dollars without a fight.

He made the turn at the landing between the second and third floors but froze as he heard a sharply indrawn breath in front of and slightly below him. Someone was coming up the stairs toward him.

"Jake?" a familiar voice said. "Jake, is that you?"

She had to have heard him. She knew he was there. But she might not be absolutely sure of his identity. He might have been another of Foster's men. If he spoke, there was a good chance she would aim at his voice and open fire.

"Jake, if that's you, you have to help me. I don't want to do this anymore. It was all a terrible mistake, and I'm so sorry." A pleading note entered Natalie's voice. "Please, Jake, I'm putting my life in your hands."

"Natalie," he said. He couldn't hold it back. Her name had formed on his lips before he could stop it.

Muzzle flame ripped through the gloom in the stairwell. The gunshot crashed against his ears.

The bitch!

Jake triggered three swift shots before he realized something was wrong. As he heard a soft cry, he realized what it was. The shot fired at him had come from lower down on the steps than Natalie had been when she was talking to him.

That meant someone else had fired it. The two of them weren't alone in this stairwell.

That didn't mean Natalie actually regretted what she had done and wanted to turn on Foster. Maybe she had just been trying to get him to talk so the other gun-wielder could zero in on him. That seemed more plausible than her having a change of heart.

He pressed himself back in the far corner of the landing and kept the pistol pointed down the shadow-choked stairs. The shot fired at him hadn't struck him, and he hadn't heard the slug hit the wall or ricochet off anything. A cold ball formed in the pit of his stomach as he realized where it might have gone.

A faint moan came from somewhere down the stairs. Then a grated curse in a man's voice. Jake heard sounds like somebody trying to climb to his feet. A hand slapped quietly against the wall for support.

"Bitch," the man muttered. "Could've told Matthias . . . not to trust her. Traitorous slut . . ."

Unsteady footsteps started up the stairs. Jake stayed where he was and waited, although that was difficult now.

The steps stopped. Jake made out a shadowy form bending over something on the stairs. Then he heard the man mutter, "The girl! But if I hit her—"

"That's right, you bastard," Jake said. "You missed me."

Flame licked from the Glock's muzzle as Jake fired three more times. The bullets ripped through the man on the stairs and flung him backward. He went down the stairs to the second-floor landing in a wild, out-of-control tumble. When he stopped, Jake didn't hear him moving anymore.

Taking the stairs two at a time, Jake went down until he came to Natalie's crumpled shape.

A part of him still didn't want to trust her. A rattlesnake could still sink its fangs in you even after the scaly son of a bitch was dead. But Natalie wasn't moving, and as Jake stuck the gun behind his belt and knelt on the stairs to take hold of her, he could tell how limp she was.

But not dead. He moved his hand to her throat and found a pulse there. It was fast but fairly steady. Jake lifted her, held her against him, and explored her body for wounds. His big hand found the wet, sticky spot on her back, a little below her right shoulder. There was no matching exit wound on her front. The bullet was still in her.

If it hadn't struck a bone and bounced around to do a lot of internal damage, the wound might not be a fatal one. Natalie needed medical attention, though, and pretty quickly. He gathered her in his arms and stood up.

As he started back up the stairs, she stirred slightly against him and murmured, "Jake?"

"Yeah, I've got you," he said. "You're gonna be okay, Natalie. Lucy. Whichever."

"Not . . . Lucy. That was . . . Matthias's . . . idea. I'm . . . Natalie . . . What happened?"

"One of Foster's men shot you in the back. I'm going to get some help for you."

"Guess he . . . didn't really trust me . . . after all. I told him I'd come after you . . . kill you . . . but I was lying to him. Just wanted to tell you . . . how sorry I am . . . about lying to you. But not all of it . . . was a lie . . ."

He didn't want to get into any of that now. This wasn't the time or place, and besides, he wasn't sure he would ever believe her again. But he didn't want her to die, either, if there was anything he could do to save her life.

She didn't seem to weigh much in his arms as he climbed the stairs. When he reached the fourth floor, he balanced her against him and opened the door, then called, "Pierce! Doc!"

Pierce and Montambault came running from somewhere else on the floor. When Montambault saw the woman and the large bloodstain on the back of her shirt, he exclaimed, "Oh, my God! What happened? Is that . . . Dr. Burke? Oh, no!"

"Hold on, Professor," Pierce said. "You don't know what happened down on the lower level. She's one of them."

"I don't care about any of that right now," Jake said. "She's hurt, and I don't want her to bleed to death." He carried Natalie over to one of the desks, cleared it with a swipe of his arm, and carefully laid her facedown on it. "One of you get over here and put some pressure on this wound."

Pierce and Montambault looked at each other. The professor's eyes were huge with apprehension. Pierce nodded in resignation and came over to the desk. Jake had already ripped a large piece off the tail of Natalie's shirt and folded it into a pad.

"Hold this on there," he told Pierce. "Don't be afraid to press down on it. The most important thing right now is stopping the bleeding. Doctor, you take a look around and see if you can find some alcohol, something like that. A bottle of booze will do if anybody's got one stashed in their desk."

"I'm sure that's not the case," Montambault said. "But there may be a first-aid kit somewhere up here. I'll ask the people who work on this floor. Someone will know."

Jake nodded and said, "You're doing good work, both of you. Now I need to get back to what I started." He reached out, touched Natalie's shoulder for a second. She appeared to be unconscious now. "Killing the rest of those sons of bitches."

Chapter 40

Matthias Foster paced back and forth, his anger visible in the quick, catlike strides. His last radio check had gotten no response from the administration building, as well as two of the other buildings his men had taken over. That could only mean the situation was continuing to deteriorate.

He was starting to think that he had spread his forces too thin. Maybe it would have been better if he had concentrated on the library and brought all of his men here. He would have had fewer hostages that way, but the chances of holding out would have been better.

The other scenario had seemed so much more dramatic, though. Taking over an entire college campus and threatening to blow it off the face of the earth . . . ! That was the sort of thing legends were made of. If he was able to pull this off, his name would go down in the annals of terrorism, right next to Osama bin Laden.

Of course, in reality he was more like D. B. Cooper, he supposed—a guy who got away with a fortune through sheer daring and audacity. And like Cooper, if he pulled this off, he would never be seen or heard from again.

Now, though, with things going wrong, it felt like all that was slipping away from him, and that angered Foster. He paused in his pacing, lifted the radio to his mouth, and called the language-arts building, where three of his men had been in control of eighty-seven hostages, the last time he had checked in.

"Marc?" Foster said. "How's it looking there? Marc?"

This time there was no response. Foster cursed and was about to lower the radio when it suddenly crackled to life.

"This isn't Marc," a strange voice said.

The resonant voice belonged to a man. It held just a trace of a Southern drawl, almost indistinguishable but there. Foster's hand tightened on the radio as he said, "Who's this?"

"Somebody you don't want to know, Matthias. But I have a feeling we'll be making each other's acquaintance before the day is over."

"Rivers? Rivers, is that you, you son of a bitch?"

"Not . . . exactly."

"Where are my men?"

"Hell, more than likely," the answer came. Foster expected that, but it felt like a punch in the gut anyway. Things were getting worse all the time.

But he still had cards to play. He said, "I guess you got everybody out of the building?"

"It's just me now," the man said. "But I'll be coming for you soon."

"I don't think so, asshole."

Foster's other hand dived in his pocket and came up with the radio he used as a detonator. Each of the bombs had a specific frequency, ones that were off-limits for normal voice communication. One-handed, Foster changed the switch on the hand-held unit to the frequency of the bomb planted next to the language-arts building. He thumbed the transmit key and with satisfaction heard the heavy thump of the explosive going off across campus. That was enough to make the hostages here on the lower level of the library scream and yell again. They probably thought they were next.

Not yet, but soon, maybe. Foster had long since decided that if he put his plan into action, he would never be taken alive.

But with any luck, he wouldn't have to worry any-more about whoever had been disrupting things. There was a possibility the blast hadn't killed him, but in all likelihood, it had.

A smirk was forming on his face when the radio crackled again. That same voice drawled, "I never said I was still *in* the building, Matthias, just that all the hostages were out. I'm still coming for you, once I've finished with all your flunkies."

Foster jerked the radio up to his lips, but he was too filled with rage to form words. Instead, he let out an incoherent sound that was half-growl, half-shout, and flung the radio away from him. It bounced and slid across the floor.

He stood there for a long moment, trembling inside from the depth of his anger. He hadn't heard anything from Natalie since she had gone up the stairs after Rivers . . . or from the guy he'd told to follow her, since he didn't fully trust her. Had something happened to them? Could things really get any worse?

Foster took a deep breath and looked around, studying the frightened faces of the hostages. He had only two men besides himself left on this level, and he'd had to pull one of them down from the first floor. Those weren't good odds. If the hostages ever decided to rush them, it wouldn't end well for Foster and his allies.

Fortunately, the chances of that happening were insignificant, in his opinion. These were college students and staff, after all. They had been thoroughly indoctrinated in the same sort of progressive claptrap he had once believed himself. They considered themselves superior, the elite who were too smart, too "woke," to ever embrace violence. Unless, of course, it was as part of a mob, preferably in hoods so their identity would be safe and they wouldn't get in trouble with the law or with Mommy and Daddy. The college administration would let them get away with anything, that was a given—the "inmates" had long since taken over these particular academic "asylums"—and chances were, their families would, too, but there was just enough of a chance that wouldn't happen that they would want to be careful. The resistance was super important, but not at the expense of tuition, housing, and a mega-generous allowance.

So, not much chance of this bunch risking their lives by fighting back. They were used to being sheep, being told what to think and do every moment of their waking lives by the government and the media, and sheep they would remain. Scared little sheep.

Foster stalked over to the radio, picked it up, and keyed the mic, saying, "Natalie? Natalie, are you there? Answer me, damn it!"

Jake had taken Natalie's radio and stuck it in his pocket before he started down the stairs. He heard Foster calling on it and was tempted to answer, just to throw a surprise into the son of a bitch.

He decided not to. Better to let Foster stew in his own juices for a while and wonder what had happened to Natalie.

Jake wondered himself how she was doing. Liberal or not, Pierce seemed halfway competent, and Montambault had proven not to be completely worthless. Jake would have hated to place his life in the hands of either of them, but he supposed they were better than nothing. Maybe somebody among the freed hostages had some medical experience. Kelton College had a pre-med program, he seemed to recall.

He shoved his worries about Natalie out of his head. It hadn't been much more than an hour since she had shoved a gun in his side and threatened to shoot him in the heart, so no matter what he had believed he was starting to feel for her, he didn't owe her a damned thing. He could have left her to bleed to death on those damn stairs and not felt a thing.

Maybe if he told himself that lie often enough, he might come to believe it . . .

More pressing concerns took precedence. He had cleared Foster's minions from the third and fourth floors, but that wasn't true of the first and second. He didn't know how many gunmen were on those floors.

The second floor wasn't that important now, Jake decided. He could afford to bypass it, because whoever was posted there wouldn't be able to come to Foster's aid right away if shooting broke out on the lower level.

The same couldn't be said of the men on the first floor. They could reach the lower level quickly just by bounding down one of the escalators, which were stopped now because the power was out. If he could deal with them, Jake thought, then Foster wouldn't have any backup left. He would be alone with however many of his men he had left—and that couldn't be many by this point.

But Foster still had guns and plenty of ammunition and dozens of innocent hostages. If he and his men opened fire, they could slaughter many of the prisoners before they were overwhelmed. Jake wanted to prevent that if possible.

The threat of the bombs still remained. Jake thought he had heard something as he was stealthily descending the stairs, something that might have been an explosion somewhere else on the campus, but in the stairwell it was difficult to be sure. If Foster's men really had planted bombs all over the campus, the amount of damage they could do in human lives was incalculable. Jake's doubts wouldn't mean a damn thing in the face of that awful reality.

So Foster had to be stopped, and he had to be stopped before he could trigger any more explosions. Jake was running out of time and he knew it.

So whoever was on the second floor could wait until later. Right now, he needed to take out any of Foster's men on the first floor, then move on to the lower level.

There weren't many shelves on the ground level, because mostly it was devoted to circulation, with self-serve checkouts and a long counter where books reserved online could be picked up, overdue fines were paid, and other tasks like that were handled. Even in this digital age, there was still a need for human beings to do some things, just like there were still plenty of print books in the library.

There were also more than a dozen rows of computer stations that students could use. Everybody had the Internet on their phones and tablets, of course, but sometimes you still needed a good old-fashioned desktop and printer.

A portion of the first floor was also given over to displays of sculpture and artwork. Kelton was proud of its arts program and showed off many works by students past and present. The front wall was mostly glass, giving the place plenty of light and a very airy feel.

Jake had spent enough time in the library to be aware of all this. Just as a matter of habit, he constantly studied his surroundings, and he had the sort of brain that once something was noted in it, he tended not to forget. He had no real reason for doing that, other than he liked to be prepared for whatever might happen. He had never forgotten a quote he'd heard attributed to General James Mattis: "Always have a plan to kill everybody in the room." That sounded like good advice to Jake, even though it came from a Marine.

The stairwell entrance was in the back of the room, beyond the art display area, next to the snack bar. If Jake had been charged with keeping the hostages under control, he would have herded them all into the snack bar, well away from the windows where police snipers might be able to get a shot. You wanted prisoners in as small an area as possible, especially if you had a limited number of men to keep them under the gun.

Knowing that, Jake wasn't surprised when he leaned toward the door, listened closely, and heard a man saying in a loud, irritated voice, "Sit back down, mister! I want you down on that floor along with everybody else."

"You're never going to get away with this," another man said in a peevish tone. "The cops are going to storm this place any minute, and when they do, you'll wind up dead! You may have started with high ideals, but now you're just common crooks!"

The second voice was familiar to Jake, and after a moment he placed it: Cal Granderson, one of Frank McRainey's campus cops. The most annoying member of McRainey's force, in fact. Jake remembered seeing Granderson on this floor when he came into the library. The guy had gotten swept up with the other hostages.

In a way, that was surprising. Jake would have expected Granderson to try some sort of grandstand play that would get him killed. Clearly, that hadn't happened.

But it might yet, because Granderson was still mouthing off to the guards.

"The best thing you can do is throw down those guns and surrender. I'm an officer of the law. I can guarantee your safety. I'll see to it that you don't get mowed down when the SWAT teams come in here."

"Officer of the law, my ass! You're a cheap rent-a-cop with delusions of grandeur. Now sit down, or I'm gonna bust your head again—"

In his anger, the gunman must have gotten too close to Granderson, because a third man suddenly yelled, "Hey, look out, he's gonna—"

A shot roared, drowning out whatever else the man was trying to say.

Jake knew instantly that he was never going to get a better distraction than this. He yanked the door back and bulled out into the open as he lifted the 9mm in a two-hand grip.

Chapter 41

Jake instantly took in the scene playing out before him. Cal Granderson, in his campus police department uniform, was wrestling with a husky Hispanic man over a gun. The second guard was off to the side in front of the snack bar, nervously jerking both his gaze and his pistol back and forth between the desperate struggle and the prisoners he wanted to keep under control. Jake figured the shot had come from the gun the two men were fighting over, but he didn't see any blood on Granderson or the other guy, so he hoped the bullet had gone wild.

The way Granderson and his opponent were twisting and staggering around, Jake couldn't risk taking a shot in their direction. But the second guard was a different story, so he called, "Hey!"

The man turned his head first, to look over his shoulder, and then his eyes widened as he spotted Jake standing there drawing a bead on him. He tried to jerk around and bring his gun to bear, but the Glock in Jake's hands had already spouted flame. The 9mm slug smacked into the middle of the guy's forehead and blasted right on through his brain to hit the suddenly blood-splattered wall on the other side of him. His knees buckled, dropping him into a crumpled heap.

Granderson and the man he was fighting with had to have heard Jake's shot, but neither could afford to take their attention away from their battle. Granderson had both hands clamped around the man's wrist. He wrenched on it, trying to get him to drop the gun, but as he was doing that, the man used his free hand to hammer punches at Granderson's head. Granderson hunched his shoulders as much as he could, trying to protect himself, but his head was bleeding from several cuts that had been opened up already.

This would have been a good time for the now-unguarded hostages to rush forward and overwhelm the gunman through sheer force of numbers. Considering the way that most of them were hiding under the snack bar tables, though, whimpering and crying because guns were going off, Jake knew that wasn't going to happen.

He bounded forward and chopped the gun in his hand down at the head of the man fighting with Granderson. The blow landed with a solid thud. Granderson grabbed the man's gun and jerked it free. He slashed upward with it and crashed it against the man's jaw. Jake heard bone crunch. The man staggered back a step and sat down hard, making grotesque noises as he clutched at his shattered jaw. Jake shut him up and laid him out with a swift kick to the head.

Then he nodded to Granderson and said, "Good work."

Granderson didn't seem to be in a mood to accept

the compliment graciously. He said, "I had him! I would have put both those bastards down if you hadn't stuck your nose in, Rivers!"

"You're welcome," Jake said wryly. "How bad are you hurt, Granderson?"

"I'm fine," he snapped. "A little banged up, that's all."

Jake looked at the group crowded into the snack bar and asked, "How about these other folks?"

"I don't think anybody is hurt. When this started, it all happened so fast, nobody had time to put up a fight."

Yeah, that was it, Jake thought. Just not enough time

Granderson checked the magazine in the gun he had taken away from the now unconscious man, then slid it back into place. As he started to turn away, Jake said, "Wait a minute. What are you going to do?"

"There are still a lot of people being held downstairs," Granderson snapped. "I'm going to rescue them and apprehend the guy responsible for all this."

"That's sort of what I had in mind, too."

A sneer curled Granderson's lips. He and Jake might have been fighting as allies only moments earlier, but that didn't mean his feelings had changed. Clearly, he still didn't like Jake—and the feeling was pretty much mutual.

"You're not going to suggest that we work together, are you?"

"That might be better than getting killed," Jake said. "*Might* be. Listen, though, the first thing we need to do is get these other people out of here, just in case Foster really does have a bomb planted somewhere in or around the building."

Granderson looked like he wanted to argue, but he nodded grudgingly and said, "Yeah, you're right." He turned and waved the hand holding the gun at the hostages. "Come on, you people. Get out of here while you can."

"But . . . but is it safe?" asked a male undergrad with multiple piercings on ears, nose, and lips.

A girl with pink hair said, "We should stay where we are until someone from the government tells us to leave."

"*I'm* from the government!" Granderson burst out in obvious frustration. "See? I'm wearing a uniform and everything!"

"The administration needs to issue a statement and address this," added a middle-aged man who Jake pegged as a professor. "This campus is supposed to be a safe space and a gun-free zone." He looked pointedly at the pistols Jake and Granderson held. "Neither of you should have those. You should turn them in to the authorities immediately."

Granderson looked over at Jake and said, "Are they insane?"

Jake just shrugged.

"That's the college experience for you these days," he said.

Then he walked over to the group cowering inside the snack bar and went on, "Listen, folks, I know you're scared, but this is your best chance to get away from here before anything else happens. All you have to do is stand up, walk to the entrance, and go outside. There'll be cops waiting out there somewhere close by, and when they see you coming out, they'll hurry to help you." He paused, thought for a second, and then added, "You can just go with them, and they'll tell you what to do."

Several faces lit up at the phrase "tell you what to do." Jake kept his face impassive. He didn't want them seeing what his opinion of them really was. It was more important to get them to safety.

He wasn't one to smooth-talk anybody, though. Never had been. If they didn't grab this chance while they had it, then it was on them.

A couple of people stood up, sidled nervously forward, then broke into a run toward the entrance. That opened the floodgates. All the former hostages scrambled up and fled.

Jake turned to Granderson and nodded.

"Let's go put an end to this," he said.

The past twenty minutes or so had been dizzying. Reports had come in to Walt Graham from all over campus about how, in one place after another, freed hostages were emerging from the buildings where they had been held prisoner. Most of them were quite shaken, but they were all right other than a few minor injuries.

The same couldn't be said of the terrorists who had tried to take over Kelton College. Nine bodies had been recovered already, along with a couple of men who were badly injured but might live.

It was almost as if some crack antiterrorism unit

had swept through the campus, wiping out the bad guys and freeing the innocent people.

But instead, all the former hostages told the same story, of how a lone man had killed their captors with stunning and brutal efficiency. Not a young man, either, but one who might have been anywhere from fifty to seventy years of age . . . although he moved like a man much younger.

Graham was back in Frank McRainey's office, along with Theresa Vega, Chief Hartwell from Greenleaf, and McRainey himself. Vega was upset and said, "What the hell is going on here? Somebody has to be lying. One man couldn't have done all of this!"

"All due respect, Agent Vega," McRainey said, "but you're wrong. I saw the guy, talked to him. If I've ever run into anybody who absolutely *is* capable to taking out this many terrorists and freeing that many people, it's the man who was here earlier."

"Dog," she said. "Is that what he told you to call him? Just Dog?"

"That's right."

Vega looked over at Graham and went on, "And he's supposed to be some sort of super-vigilante working for the government."

"Nobody ever said he's super," Graham responded. "Just very good at what he does. I don't *know* that the legendary Dog is back . . . but that would sure make some of this a lot easier to accept."

Vega just shook her head and turned away. She wasn't going to be convinced. Some people were like that, Graham reflected.

Hell, maybe he just *wanted* to believe that Dog

was back. Who *didn't* like to see a legend return just in time to save the day?

One of McRainey's officers, the young man called Bagley, hurried into the office after knocking on the door but not waiting to be told to come in.

"Hostages are running out of the library," he said excitedly.

The two federal agents and the two police chiefs stiffened as they looked at Bagley. McRainey said in a strained voice, "All of them, Jeff?"

"No way to know that, Chief, but some of them, for sure. I'm told none of them appear to be hurt, at least not much."

"Thank God for that," McRainey said.

Vega looked at Graham and said, "You think this is more work by your mysterious Dog?"

"I don't know," Graham replied with a shake of his head. "But let's get over there. Maybe we can find out."

Too much time had passed. Matthias Foster had a very strong hunch that Natalie wasn't coming back, and neither was the man he had sent to follow her.

He hoped she was still alive. At least, he *thought* he hoped that. But he wasn't really sure. She was beautiful, no doubt about that, and she had seemed devoted to their cause. Not devoted enough to go ahead and fall in bed with him, as he had assumed she would, but there would be plenty of time for that once they were filthy rich and far away from here.

Now it was beginning to look like none of those

things was ever going to come true. When shots blasted from the library's ground floor, clearly audible right up the escalator, the certainty that he was screwed grew even stronger in Foster.

Earlier, he hadn't been able to raise any of his men on the third and fourth floors. Now he lifted the radio to his mouth and called, "Phil? Are you there?"

He could have just stepped over to the escalator and yelled up the unmoving steps, he thought bitterly. That's how close ruin had crept to him.

Of course, Phil didn't answer. Foster didn't waste time trying him again. Instead, as a thought occurred to him, he switched frequencies, keyed the mic again, and said, "Lamar?"

"I'm here, Matthias," a slightly breathless voice came back. "What the hell is going on? There's been shooting above us, and now below us—"

"You and Tanner are all right?" Foster interrupted him.

"Yeah, we haven't had any trouble here. Matthias, maybe we'd better start trying to come up with some sort of exit strategy—"

"There are only two exits from this, you know that. Victory or death." Foster laughed. "Isn't that what somebody said at the Alamo or somewhere? I know I remember hearing that in some history class."

"Yeah, but it's all going bad on us!"

"Get it together, Lamar," Foster snapped. "We may have to make a stand. I want you and Tanner down here now. Forget about the hostages you have there. Use the elevator and come straight to the lower level."

"Are you sure—"

"Just do what I told you, damn it!" Foster said. With an angry, frustrated snap of his wrist, he threw the radio away from him.

He had two men left down here. If Lamar and Tanner could reach the lower level, that would make five of them against whatever the authorities could throw at them. Would the authorities actually attack head-on, though? He had set off two bombs already. Was that enough to convince the cops and the Feds that the entire campus was in danger?

Or did they need another demonstration?

Foster's hand stole into his pocket. The fingers curled around the detonator. This one was separate. None of the others in the group, not even Natalie, knew about it. They were aware that he had been able to get hold of enough explosive to build only three working bombs. The others were decoys, intended to keep the bomb squad busy checking out the work done by the "groundskeepers" that morning . . . and to keep the cops worried, so they would hold back in order to prevent a possible holocaust.

Two of the three bombs they knew about had already been detonated at different corners of the campus. The remaining working device was planted at another corner.

But what no one knew except him was that ever since he had gone to work as a groundskeeper, under the name Rick Overman, he had been planting charges around the library's foundation, one at a time, so nobody had ever noticed. He had gotten his hands on a lot more C4 than he'd ever let on to the others. They believed the bomb threat was largely a bluff.

Foster wasn't bluffing, though. From the start, he had known that he would either get what he wanted—the money, along with the freedom and power it would give him—or he would wreak his bloody vengeance on the world in a way that would never be forgotten.

All it would take was for him to open the detonator and press the button. The charges around the foundation would detonate, and the library would come crashing down onto itself, killing everyone still inside—including Foster.

But that was all right, if it came to that. Foster caressed the cold metal smoothness of the detonator and whispered to himself, "Victory or death."

Chapter 42

Jake knew Granderson still didn't like him, but the guy got caught up in planning their next move and didn't seem to mind too much working with Jake to take down the rest of the bad guys.

"Once the cops outside see those hostages escaping, they're gonna come rushing in here to clear the building," Granderson said. "So if we're gonna get the son of a bitch who's behind this, we don't have very long."

The same thought had occurred to Jake. He nodded and said, "If Foster's telling the truth about being able to blow up the whole place, or even just part of it, he's more likely to push the damn button if he sees a bunch of SWAT types running in here. Two guys might have a better chance of taking him out."

"Two guys like us, eh?" Granderson sneered. "Doesn't make us friends."

"Damn right. Come on."

Jake figured he and Granderson would go down the stairwell, but as he turned in that direction, his gaze happened to land on the small elevator tucked into a corner. The library was an old building that had been remodeled numerous times over the years, so he figured the elevator had been added at some point to make it ADA-compliant.

The really interesting thing about it, though, was that the downward-pointing arrow on the panel above the doors was lit. That meant the elevator was descending from an upper floor.

The implications of that burst through Jake's brain like an explosion. He snapped, "Come on!" at Granderson and broke into a run toward the elevator.

If the campus cop wondered what was going on, he didn't hang back to ask questions. He just charged after Jake, who lunged forward to stab a finger against the elevator button.

Just in time, too. Another second and the elevator would have been past ground level. But Jake had been able to catch it, and with a little *ding,* the light above the doors came on. They started to slide open.

A man inside was already desperately pushing a button to close them again. The doors came to a jerky stop when they were only half open. That gap was wide enough for Jake to look into the small, enclosed space and see two men standing there, a tall, rangy black guy and a shorter, stockier white guy with a brush of red hair and a close-cropped beard. Both were armed.

Reactions on both sides were almost instantaneous. They had to be, because the doors had started to slide closed again. Jake and Granderson crouched and poured lead into the cubicle. The men in the elevator returned the fire. The roar of shots was too loud for Jake to hear anything except that, but he *felt* the disturbance in the air as slugs whipped past his ears. More than once, a hot breath blew against his cheek.

Then he stuck a foot out at the last second to stop the doors from closing and prevent the elevator from continuing its descent. The echoes of the gun-thunder died away into a hollow silence. Jake kept his pistol leveled at the opening. He had kept count of his rounds and knew he had two shots left.

"Push the button again, Granderson, so the door will open," he told the campus cop.

"I'd . . . like to," Granderson said in a strained voice, "but I don't think . . ."

Jake threw a quick look at his ally. Granderson had gone down to one knee. He had a forearm propped on that knee as he leaned forward. The gun was in that hand. The other hand was on the floor to help brace him. Bloodstains spread on his shirtfront in a couple of different places.

"Damn it," Jake grated. "How bad—"

Granderson was breathing hard. He pointed his gun at the elevator doors and said, "You just . . . open 'em up. I'll be . . . ready."

Jake kept his foot in place and stretched to the side to push the button again. The doors began to open. As they did, he stepped back hurriedly and brought his pistol to bear, too.

There was no need for that. The two guys in the elevator were both dead, shot to pieces.

"They have to be Foster's men from the second floor," Jake said. "They were the only ones left upstairs. When I saw that the elevator was on its way down, I knew it must be them. He was trying to get them to rally with him on the lower level. He's going to make his last stand down there."

"Give me . . . a hand. Foster must've heard . . . all the shooting. If I take the elevator . . . on down . . . he'll be waiting to see . . . if it's his guys or somebody else . . . who gets out."

"You'll run right into a swarm of bullets if you do that," Jake protested.

"Won't matter. Blood's already leaking . . . into my lungs and guts. I won't make it. But I can distract him . . . and anybody he's got left on his side . . . while you hit them . . . from the other direction."

"Blast it, you just want to make some show-off play and be the hero—"

"Why . . . shouldn't I be?"

"Because you're such an asshole!" Jake burst out.

"Yeah? Well, so are you, Rivers!"

They stared at each other for a second, then both men laughed.

"You gonna . . . help me or not?" Granderson demanded.

"Yeah, yeah, hang on." Jake took Granderson's arm and helped him onto the elevator. He had to use his foot to push aside one of the bloody corpses as he did so. Granderson propped himself up against the car's back wall.

Then he nodded to Jake and said, "When you hear the shooting . . . you'll know."

"Yeah. Good luck, Granderson."

"Don't need it anymore . . . as long as I can keep

breathing . . . long enough to get down there. Push the button for me . . . will you?"

Jake thumbed the lower-level button on the control panel and stepped back as the doors closed. His last sight of Granderson was of the campus cop grinning as he hunched forward a little with blood soaking the front of his uniform shirt.

Foster left one of his men, a guy called Alec, watching the hostages and told the other one, Reese, to come with him as he headed for the elevator to meet Lamar and Tanner.

Before they got there, a storm of gunfire broke somewhere up on the first floor, with at least two dozen shots being fired in ten seconds. Foster stopped short and tensed, then stared at the elevator. Above the doors, the down arrow was still lit. It had been on its way to the lower level but must have stopped for some reason on the first floor.

Whoever was to blame for everything else going wrong had stopped the elevator, too. Foster was sure of it. And that couldn't be anybody else except Jake Rivers.

Why hadn't he had Rivers killed when he had the chance? Was that one mistake going to ruin everything?

Foster heard the faint rumble as the elevator began to descend again.

He made a curt gesture to indicate that he and Reese should split up. Foster went left, Reese to the right, as they approached the elevator. Foster held his gun ready in front of him in a two-handed grip as he said quietly, "Be ready when that elevator opens. It might be two of our guys in there . . . or it might not."

"I'm ready, Matthias," Reese said, but he sounded tense and worried. As the long day had gone on and more and more things went wrong, the worry and uncertainty had spread through Foster's group. Foster had to give them credit, though: as far as he knew, none of them had deserted him.

A faint *thunk* sounded as the elevator came to a stop at the bottom of the shaft. The doors slid back . . .

Even though Foster was ready, he still jumped back slightly as a bloody, grinning apparition lurched toward them. The thing held a gun that spat fire at them as he stumbled forward. Foster barely had time to recognize the blood-sodden clothing as the uniform of a campus security officer before he was returning the fire, along with Reese. Their bullets pounded into the campus cop and threw him back across the elevator car to hang against the rear wall.

There was no way the guy could still be alive, but Foster would have sworn that his grin widened even more, just for a second, and his eyes burned even brighter with hate and something else . . .

Triumph?

Another shot blasted somewhere behind them, and Reese pitched forward with half of his head gone. Foster whirled around and saw Jake Rivers at the bottom of the escalators. He threw himself aside as Rivers fired again. The shot went wide because of Foster's quick reaction.

"Stop him!" Foster yelled at Alec, who was staring openmouthed at Rivers. "Shoot the son of a bitch!"

Foster had drilled the men enough that they were obedient, almost like a military unit. Alec clapped his mouth shut and brought up his gun, and Jake Rivers shot him in the chest, knocking him back toward the hostages with arms and legs flailing. His body landed on some girl with purple hair who started screaming and panicking, and a second later chaos had that area firmly in its grip as the panic spread.

Foster didn't care. His options had suddenly narrowed down to one—but he wasn't *out* of options. He dashed toward the stacks, deliberately taking a path that would carry him in front of the hostages so Rivers couldn't shoot at him without a miss striking the innocents. Just as Foster expected, Rivers held his fire and came after him on foot.

Once he reached the stacks with their narrow, claustrophobic aisles, Foster would either get the drop on Rivers and kill the meddling bastard once and for all . . . or he would push the button on the detonator and set off those charges of C4.

Either way, Jake Rivers was going to die in the next few minutes.

The only question was how many others were going to die with him.

Chapter 43

As Jake ran after Foster, he glanced toward the elevator. Cal Granderson sat at the back of the car, having slid down it leaving a bloody smear on the wall. His legs were extended out in front of him. His feet just reached the track where the doors ran and kept them from closing. Jake caught a glimpse of the young man's face, which seemed strangely at peace considering the state of his bullet-riddled body below.

Jake didn't have time for anything else. He had to deal with Matthias Foster. Every instinct in Jake's body was screaming at him that the threat wasn't over. In fact, the worst might still be to come.

Jake reached the spot where Foster had disappeared into the stacks. He paused long enough to glance over his shoulder. Some of the hostages had realized there was no longer anything stopping them from getting out of here. They stampeded toward the escalators, and the others began to follow them, tentatively at first and then in more of a rush.

A shot cracked and a bullet whined off a metal shelf only a foot or so from Jake's head. He had taken his attention off the enemy for too long. He couldn't afford to do that. Crouching, he caught a flicker of movement at the far end of the long, narrow aisle and snapped a shot that way in return.

Then, instead of charging along that aisle, he darted two over and headed down that one. He moved as quietly as possible, not wanting Foster to be able to track him by sound. Foster would be doing the same thing, he knew. Keeping quiet and trying to get the drop on him.

But maybe Foster didn't have the patience for that, because he called, "Rivers, you hear me?"

Jake stopped in his tracks but didn't say anything.

"I know you're there, you big son of a bitch. It's not like you'd give up after coming this far and killing so many people." Foster laughed. "Just how many *have* you killed today, Jake? You think you're the hero and I'm the bad guy, but I'll bet you've got a hell of a lot more blood on your hands than I do!"

Foster was wrong about one thing: Jake didn't think of himself as a hero. Just a guy who could recognize when something needed to be done and who possessed the resolve to do it. He wasn't really thinking about what Foster was yammering about, though. He just tried to home in on the voice. It sounded like it came from a couple of aisles over.

Jake looked at the shelves beside him. They were ten feet tall, so that a member of the library staff had to bring one of the rolling ladders and climb on it to retrieve volumes on the top shelves. The ceiling was twenty feet tall, though, so there was a ten-foot gap between it and the top of the shelves.

Jake tucked the pistol into the waistband of his jeans at the small of his back and pushed in some books in several places. That didn't make any noise, and neither did he as he used the handholds and footholds he had created and started to climb.

"Well, all that's going to change," Foster went on. "It won't be long now before the big body count will belong to me. I can't blow up the whole campus, I might as well admit that now, but you know what, Jake? I can call you Jake, can't I, since we're about to be blown to atoms together? I *can* blow this library sky-high. The detonator is right here in my hand, Jake. All I have to do is push it."

Jake froze where he was. He didn't want to give away what he was trying to do, so he dropped back to the floor, landing lightly, and called, "Don't do it, Foster."

That brought another laugh from the terrorist. Or madman. Pretty much the same thing.

"Now you talk to me! You don't want to be blown up, do you?"

"I don't really give a damn about that," Jake said. "I just don't want you to die thinking that you're some sort of infamous mass murderer. You and me are the only ones left in this building. You blow it up, and we're the only ones you'll kill."

That was a bluff, at least as far as he knew. Pierce and Montambault were still upstairs with the other hostages he had freed earlier. He supposed it was possible someone had been watching from a window and had seen the others fleeing, leading them to come downstairs and get out, too, but Jake had no way of knowing that. He'd had his own hands too full to keep up with anything else.

"What?" Foster snapped. "You're lying!"

"No, I'm not. I don't know who else you might've killed earlier, but blowing up this library won't get any more victims except a couple of nobodies . . . you and me, pal."

As he said that, Jake wondered about Natalie. Was she still alive, or had she succumbed to her wound? Was she upstairs, or already in custody? Jake hoped she survived. Not so much for her sake, although he had a hunch he'd always have a soft spot for her, but because she might be the only one left who could tell the authorities any details about Matthias Foster and his crazy, evil plan. That might help keep someone else from doing something similar in the future.

Foster was muttering something. Jake could make out a few vile obscenities, but the rest was an incoherent jumble.

Finally, Foster called, "Don't try to talk me into surrendering. I'll never be taken alive. Victory or death!"

"Colonel Travis at the Alamo," Jake said. "Don't dirty up the words of a noble man, Foster." He paused. "If you don't want to be taken alive, forget about blowing anything up. Put that detonator aside, step out, and face me. Just the two of us."

Foster laughed.

"Head to head? *Mano a mano?* Just like the showdown in every bad book ever written and every bad movie ever made? So that you'll have the chance to deliver some classic badass line like *Yippee-ki-yay—*"

"Screw it," Jake muttered. He swarmed back up the shelves, flung a leg on the top, powered up, leaped to the next one, sure now from the conversation where Foster was, and dropped on top of the nutjob while Foster was trying to dig that detonator out of his pocket.

He hoped the jolt wouldn't make it go off.

Foster screeched curses, hammered fists at Jake's head, and tried to ram a knee into his groin. Jake was taller and heavier, but Foster battled with the strength of a madman and the cramped quarters didn't help, either. Foster chopped a glancing sidehand blow across Jake's throat, and while it wasn't powerful enough to crush his windpipe, for a couple of seconds Jake couldn't breathe. Foster pulled back and managed to jerk something from his pocket.

Jake tackled him, and as they both crashed to the floor, the little box slipped from Foster's fingers and bounced and slid away. He tried to scramble after it, but Jake grabbed him and swung him to the side, crashing him into the shelves. Foster kicked at him, caught him under the chin. That rocked Jake's head back and made the world go black for an instant.

Foster got loose, went after the detonator. Jake snagged an ankle and upended him again. Foster's hand hit the detonator and sent it skidding underneath one of the heavy shelving units. Foster screamed in frustration.

Since he couldn't get the detonator, he scrambled to his feet and ran.

Jake caught up with him in the study area with its comfortable furniture, where he and Natalie had met earlier that day, even though it seemed like days had passed since then. A diving tackle brought both of them crashing down on the carpet.

Foster fought like a wildcat. He was strong, wiry, and had blinding speed. Jake was extremely fast, especially for such a big man, but Foster was even quicker. He got a hand on Jake's face and gouged at his eyes enough that Jake was blinded momentarily. He came up on his knees, pawing at his eyes with the back of his left hand.

Foster leaped to his feet and clawed at the pistol he had stuck behind his belt earlier. Jake's vision cleared enough for him to see that. He reached for the gun at the small of his back, drawing faster than he ever had. Sometimes real life just played out like a book or movie.

Final shoot-out.

The shots crashed together. Jake felt the impact against his chest and went over backward. As he fell, he watched through eyes gone hazy again as Foster stumbled back and forth, trying to stop the blood that fountained from his bullet-torn throat. He couldn't do it, of course, and after a second the gory stream slowed as his heart began slowing to its inevitable stop. He fell forward, and the blood began to form a slowly spreading pool under him.

Jake lay there, mostly numb. He was only vaguely aware of the tactically armored, heavily armed figures that began to swarm around him a few moments later. He heard some sort of erratic thumping, like the sound of distant drums, and wondered if that was his heartbeat.

Then that went away, and so did he.

The death toll of innocents that day at Kelton College was sixteen. It could have been much higher. Easily could have been.

Twenty-three terrorists were killed. Five were taken into custody, including Dr. Natalie Burke, who was expected to recover—under heavy guard, of course.

Walt Graham and Theresa Vega questioned all the surviving members of the group and eventually were convinced that they'd gotten them all. Nobody else was lurking out there, waiting to wreak bloody havoc on Kelton College.

The campus was closed for two weeks to allow repairs to be made and all explosive devices to be removed. Getting rid of the bombs didn't take nearly as long as cleaning up the blood and the bullet holes.

Counselors provided by the college were overworked as they tried to help the students deal with the trauma they had gone through. This had been a *macro*aggression, and some of those already easily triggered snowflakes would never get over it.

That was the trouble with being a snowflake. You melted if things got the least bit warm.

Dr. Alfred Montambault tendered his resignation from the faculty. He planned to go on a trip to France, to see his ancestral homeland and allow his nerves to recover, he said.

Pierce Conners remained enrolled, but he told the other members of his study group that he thought he would be studying on his own from now on.

President Pelletier worked almost around the clock trying to keep the college's wealthy patrons—many of whom had children who'd been affected by the crisis—from pulling all their funding. Cordell Gardner could have led the charge by dropping his donations, and that might have been the death knell for the school. Instead he helped Pelletier keep the place open . . . on one condition.

"At least it's not a damn statue," Jake said as he looked at the plaque with his name on it mounted next to the entrance of the Burr Memorial Library.

Frank McRainey said, "Hey, your grandfather told me he thought about making them rename the whole library, but he decided the plaque was enough, since you didn't die and all."

"Yeah, staying alive fouled it all up, didn't it?"

Jake still had a few twinges in his chest now and then from the bullet that had ripped through there, but it hadn't hit anything too vital. The minor pains would go away in time. Probably.

He went on, "You know, Granderson ought to have a plaque, too."

"We'll put something up in the station for him, don't worry." McRainey gave a slow shake of his head. "He sure was an unlikable kid."

"Yeah, he was," Jake agreed, nodding, "but when the time came, he did what he had to do. Proving that assholes can be heroes just like anybody else."

"And a good thing, too, since most of us fall into that category at least some of the time." McRainey put a hand on Jake's shoulder. "Are you really not coming back as a student?"

"That's right. I'm just not cut out to be in college these days, Chief."

"You could be a campus cop . . ."

"Oh, no. Spend every day dealing with these . . . No, just no."

"All right." McRainey stuck his hand out. "Come back to see us sometime, anyway."

"Sure, I'll do that," Jake said as he shook hands, even though he knew he wouldn't.

McRainey headed off. Jake decided he would take one more walk around Nafziger Plaza, since it was a really beautiful autumn day, before he left for good. Classes had started again at last, and although a subdued atmosphere still hung over the campus, it was starting to get back to normal.

Jake had walked halfway around the plaza when he became aware that a man had fallen in step beside him. Funny, he hadn't heard the guy come up at all. Even more surprising, when Jake glanced over, he recognized the man from Keith Randall's gun range.

"Mr. Rivera," he said.

"Not quite, Jake," Rivera said.

"We haven't been introduced, so I guess Keith told you my name like he told me yours."

"Not exactly. I've known who you are for a long, long time, Jake. And the name's not really Rivera, although I've gone by that for almost as long. It's

Rivers, just like your mother's name. And your grandfather Big Joe's name."

Jake stopped and frowned over at the older man.

"What the hell are you saying?" he demanded.

"I'm Barry Rivers. I'm your uncle."

CHAPTER 44

A long moment of silence passed, and then Jake said with more than a hint of anger in his voice, "The hell you are. My uncle Barry is dead."

The older man shook his head.

"That's what the world has believed for a long time, but it's not true."

"He was killed in an explosion, along with his wife," Jake insisted. "It was some sort of mob-related thing. My mother told me about it."

"And as far as Donna ever knew, that was the truth. Only a handful of people, including the president at the time, ever knew it *wasn't* true. That's the way it had to play out."

"You're claiming the whole bomb story was a fake?"

A shadow seemed to pass over the older man's weathered face.

"It wasn't a fake," he said in a low voice that held an angry growl somewhere inside it. "The explosion was real enough. It killed my wife, Kate, and it came awfully damned close to killing me. But not quite. I lived . . . if you can call it that."

"I've seen pictures of Barry Rivers," Jake said stubbornly. "You don't look like—"

"The blast tore up my face, and when the doctors put it back together, I didn't look exactly like I used to. I think you can still see a hint of the old me here and there, if you know where to look, but most people never would. And you never saw me when you were a kid. I was . . . dead . . . before you were born. So was your Uncle Paul. He died in that insane asylum. Where he belonged, I might add."

"I'm not sure he's the only one who belongs in an asylum."

The man who claimed to be Barry Rivers chuckled.

"Why don't we go sit down on that bench over there?" he suggested as he nodded toward a concrete bench under one of the trees. "I'll tell you all about it."

Jake hesitated. While he was in no way prepared to accept this guy's story, neither did he believe he was in any sort of danger. The man seemed to have an aura of menace about him, but Jake could tell that it wasn't directed toward him.

"All right," he said. "But I warn you, I'm not going to believe a word of it."

So for the next half hour, Jake sat there mostly in silence, asking a question only now and then, as the man told him about being funded and equipped by the government to become a sort of one-man strike force free to travel the country and right wrongs wherever he found them. Taking advantage of his background as a trucker, "Barry Rivera"—his new identity following the supposed death of the old one—had used a specially equipped Kenworth in his justice journey. An eighteen-wheel avenger, someone had dubbed him when the rumors began to rise of a mysterious trucker who dealt death to all sorts of evil people. Others called him the Rig Warrior.

Anytime someone asked Barry who he was, though, his answer was the same.

"Call me Dog. Just Dog."

Now, sitting on the bench in Nafziger Plaza, Jake heard the unmistakable ring of truth in what this man was saying . . . no matter how much he wanted to disbelieve it.

"That went on for years," Barry said. Already, Jake couldn't think of him by any other name. "Lots of years. So much blood that sometimes it seemed like I was wading in it up to my neck. Only real friend I had was Dog. The real Dog. Big, mean-tempered critter who wound up one of the best friends I ever had. Things were never quite the same after he passed. In fact, I hung it up for a while. Found a place in Arkansas, way back in the woods, on top of a mountain, so isolated nobody could ever find me. That's what I thought, anyway." Barry shrugged. "But trouble always has a way of finding a man, and I got dragged back into the game.

"All the while, though, I kept tabs on what little family I had left. My sister . . . and you. Of course, I had to do it from a distance, since nobody was supposed to know Barry Rivers was still alive. But I saw you at least a dozen times over the years. You just never knew it. I could tell you were growing up into a fine young man, though. No surprise. You've got good genes on both sides."

Jake grunted and said, "You could never tell that by my father."

"Well . . . even the best of genes skip a generation now and then, I guess. Your father wasn't a good man. But you are, Jake."

"You've been hanging around this part of the country for a while. What are you doing here?"

"I'm semiretired again. The government calls on me to do a job now and then. And if I see something that interests me, I'm free to poke into it. Mostly, though, my time is my own, and I'll admit, I've been keeping an eye on you." Barry grinned. "I wanted to see how a throwback like you was going to fit in on a modern college campus. Not well, from what I gather."

"So I'm a throwback, am I?"

"You're the kind of guy who's been getting in trouble because of rules and regulations made by weaker men for thousands of years, Jake. And by weaker I don't mean physically. You've got the sort of code that men used to have, a true sense of right and wrong that won't let you stand by and do nothing while innocent people are suffering because of evil. You bull right in and take action, even if it puts you at risk. You're *more* likely to jump into something if it's dangerous, because that means you're fighting for something that's actually worthwhile."

"You seem to think you know a hell of a lot about me."

Barry smiled faintly and said, "I told you I've been keeping an eye on you. I wasn't surprised you kept getting in trouble here. I wasn't really expecting to find you in the middle of a hostage situation fighting terrorist assholes, though. It was their bad luck you were around." He paused. "I hope you don't mind that I pitched in a little, too. I knew they were scattered around the campus and you couldn't be everywhere at once."

"Wait a minute," Jake said. "I heard rumors about how some mysterious guy killed some of Foster's men and freed a bunch of hostages. The official story downplays that, but too many people have said they saw it happen. Are you telling me that was you?"

"Just mopping up, really," Barry replied with a shrug.

"Damn." Jake shook his head. "This is a hell of a lot to dump on a guy."

"Yeah, it is. But you're strong enough to take it."

They sat there in silence that stretched for several minutes while the campus population continued bustling around them. Life went on. Finally Jake said, "I think I believe you."

"Good. I hoped you would."

"But why? Why tell me all this?"

Barry took a deep breath and said, "After all these years, I wanted to look my nephew in the eye and have him know that we're family. Maybe I'm just gettin' sentimental in my old age. For a long time, family meant betrayal to me. Your Uncle Paul was responsible for a lot of pain and heartbreak for me and a bunch of other people. But I finally realized that you can't turn your back on your whole family because of what one person does."

"Does that mean you're going to reach out to my mother, too?"

"One thing at a time, kid," Barry said. "Anyway, that's not the only reason. I've got a practical motive for talking to you today, too."

"And what's that?"

"What do you plan on doing with your life, Jake?"

The question was one Jake had no idea how to answer, not at this point, anyway. He shook his head and said, "My grandfather thought I ought to go back to school. That didn't work out so well. I guess I'll get a job of some kind—"

"Work with me," Barry said.

Jake frowned at him.

"You mean . . . for the government? You said just a few minutes ago that I don't handle rules and regulations very well, and who has more of those than the government?"

"It's not exactly the same," Barry said. "When they come to me and ask me to do a job—*ask* me, not tell me—I have a free hand. Because there's nothing official involved, and that lack of a traceable connection gives them complete deniability. They say, 'We think this is a problem,' and if I agree with them, I go and take care of it however I see fit. That's the only way I'll operate. But that doesn't mean I couldn't use a hand now and then." He chuckled. "And believe it or not, I'm not getting any younger. There'll come a time when I can't do this work anymore. But it'll still need to be done, take my word on that. There'll always be evil in the world, Jake, which means there'll always be a need for men to fight it."

Jake couldn't argue with any of that. He had to admit that he was intrigued by Barry's proposal. A job like that might well get him killed . . . but he wouldn't die of boredom.

When Jake didn't say anything for several moments, Barry went on, "I still have that place in Arkansas. Thought I might head back up there for a while, do some training. You want to come along?"

Jake took a deep breath and then said, "I suppose we could see how it goes."

A grin split Barry's face as he nodded.

"Good. That's what I wanted to hear."

He stood up and started walking along the concrete path at the edge of the plaza. Jake fell in alongside him. The tide of campus life ebbed and flowed around them. After a moment Jake said, "Dog, that's your code name, right?"

"Yeah."

"Do I get a code name?"

Barry squinted over at him, said, "You're as big as a horse. How about Horse?"

"No," Jake said, shaking his head. "Not Horse. That's not a good code name." He thought about it. "Now, Stallion, maybe . . ."

"I don't think so." Barry clapped a hand on his nephew's shoulder as they walked off into the pleasant autumn afternoon. "We'll work on it."